I0726235

Found in Translation
Coddiwomple Universe

by Lea Carter

Copyright © 2022

Cover design by Daniel Manfredini.

This is a work of fiction. The characters, names, incidents, places, and dialogue are products of the author's imagination, and are not to be construed as real.

ISBN 978-1-951248-20-8

Shout-out to everyone that made this story possible. I won't go naming names, but I hope you folks know who you are: my betas, my artistic advisers, the folks that tell me I can do this—even when I act like I don't believe you, I heard what you said.

Special mention to the writers, cast, and crew of *The Rational Life*, who inspired me to write this.

Chapter 1

Natua wiped ink-stained fingers on a damp rag, then wiggled them to dry them. The desert air in Marroi needed only a moment to do the job and she was able to turn her attention to stacking the pages she'd finished earlier.

It hadn't been easy, translating a forty-page contract between Nebarma Stables, one of the four major dragon training houses, and their primary suppliers from Guag to Marroi. Ah, but it was worth it. She'd finished with time to spare.

"Head Translator."

She jerked in surprise when Pyr, one of the office messengers, popped into her doorway. Gathering her wits, she smoothed out the pages she'd crinkled. At least she hadn't thrown them across the room this time.

"Goodness, Pyr. Are all your assignments so important that you forget to knock?" Whatever had brought him to her door, it couldn't be good. She'd learned early on that the office messengers knew everything that went on at Itzuli Communications. Today Pyr's expression was barely a three out of ten on the smile scale.

"Mirko wants to see you."

"Manager Mirko." Natua's heart sank even as she gently corrected him. No one liked Manager Mirko, who unhappily had been left in charge when Director Rysl retired two years ago. If she and her peers were soap bubbles, Mirko was a prickly pear waiting to pop them.

Pretending to focus on arranging the rest of the pages in the correct order on her metal desk, she asked, "Did he mention why?"

"Not a word." Because he liked her, Pyr walked the few steps to her tiny desk and offered, "Better let me finish that. I've the feeling he wants you sooner than later."

"Right." She surrendered the project to him. Out of habit, she tugged on the hem of her blouse to straighten it as she got to her feet. "When it's ready, please take that straight to the copy center."

Pyr made a face. "I'd rather run a bundle out to the edges," he muttered.

Natua raised an eyebrow inquisitively. Office messengers didn't often have errands that took them outside of the building, but she knew that deliveries to the far edges of town was a run they all dreaded.

"What, and be out in the heat of the day?" Partly out of curiosity and partly to delay the inevitable, she teased, "Don't tell me you're afraid of Supervisor Gusari?"

"Not him, not exactly." And yet, he shuddered theatrically.

Sensing an undercurrent of genuine…disgust, Natua cocked her head at him. "What is it, Pyr? What's actually going on?"

Pyr considered, then waved her off. "Mir…um, *Manager* Mirko doesn't like to be kept waiting."

"Pyr." She waited until he looked her in the eyes. "Come find me at lunch and we'll talk, alright? If something's wrong at the copy center, I really want to know."

Pyr nodded and grinned at her retreating back. He surely did like her. She might be a foreigner *and* a head translator, but she had a good heart.

The sound of Natua's hard-soled Lurrakian boots on the stone floors kept her company as she strode through the corridors to the main offices. From the corners of her eyes, she could see junior translators looking up from their work to watch her as she passed and she heartily wished she'd worn her soft Marroi slippers instead.

Marvelous. Now the entire translation staff wanted to know what this was about.

Ordinary assignments were delivered by office messengers, as were paychecks and other trifles.

Occasionally Korrez, Mirko's personal secretary, tried to mingle during rest periods or lunch. Korrez might bring them good news if there was any, but he also carried all that he heard right back to his master. He was tolerated only out of fear for his position at Mirko's elbow.

"Translator." Korrez set aside his work with a too-bright smile. "You're here early."

"*Head* Translator," she reminded him for the thousandth time. Ignoring his invitation to engage him on the subject of her prompt arrival, she waited for him to do his job and announce her.

"Manager Mirko is busy at the moment." Korrez made a show of checking his appointment pad against the elaborate sandglass on the wall. "My fault, I'm afraid. We never dreamed you would abandon an unfinished translation. Especially when there's so little time left until the deadline." If anything, his grin broadened.

"Another deadline?" Pretending not to realize he meant the contract she'd already finished, she shook her head and somehow managed to stifle an unladylike snort at his use of the plural pronoun *we*. Was Korrez truly so deluded as to think Mirko was loyal to anyone but himself? "Perhaps it's time we hired replacements for our translator pool." They'd lost six translators since Mirko took command and had only been able to fill three of the slots. "Still, now that I'm done with the Nebarma translation, I'm happy to help with this new predicament. Is that why he wants to see me?"

Korrez's mouth opened and closed a few times while she spoke, either because she spoke too quickly to interrupt or because he couldn't decide how to answer.

"Head Translator Prezio." Mirko's silky voice came from his office, where he'd obviously been listening to their conversation. "Come in."

Natua walked past Korrez without a backward glance. She entered Mirko's office with her head high and shoulders back in the best Lurrakian fashion.

The heavy wooden desk in the center of the room dwarfed the man lounging behind it. His jet-black hair was ruthlessly combed straight back, making his angular nose seem even more so. His fingernails, worn as long as was popular amongst Marroi men, boasted to the world that here was someone who did not have to work with their hands for a living. Not even as a translator.

Natua self-consciously closed her owns hands slightly to hide her nails. As hard as she tried, and as short as she kept them, they were forever ink-stained in some form or fashion.

"So." Mirko's lips curved at the corners, giving his narrow face an odd, downward-pointing arrow appearance. "The translation of the contract for Nebarma is completed. Excellent." He paused, as if expecting her to respond, to mistake his statement for a compliment. When she did not, he continued. "Word of our good work will spread from one end of Koroa to the other. Just in time for the royal wedding." His tone was that of a small boy rubbing his hands in gleeful anticipation.

"Yes, sir." It was easy to agree with that. Being *the* trusted translators for four of the largest concerns in the entire capital city of Koroa should guarantee that Itzuli Communications would be stretched to its limit to keep up. Add to their ordinary workload the myriad documents required for the upcoming royal wedding, which happened to include the first international royal bride in living memory, and Natua wanted to sleep for a week.

An idea struck her and she smiled. "This would be an ideal time to hire additional translators." She held her ground when his gaze snapped from whatever glorious future he was imagining to her face.

"Ah, good." Straightening, he scowled at his fair-haired nemesis. "For a moment, I feared you would not make your usual attempt at instructing me on how to do my job."

"That isn't what I meant at all." She began to speak, but he cut her off.

"And I'm sure you will be elated to learn the time has at last arrived wherein I agree." Picking up a list of names, he tossed it to the other side of his desk. "They start tomorrow."

"Splendid. We'll need a full staff when the wedding translations begin to flow in." Of course, he would wait until absolutely the last minute to tell her. She'd have to completely rearrange her schedule so she could be there to welcome them, get them settled, start their training, etc. Her gaze swept the list and she frowned, puzzled. "There are four names here."

"Are there?" He made a show of retrieving the list and inspecting it. "Yes, of course there are. How stupid of me." Dropping the list again, he gave her an oily smile. "Three to fill the empty slots. And one to replace Translator Japoni when he becomes Head Translator."

"Japoni?" It should've been a pleasant surprise. She knew he was a hard worker and that his family would receive enormous benefit from the raise that came with the new title. Yet something felt…off. Generosity was completely out of character for Mirko.

"You disapprove?" The question came quickly, sharply, as if he hoped to startle her into an admission.

"On the contrary," she shot back. "Head Translator Japoni will be a credit to Itzuli Communications. He always has been."

"Good, good." Now Mirko did rub his hands together. "I'm glad you support the decision. I was worried you might resent being transferred."

His meaning hit her like a bucket of ice water. She clamped her lips together to keep a dozen shocked questions from spilling out. They backed up in her throat, making it hard to swallow.

"I've given it a great deal of thought and there is no one better suited to whipping the copy center into shape than you, Head Translator." Mirko didn't put much effort into sounding sincere. She might be able to do it; she might not. He privately hoped she would give up and move on to…well, he didn't care where she went when she left Itzuli. Just so long as she left.

"Here is a list of deficiencies." He held out a thick packet of papers. "Starting tomorrow you will work with Supervisor Gusari to set things in order."

Carefully, she took the packet from him. Its weight settled into her hand like a boulder in her stomach.

"You have two months to make a ten percent improvement in efficiency." He sighed doubtfully. "I only hope it's enough time." His hard amber eyes scanned her face, eager for her next reaction. "If we can't improve what we have, I'm afraid we will have to begin terminating scribes."

"Terminating?" The word exploded out of her like a ripe teryn nut left too long in the fire. "What good is it to hire more translators only to terminate scribes? Are you looking for new ways to fall behind? Or will you have highly trained, highly *paid* translators do their own copying?"

Lowered wages last year had cost them some of their best translators and was a sore point with Mirko that she wouldn't have brought up under ordinary circumstances.

If not for the delightful anticipation of watching her suffer through her time with Gusari—and failing dramatically—Mirko would've terminated *her* right then. How dare she stand there and question him in that tone of voice? In his own office!

"Two months, Prezio. Or we will see if new scribes are the solution. Without you." Snatching up the nearest piece of paper, he stared at it with such intensity that she knew she was dismissed.

Her temper barely in check, Natua stalked out of his office and back to hers. As she had no door to close when she arrived, she leaned against the shelves to the right of doorway, hidden from view unless someone entered the room.

The walk had cooled her off, but also gave her time to think of more questions. What would it take for her to get her regular job back? Just the ten percent improvement? Or was Mirko really willing to jeopardize the future of Itzuli Communications in his bid to get rid of her? Should she be flattered or just angry that he was so…so…

So what?

Her shoulders drooped. Of all the irrational ideas. Granted, she didn't believe Mirko's supposed reasoning for making her, a mere translator, responsible for setting things right at the copy center. However, that didn't automatically mean this was part of some extravagant plot to ruin her.

And yet, how much good could she do? It wasn't as if Mirko had put her in charge, given her the power to actually effect change. No, she'd share that with Supervisor Gusari.

Willing away the cold shiver that the thought of working closely with the man brought, Natua drew her first deep breath since hearing that Mirko wanted to see her. Something crinkled, bringing her attention to the packet Mirko had given her.

Taking a seat, Natua opened it and began reviewing the contents. There wasn't enough room on her tiny desk to spread things out and get a better look at what she was supposed to *fix*. She'd have to take the packet home with her and study it more closely there. Still, two things stood out like draft dragons in a flock of the lean, diminutive gezi dragons.

Item one: In theory, the copy center should be self-sustaining. Itzuli Communications took a number of contracts each year that involved producing and distributing hundreds of copies of documents: training manuals; blank forms for import-export businesses to fill in; invitations; that sort of thing. This type of work supported the copy center even when there weren't jobs like the contract she'd sent over that morning. Yet somehow, the copy center was showing a sizable deficit.

Item two: Evidently there was a huge discipline problem at the copy center, if the sheer volume of Gusari's written grievances was any indicator.

Natua briefly wondered if she held the original complaints or if Gusari had ordered some scribes to make a copy for her. What an unpleasant task that must've been.

She rubbed her arm when the cold shivers returned. It didn't make sense that she felt so strongly about working with him. She'd met the man exactly once, at the celebration for Director Rysl's retirement. Surely it was unjust of her to think she'd seen only greed in the man's eyes as they toured Rysl's beautiful home and visited his lush garden.

True, Gusari's muddy brown eyes almost bulged out of his head at the size of the firestones positioned around the property, but it had taken her by surprise as well. Here in Marroi, where wood was scarce and firestones largely too expensive, most homes and even businesses were lighted by dragonglass skylights during the day and lamps filled with concentrated toyn juice at night.

Sighing, Natua riffled through the pages of complaints. Once she got to know Gusari better, her bizarre dislike of him would surely fade. In the meantime, there were a lot of repeated names here.

Taking out blank paper and ink, she began making a list. She included a column for names; a column for the type of reported infraction; and for a few individuals, a set of lines representing the number of times the infraction was repeated.

Three names stood out from the rest—Mirn, Kaloe, and Wiot.

Setting the list aside, Natua frowned at it while she wiped ink from her fingers. Some of the complaints were more serious than others. Persistent tardiness or being caught sleeping during work hours, for example.

Yet this Kaloe, um… She consulted the report. Kaloe Tetsu, that was it. He was on report dozens of times for what sounded like little more than a bad attitude.

A knock at the door made her look up. Pyr stood there, arms wrapped loosely around an empty wire crate. The expression on his face drew Natua to her feet.

"Pyr! What's happened?" Dread pooled in her stomach when he swallowed hard before answering.

"Korrez told me to bring you this." He lifted the wire crate, but didn't offer it to her. Blurted, "Did they actually terminate you?"

"*What?*" For a sick moment, she wondered if they had. In this company, the plain wire crate was a badge of dishonor, given to ex-employees to take their things home in. When Natua got her promotion and moved into her current office, the other translators had each cheerfully carried a book or two for her, making the transition almost celebratory. But she wasn't… Oh!

Her lips tightened as she remembered. *Starting tomorrow you will work with Supervisor Gusari to set things in order.*

Aloud she said, "I haven't been terminated." The poor lad still looked so shaken that she beckoned him into the room. "I'm temporarily assigned to the copy center. That's all."

It would've been nice of Mirko to mention that he expected her to relocate. Temporarily, of course. Perhaps he'd thought it was obvious? After all, what could she contribute from an office in a different building?

She didn't actually believe that, so she kept it to herself. Smiling at Pyr, she motioned for him to put the crate on her desk.

"It looks like I won't be able to have lunch with you today." Pulling her personal dictionaries from the bookshelf, she laid them carefully in the crate. "But if you'll help me put a few things together and carry them over, you can tell me about the copy center while we work."

Chapter 2

Pyr offered to carry her crate over for her and she agreed, suddenly feeling every stress-filled hour of the last few days. It would be better to start fresh with the copy center tomorrow, she assured herself as she left the building to start walking home.

And, in the meantime, she had a lot to think about.

Supervisor Gusari was a hard man, almost cruel; he never asked when he could order and was rumored to deduct the novices' pay for any excuse. Those who dared to be tardy, even by minutes, were docked a full hour of wages. The room was kept dark. The tools were inferior.

Natua had heard most of it before in the whispers of the breakroom, but had dismissed it as rumor and wild exaggeration. Tomorrow, she would see for herself how much of it was true.

Lurrak, Natua's homeland, had laws governing the way businesses treated their employees. Did they have such laws in Marroi?

She bit her lip, a little surprised to realize that she'd never checked. She'd been hired and moved to Marroi immediately after completing her university courses, where she'd worked happily for the last six years.

The copy center might be a dark stain on Itzuli Communications' records, but the translators were treated well. Perhaps that was because, unlike the scribes and novices, translators often interacted directly with clients?

The cobblestones under her feet changed to larger stone slabs, buried in the sand and worn smooth by years of use. Turning to her left, Natua entered the 'foreign' quarter. Orange, mud-brick buildings of the Marroi middle class gave way to the dull gray stone of the residences created specifically for those unaccustomed to the desert heat.

A night alone sounded good right now. Tired from

work, she could almost be grateful that her mother had accepted the invitation to spend a few days with one of the other Lurrakian families in the quarter and wouldn't be back until tomorrow.

Instead of having to choose between fending off or surrendering to a hot Lurrakian meal, which would make her lethargic, Natua could eat a little fruit and cheese while she went back over the reports from Mirko. Then off to bed and…

The sound of off-key humming smote Natua's ears when she opened the front door. As hard as she fought it, her heart sank. What kind of a daughter was she? Taking a deep breath, she eased the door closed.

"Mother, is that you?"

"Natua! There you are." Kume bustled out of the kitchen area, wiping her hands on her apron. "I should be cross at you for being so late. And," she put her fists on her hips, "for cluttering up my kitchen with all of that foreign food."

"*That* food?" Natua braced herself. "You didn't throw it away, did you?"

"Well, not all of it." Wrinkling her nose, Kume told her, "Just what had gone bad. The fruit's quite nice, if a little different from what we're used to." Pivoting, she disappeared into the kitchen. "I thought we could have some with our supper."

"Mother." Natua followed her, shoulders rigid with tension. "That food was perfectly good. I only bought it last night."

"You poor dear. Why, if only I'd taught you to cook, you wouldn't have had to resort to buying it at all." Kume hung up the apron and gestured toward the sink with a long-suffering sigh. "Now, wash your hands and we'll eat."

Gritting her teeth, Natua set the reports down and obediently washed her hands. "I didn't *resort* to it, Mother. I like Marroi food."

"Oh?" Kume, once again out of step with the woman her daughter had become, foolishly vented her frustration on Natua. "I suppose that means you don't like my cooking anymore. I suppose you're sorry you brought me with you! You didn't have to, you know. I could've had a very nice room with the other widows." It was an idle boast, to be sure. Widowed for over nine years, Kume couldn't bear the thought of being separated from the last living member of her own little family. Still, she said the words, hoping to hear her daughter answer that she felt the same.

Natua closed her eyes. She hated this part of the argument. Her mother wasn't completely wrong. She would've been welcomed by the other widows. But would she have been happier there than she was here, in Marroi? With Natua? That was the question that Natua couldn't answer. Or stop asking herself.

"I could never have left you, Mother." Frustrated yet defeated, Natua forced a smile before turning around. There was no reasoning with Mother when she was in this mood. "I would've worried the whole time. Now, come. Let's eat while it's fresh, alright?"

"Hmmph. We can't eat yet." Kume hid her disappointment at, to her ears and heart, being called an obligation, behind a haughty toss of her head. "We haven't any bread."

"Bread?" Natua looked at the table—really looked at it for the first time since entering the kitchen. A dish of fruit sat between two soup bowls on the small, round table in the corner. A sidelong glance at the stove confirmed it. They could've roasted ripe, juicy truip on a stick in the sunshine that noon and her mother was serving boiling hot soup for supper.

Kume sniffed emphatically.

Natua's shoulders sagged. "I'll...I'll go buy some."

The cobblestones felt harder and rougher under her thinly soled slippers on the way to the market than they had ten minutes earlier on her way home. Sweat trickled down one cheek and she discreetly wiped it away. At that moment, she could only wish that the trouble at the copy center was her biggest worry.

Ahead of her, brightly colored tents and gaily decorated metal stalls stretched as far as the eye could see, filled with vendors offering everything from fresh goat cheese to dragonglass. She hardly ever ventured into the marketplace, but the shop where they bought their groceries was closed, so her choices were limited.

Still, there was the stall where she'd purchased supper last night. If they didn't sell bread there, they should at least know where she could get some.

The only problem now was that the stall was on the other side of the marketplace. Unwilling to weave her way through the hubbub, Natua wearily started walking around it.

The cries of the vendors vied with the rattle of carts for dominance, adding to Natua's tension until her head began to throb.

"Where do you think you're going?" demanded a deep voice, startling Natua into coming to an abrupt halt. "Thought you were going to get away, did you?"

Thoroughly confused, Natua turned to face her accuser.

Less than ten feet away stood a young man, glaring down at a young woman Natua didn't recognize. He held her by one arm while he lectured her, his voice loud enough that Natua could hear him quite clearly.

"You can't keep doing this. You made a commitment, the same as me." Kaloe Tetsu kept a firm grip on Anella, his younger cousin, despite her best efforts to shake him off.

"Let me go," whined the girl, tugging at her arm. When that failed, she tried kicking him in the shins. She landed a blow and promptly began hopping on one slippered foot. "You big bully!"

Kaloe groaned inwardly. She got hurt kicking him and *he* was the bully? Unbelievable.

What's going on?" Natua blinked. She felt as surprised as they looked when they turned to stare at her.

"Help!" Anella pleaded. "He's hurting me!"

"Mind your own business." Kaloe advised the stranger as politely as he could. Returning his attention to Anella, he scolded, "Don't you think it's about time you grew up?"

"Just a moment." Natua took a deep breath. This was more important than her headache, or even the perpetual argument with her mother. "I don't know what's going on, but is it so desperate that you have to resort to holding her captive?"

Kaloe gritted his teeth. He liked to think of himself as a pretty even-tempered man, but after nearly two weeks of his cousin ducking out instead of helping with the work, he could feel his control starting to slip. "I already told you. Mind your own…"

"Do I need to call an officer?" Natua took a determined step forward.

"What?" Forgetting Anella for a moment, Kaloe turned to face the interloper. He regretted the action instantly, for his cousin wriggled free, sprinted into the crowd, and disappeared. "Now look what you made me do."

"It's for the best." Natua experienced a twinge of wistfulness as she watched the girl run away from her troubles. Temporarily, anyway. "When your wife comes home later tonight, you can calmly discuss what happened, within the privacy of your own home. Instead of making a public spectacle of yourself."

Kaloe watched, speechless, as the stranger walked away. *His wife?*

The sound of chuckling drew his attention to where the old woman who sold discs of honey candy stood. It was obvious that she'd witnessed the whole fiasco.

Now she wagged a wrinkled finger at him. "She has spunk, that one. Not your ordinary 'kanpotarrak'."

The word gave him pause. There were over a dozen ways to say 'outsider' in Marroi, but 'kanpotarrak' was probably the most respectful. After a moment's reflection, he realized why she'd chosen it.

The stranger who'd accosted him might have hair as golden as the southern sands and eyes as light as smoke, but she'd spoken in Marroi. Fluently.

Unsettled, Kaloe ran brown fingers through thick black hair. Well, what did it matter? He had to go help his aunt close the stall for the night.

Oh, how glad he would be when his uncle's broken leg got better. His poor back, already aching from a day spent hunched over while he copied documents at his full-time job, fairly whimpered at the thought of loading the cart with leftover goods tonight—only to add new goods in the morning and unload it all at the stall the next morning.

Natua, meanwhile, bought her bread and began the long walk home. Somehow, her short excursion took so long that 'everything' was ruined by the time she returned.

"I suppose it's just as well." She cringed away from her mother's narrow-eyed gaze. "What I meant to say is that I'm much too tired to eat right now. Anyway, it's soup. It can't be too spoiled, can it?" Seeing her mother's face stiffen, Natua made one final effort. "I'd love to have some for my lunch tomorrow."

"What kind of a mother do you think I am?" Kume grumbled louder than necessary, for now that her temper had cooled, she thought she was rather a poor mother. She'd barely let Natua walk in the door before starting in on her. They hadn't even hugged, or said they'd missed each other. Somehow the thought made her positively waspish as she plowed relentlessly ahead, "The very idea of my sending you to work with nothing but burnt soup and stale bread for your lunch. Why, sometimes I don't think you care a bit about me."

Thoroughly bewildered, Natua opened her mouth, then shut it again.

"Oh, never mind. You look awful. Go up to bed and try to sleep." Her mother pulled her graying hair back in a severe bun. Determined to prove to herself that she wasn't completely useless, she attacked the pile of dirty dishes she'd created. "Not that anyone can sleep in this heat!" she muttered.

Natua left her banging dirty dishes and pots in the kitchen. "Sometimes," she told her reflection as she massaged liaora oil into her temples to ease the ache, "I do believe Mother must enjoy being miserable."

Unlatching the pane of blue dragonglass, she opened it inward. After a careful inspection of the protective layers of thin mesh and, three inches further out, the grid of heavier wire, she left the window open to improve circulation. Bugs weren't too much of a problem, even in the cities of Marroi, but the knee-high gezi dragons that roamed the streets were notorious for sneaking into houses in search of food to steal.

Lying on her side, Natua took slow, deep breaths. Their neighbor's garden boasted night-blooming lurrin flowers that were as large as saucers when they unfurled. Something about their soft, sweet scent always calmed her mind, allowing her to get some badly needed rest.

Breakfast was strained the next morning, and Natua seized on an excuse to leave early.

"I'm working at the copy center for a little while," she explained as she gathered her things. "It wouldn't do to be late."

Her escape was foiled when her mother asked, "Is that a promotion?"

"No." Natua scrambled for an answer that wouldn't worry her. "It's an opportunity to help the company. Shouldn't last more than," she swallowed, "two months. I don't think."

Kume's eyes narrowed. "I suppose you'll be working late again."

"Oh." Natua grimaced. She hadn't thought of that. "I probably will." Seeing Kume's mouth beginning to turn down, she quickly offered, "Don't worry about making supper for me tonight. I'll get something from one of the food carts."

Kume's only answer was a tight-lipped nod before she turned and began clearing away the breakfast dishes. Sometimes it seemed she might as well have stayed in Lurrak, for how little she saw of Natua.

Natua fought back an overwhelming desire to help her and headed once more for the door. "Perhaps…" Was her mother sad because she'd be eating alone? "Perhaps we could invite the Motruns over for supper. In a few days, I mean. Once my schedule has settled down."

Kume perked up. "We could ask them."

"Wonderful." Natua let herself out and started for the office.

Her steps were heavy with concern, both for the day ahead and for the mother she'd just left behind. The prospect of giving a party, even such a small one, should put Kume in a better mood.

Was it her imagination, or had Kume been more out of sorts than usual of late? And why?

Natua spent every ounce of energy she could spare on her walk in trying to think what might be bothering her mother, but was no closer to an answer when she arrived. The one thing she could always count on to make her mother sad was the anniversary of her father's death, and that was seven months away.

Habit nearly had her turn in at the front door of the large, stone building that housed Itzuli Communications, but she resolutely walked past it and around the corner.

The ugly, squat building that housed the copy center stretched out before her like…like the dirty, discarded slipper of some square-toed giant. It appeared to be made of some sort of metal that she didn't recognize. Metal that might've been white once, before howling sands dug pin-sized holes in it and dust and grime were allowed to collect on it.

When she opened it, the door screeched like a housewife discovering a gezi dragon plundering their kitchen. Stepping into the wide, open room, she did her best to ignore the snickers coming from the section off to her left, a sunken area crammed with long tables. Dozens of scribes hunched over their work, only their backs or the tops of their heads visible from where she stood.

"Translator. Welcome." Gusari rose from his desk and hurried over. He wasn't a tall man and bad eating habits combined with a sedentary job had increased his girth so that it hung down and jiggled when he walked. "Welcome to the copy center."

"Thank you." Natua submitted to the obligatory handclasp and somehow kept a straight face despite the damp, doughy feel of his pudgy hand. "I apologize if I'm late. I didn't realize the copy center kept different hours."

"We do, we do." He nodded, looking out at the rows of scribes hunched over their work. "Have to reach deadlines."

"Yes, of course." She shifted the package Mirko had given her and glanced around, hoping to spot her desk. Surely she wasn't going to have to share with Gusari?

"Truth be told," Gusari smiled, his beady eyes nearly disappearing in the crinkles of his cheeks, "your timing is most propitious."

"Oh?" Relieved that he didn't seem to see her as an interloper, Natua willingly followed him further into the room.

"Indeed." He lowered his voice. "We've been having some trouble with the translations of late." At his desk, he shuffled through papers as if he didn't know exactly where to find what he was looking for. "Errors, you see. Mistranslations in important documents. Ah, here we are."

"*Mis*translations?" Confused, she accepted the packet he handed her. Read the document title and stared at him in disbelief as he went on.

"Quite so. And, as you can imagine"—Gusari shrugged helplessly—"shoddy translations slow us down considerably." He watched her face for any sign of embarrassment. She'd obviously recognized the papers he'd handed her, as well she should. According to the assignment sheet at the end, the Nebarma contract was entirely her work.

"Yes." Natua cleared her throat. "I can well imagine."

"May I be candid, Head Translator?" Gusari smiled blandly at the woman who'd been forced upon him. True, Manager Mirko said he'd banished her to the copy center to be persuaded to quit, but only a fool believed what they were told. Of course, Gusari had agreed and nodded—and thought it far more likely that she was a spy sent to catch him at his, ah, creative methods of lining his own pockets. He wouldn't put it past Mirko, curse the man.

"Please." She shifted to face him more squarely despite the near-maddening desire to rip open the Nebarma contract and proofread it right then.

"I know you were given a list of things that Mirko believes need fixing here." Gusari didn't miss the way her grip tightened on the package she'd carried into the room. Interesting. He'd have to arrange to get a look at its contents. "For today, at least, I think we would all be best served in having you review some of the more difficult translations. Once you've approved them, the scribes can proceed without hindrance."

"Well, I…" What could she say? And, really, what would they lose if she spent a few hours scanning translations? "I suppose I could do that. I'll start with this one."

"Oh, no." Gusari deftly retrieved the contract from her. "One of my scribes, Tetsu, was able to make the corrections. The copies are already completed and delivered."

"You delivered copies of a *legal contract* altered based on the recommendations of a scribe?" Belatedly, Natua realized that she'd spoken loudly enough for everyone to hear her.

"Back to work." As mild as Gusari's tone was, the scribes obeyed with alacrity. "We have far too much to do to sit around gawking, don't we?"

Natua's focus snapped back to the man before her.

"Forgive me, Head Translator." Gusari dipped his head abashedly. "I didn't mean to distress you. Please, accept my assurances that I personally approved Tetsu's corrections." Secretly delighted at how thoroughly he'd disconcerted her, Gusari gestured to his right. "Here is your desk. I took the liberty of setting a few translations aside for you."

A *few?* Natua counted six separate file jackets at a glance. One jackets bore three stripes, indicating that there were essentially four files inside: the original and three translations.

"As soon as you have reviewed them, they can be passed on to the scribes." Gusari bowed slightly. "And now, if you would excuse me, I am late for an appointment with Manager Mirko. I think," he raised innocent eyebrows, "he wants to know my impression of you."

Moving with more speed than Natua would've believed possible, Gusari reached the door before she could formulate a polite response to either thought.

Groaning inwardly, she took a seat at the desk he'd assigned to her. The chair promptly wobbled, nearly dumping her onto the floor.

The sound of someone chuckling brought her gaze up in time to see several heads duck down to their work again. Clearly the defective chair wasn't an accident.

Chapter 3

After over an hour of reviewing various translations for Gusari—and silently applauding her peers for their flawless work—Natua found herself unable to ignore the Nebarma contract any longer. Even from its place at the bottom of the stack, it called to her.

When she realized she'd gone over the same paragraph of another document twice, she groaned inwardly. What did she think she was going to do? The copies of the contract were already delivered, so it was too late to find and fix any supposed errors.

Yet, if Natua was being honest, that wasn't all that was driving her crazy. She'd put *so much* effort into that translation. She wanted to know what mistakes she had made!

Setting aside what she was working on, Natua dug out the contract and flipped through it. Strange. There were no editing marks on her original translation. In fact, aside from a few curious blotches around the edges, the document was exactly as she'd left it.

Perhaps the blotches were sweat spots. She dabbed at her forehead. It was much warmer here in the metal building than in the stone office building she was accustomed to. Picking up her tightly lidded water container, she opened it, added a pinch of cooling powder, and sloshed it around to mix it in. It wasn't enough to truly lower the temperature of the drink, but she held it in her mouth anyway, savoring the temporary relief and taking another look at her surroundings.

The copy center was lit primarily by the open panels in the ceiling, which also allowed the occasional breeze to cool the room. Firestones and a few air vents would've created a much more comfortable atmosphere, but of course, firestones were prohibitively expensive.

Lifting her head to relieve her neck muscles, she saw something that made her frown. The stack of files to be copied had only grown taller since her arrival. Granted, she'd added a few from her own pile, and office runners slipped in and out almost unnoticed. Nevertheless, the scribes had barely stirred or looked up from their work. How could they not be making more progress?

An excellent question. One she would've liked to ask Gusari.

Natua bit her lip. She only had two months to make a difference here. A ten percent difference, to be precise. Discussing things with Gusari first would've been ideal, but his abrupt departure made that impossible. Anyway, surely he wouldn't mind if she started trying to help?

But, first things first. Once she'd cleared up this business about the Nebarma contract, she'd be able to focus on her proper task.

"Tetsu. Come here please." As she called out for the scribe, she remembered where she knew that name from—the list of complaints! More dubious than ever about Gusari's decision to make changes based on a malcontent's recommendations, she spread the contract out. It was rather wonderful having a desk large enough to hold more than half a project at a time.

Natua was trying to imagine fitting the desk into her old office when she became aware of someone standing nearby.

"Take a seat," she instructed, assuming it was the scribe.

"I'll stand."

Surprised, she looked up and into the eyes of the young man from the marketplace! Sucking in a breath, Natua gripped the edge of her desk.

"How did you get in here?"

Charcoal-colored eyebrows rose and he answered, "I work here." He might've turned the question back on her, if he hadn't seen Gusari greet her and give her this desk. This meant the arrogant woman from last night was also the head translator that Gusari was afraid of. Interesting.

"You…*you*?" She sounded like an idiot. Shoving her confusion aside, she clarified, "You are Tetsu?" That was the important thing. If he was here as an employee, then he hadn't sought her out as a result of last night's confrontation.

"Kaloe Tetsu, yes." He folded his arms across his chest, clearly irritated. There was work to be done copying the student manuals. Work that they had to finish before the lunch break if they wanted to eat.

"And you altered this document?" She spoke more sharply than she'd meant to, unsettled both by their previous encounter and his obvious impatience with her.

Moving closer, Kaloe leaned in to try to read it.

"Here." Natua snatched a page and handed it to him, eager to get some of her space back. In Marroi, people often stood toe to toe when they spoke, something she'd given up on becoming accustomed to.

"Thanks." Kaloe accepted the page and tilted it toward the light. "It's a little hard to read this handwriting."

"Oh?" Concerned, Natua ran an anxious eye over the next page. While anyone might write sloppily when they were tired, she prided herself on her penmanship. For a professional translator, even an overly embellished curlicue was a risk.

It looked fine to her. Relieved, she returned her attention to the scribe.

"I remember this now." Kaloe tapped the paper he held. "We get a lot of boring copies here, but contracts are the worst."

Natua straightened. Narrowed her eyes at him. "Is that why you suggested making alterations?"

"No, of course not." Kaloe took a deep, calming breath. This woman, whomever she was, had a great love for leaping to conclusions. "Look, here." He pointed. "And there. No one uses those words except the printers of dictionaries."

"That doesn't matter," she protested. "So long as they are used correctly." This time it was *her* eyebrows that went up. "And were they?"

He hesitated, then reluctantly nodded. "Yes, I suppose."

"You suppose? You recommended changing the words and yet you can only *suppose* they were used correctly?" She couldn't believe her ears.

"Anyone who speaks Marroi, or at least, anyone who spoke it *fluently*, would have said the same thing," he retorted in a superior tone. "Your work loses something in translation."

Natua glared at him. "Any translator will tell you that it's not about using the most popular or even the most commonly understood word. It's about finding the most *precise* word. Especially with legal contracts." She nearly stood up to face the insolent young man towering over her. "Were you aware that this contract took over a month to draft? Eight lawyers spent hours hand-picking words, but you know best?"

"Dear me. What's this?" Having just returned, Gusari interrupted the heated discussion with some interest. "Tetsu, are you causing trouble again?"

"Supervisor. Forgive me." Natua leaned back in her chair, trying to project a nonchalance that she definitely did not feel. Something about the way Gusari was eyeing Tetsu reminded her of a predator toying with its prey. "I shouldn't have interrupted one of the scribes without discussing it with you first. Of course, we have a great many things to discuss."

Picking up her list of suggestions, she gestured to Tetsu and followed Gusari over to his desk.

Interpreting the flick of her hand as a dismissal, Kaloe shrugged and returned to his seat on the crowded bench.

"What happened?" hissed one of the younger scribes.

Kaloe reproved him with a look. Everyone knew they didn't discuss important things where Gusari might overhear them. Not even when he appeared to be completely focused on his discussion with the translator.

"Let's finish this job," an older scribe advised mildly. "I'm getting hungry."

Little was said on the copy floor until the last sheet of the training manual was hung to dry.

Natua, who was accustomed to a much earlier lunch, noticed with some relief when the scribes began reaching for their lunch pails. After listening to Gusari systematically explain why none of the ideas she'd prepared would work, she needed a break badly.

Gusari noticed, too, and grumbled something under his breath. "Excuse me." Setting aside what they'd been working on, he got to his feet. Fists on his hips, he glowered at the scribes. "You're half an hour late to lunch, eh? Well, we've still a schedule to keep. Work to complete. Those that take more than half an hour for lunch and come back late will have their pay docked."

Natua opened her mouth to speak, then closed it. Pyr's reports of bad morale and even some of Gusari's complaints about the behavior of the scribes suddenly began to make a great deal of sense to her.

"I hate to do it," Gusari told her as he retook his seat. "Unfortunately, this lot will take advantage of any generosity they are shown."

"Some people are like that." She slowly drew a line through one of her suggestions that Gusari had flatly refused to consider, then set the pencil aside. "As that is the case, we should hurry. This doesn't give us much time to chew."

She deliberately included him in his edict, then watched for his reaction.

Gusari responded smoothly, "Ah, that was for the scribes. As much as I would like to remain and oversee things, well. I have a meeting scheduled that I simply cannot postpone. One of our larger, and terribly busy, clients has been gracious enough to consent to discuss business with me over lunch…" He shrugged eloquently, the very picture of a man trapped by circumstance.

"I see." At least, she thought she was beginning to. "Perhaps I should go with you." Smiling blandly, she got to her feet as well. "I can't help improve things at the copy center unless I understand how it all works."

"An excellent idea." Gusari mopped at his face with an ever-present handkerchief. "But for one thing. As necessary as this lunch is, I have had to postpone it because there was no one of authority available to remain at the copy center." His eyebrows rose fractionally, urging her to take his hint.

Her plans took a sudden shift. So far, none of her proposals had made it off the paper. Perhaps she'd make more progress if she stopped making suggestions and started taking them. Which would be much easier if Gusari was conveniently gone for…

"I guess I can try to keep things going." Natua clasped her hands at waist level and tried for a dubious expression. "How long will you be, um," she half-laughed, "in your meeting?"

Gusari chuckled with her. "I will try to hurry back, but this is a very important client. We have many details to agree upon. An hour, possibly even two, may not be enough."

"Oh, dear." She let her gaze stray to her own lunch pail. "I mustn't detain you any longer."

Gusari muttered something polite and vanished again.

It was all she could do not to laugh once the door had swung shut behind him. She'd been underestimated before, several times in fact, but this was ridiculous.

Gathering her lunch pail, she followed the last straggling scribe out the back exit. And stopped in surprise.

It wasn't pretty, but somehow she felt lighter just stepping out of the drab copy center and into the sun. A rather scraggly looking tree and a handful of shoulder-height spiny succulents added a refreshing green to the walled-in patch of ground where the scribes were scattered, eating and talking quietly.

There wasn't anywhere to sit, really. Some knelt while others squatted, leaning their backs against the short wall that separated them from the rest of the world. With or without intending to, they had formed into tight groups.

She shivered, her hopes of pleasant, useful conversation evaporating like water spilled on hot marble. Those that weren't ignoring her were sending dirty glances in her general direction.

Making a mental note not to be quite so hard on Mirko's secretary, Korrez, the next time he showed up in the breakroom, Natua briefly debated retreating to her desk.

Of course, that would only make things worse in the long run. A leader who turned tail at the first sign of difficulty was no leader at all.

So, as gracefully as she could, Natua picked a semi-shady spot and lowered herself to the ground. The loose trousers of the Marroi palantzia made the maneuver easier and, copying the local style, she bent her knees, then bringing her feet in. Lunch pail balanced nicely on her crossed ankles, she lifted the lid.

"Oh, dear." Her stomach curled into a whimpering knot at the sight of a thick, salt-cured meat sandwich. Usually, she was able to nibble her way through the heavy lunches her mother packed for her. Usually, she ate lunch in the semi-cool break room of the larger building; not outside in the early afternoon heat.

Sadly, Natua lifted out a rather wilted-looking handful of carrot sticks. The protective layer of paper crackled as she peeled it away, yet she could tell her mother had tried dampening it to keep the carrots fresh longer.

Despite careful chewing, the carrots turned into lumps lined up in her throat like carts waiting to make deliveries. No amount of sipped or gulped water improved the situation, so that she was still suffering when the next bell rang.

Sighing, she closed her lunch pail and got to her feet, which turned out to be a much more awkward process.

No one else moved.

Unaccustomed to being anyone's direct leader, she took her time dusting herself off while she tried to figure out what to say to bring them back to work.

"Gusari makes the rules at the copy center right now." Though most of the scribes ignored her, she managed to look a few of them in the eye. "Returning late from lunch will not change the rule. It will only change the amount of compensation you receive for your work today."

That went well. She sarcastically congratulated herself as she walked back to her desk. And what, exactly, had she meant by 'right now'? Gusari was about as likely to be removed from power here as the sand outside was to turn into gold dust.

Irritated, she took a moment to stretch her shoulders. She froze at the sound of rustling behind her. Sneaking a look over one shoulder as she changed positions, she spotted Kaloe watching her from partway into the room.

"What are you doing?" he asked boldly.

"Stretching." Turning to face him, she put one elbow in the opposite hand and demonstrated a simple maneuver. "My shoulders get tight."

"And this helps?" He grimaced as he duplicated her motions.

"If it hurts, you're probably pushing too hard," she suggested.

"Oh." He eased off and nodded. "Better."

"I have to do it every day, but yes, it helps." She held the stretch as the door to the courtyard opened and more scribes filed in. Looking from them to the stack of translations she'd already reviewed, she frowned thoughtfully. Surely the rest of the translations could wait—if she could find something better to do. "Is there a senior scribe among you?"

The group parted to reveal an older man watching her, arms folded across his chest.

"What is your name, sir?" Natua observed the surprise that rippled through the others, but couldn't decide what caused it.

"Bariux."

"Will you join me, please, Bariux?" She gestured at the chair Gusari had been using. "I have some questions for you."

Seating herself, she took a quick peek at her abbreviated list of scribes with discipline problems and confirmed that Bariux wasn't on it.

"Gusari will not be happy to find me away from my copies." Bariux spoke from where he'd stopped beside her desk, his tone turning the statement into a rebuke.

"I'll take full responsibility," she promised without hesitation.

Bariux's face remained stony, but he lowered himself into the chair across from her.

For the next several minutes, she quizzed him on copy center procedure. How long had he worked there? How were copies usually assigned? Did all the scribes work on the same project until it was completed? Who checked the copies for mistakes? How many mistakes could a copy have? Which projects took the longest, and why?

He only answered the first half of the last question.

Sensing when he'd reached the end of his cooperativeness, she dismissed him and sat back to think. Though Bariux answered her questions only grudgingly, she'd learned more from him in ten minutes than she had in hours from Gusari.

Their last assignment completed before lunch, the

scribes moved directly to the next oldest assignment. It needed only twenty copies, five pages each, and no one could work on anything else until it was finished. The most interesting point to Natua was that this project needed to be copied in Tariek, one of the hardest languages on the entire planet of Jatorri. The alphabet consisted of twenty-three letters, five of which changed their written form depending on the tense and gender of the word being written. Without context to guide a scribe, mistakes would surely abound.

Going over to where the assignments sat in a neat stack, Natua began comparing their due dates. Upon finding a document that was due the next day buried five files down, she made up her mind. If Gusari didn't like what she was about to do, he could just stick around the copy center for a change going forward.

Facing the scribes, she clapped her hands to get their attention.

"Will those who are fluent in Tariek please stand?" Predictably, none of them moved. "Very well. Let me see the page you are copying." She pointed at the nearest scribe, who looked not at Bariux but at *Kaloe*. Why? "Now."

It came out sharper than she'd intended, but it had the desired effect. The lad hopped to his feet and brought her his work.

Accepting it, Natua was dismayed at what she saw. The letters specific to Tariek were carefully formed yet sloppily spaced, a clear indication of his unfamiliarity with the language. And while there were only two mistakes in the three lines, it had obviously taken him the entire time since coming back from lunch to complete those three lines.

Retaining the paper, she instructed, "Everyone with five lines or less copied, bring your pages to my desk."

There was an immediate uproar amongst the scribes, protests in various forms and at different volumes.

"Stop it!" She folded her arms across her chest, determined to win the point. "Gusari has left me in charge. We're going to try something new, that's all."

"What shall the rest of us do?" Kaloe's voice cut through the following silence.

"Continue copying your current assignment, please." Relieved and pleasantly surprised by a question she could answer—and not a little by the source—Natua gave him an approving nod.

Kaloe nodded back and dipped his steel quill in the inkwell. Ignoring the other scribes as they exchanged uncertain glances, he resumed his work as calmly as though nothing unusual had happened.

Slowly, several of the scribes picked up their copies and brought them to her desk. Each was as bad as the first she'd looked at; some were worse. Asking them to continue making copies in Tariek was clearly a waste of time.

"Alright, everyone." She handed their papers back. "Return to your seats and write 'I work at Itzuli Communications as a scribe.' at the bottom of these pages in Marroi."

"We can't do that!" One of them burst out indignantly. "Supervisor Gusari will dock us for the cost of the spoiled copy pages!"

Several of them nodded and murmured their agreement.

"I'll take responsibility." That was the second time she'd said that in less than half an hour. Goodness, what was she getting herself into? Whatever it was, she'd better have it well underway before Gusari got back. "Hurry. And bring them to me when you've finished."

Thankfully, the results were exactly what she'd hoped for. "You all write excellent hands in Marroi," she approved, smiling at them. In response, they shuffled their feet and refused to look at her. Odd.

Chapter 4

In short order, and with only mild resistance from the scribes, Natua changed the seating arrangements so that the newly formed group was able to share writing space. And the original document.

"This is your assignment." She handed them the file she'd selected.

"Two hundred copies?" They all gaped at the instructions on the outer jacket. "By tomorrow?"

"We'll never make it," muttered one of them.

"Gusari will take the refund out of our pay." Another hung his head.

"Listen to me." She folded her arms again, hoping it gave her an air of authority. "I want you to do your best work on this assignment." Tapping the pile of blank pages for emphasis she continued, "No mistakes. If we can use every page you copy, Gusari will not have the chance to dock your pay."

Resisting the urge to make another promise, she pivoted and walked away. What next? Was she going to offer to pay the scribes—out of her own pocket—to work overtime to complete the project before tomorrow?

Finding herself at another table, she picked up a completed sheet and read it, searching for grammatical and spelling errors.

"Good," she announced aloud, then moved on to check the work of another scribe. Some were faster than others, naturally, but that didn't matter. So long as the copy was correct and legible, she said nothing. Instinctively she realized she could only push her 'borrowed' authority so far, especially given that Gusari hadn't approved a single thing she was doing.

Kaloe had a sheet waiting for her when she reached his bench. Careful not to smudge the drying ink, Natua scanned quickly over the contents. By now she was familiar with the text of this page and recognized his work as among the best she'd seen.

"How long have you been at Itzuli Communications?" She'd asked this question a few times and had noticed a pattern. The sloppiest work didn't come from the youngest scribes, or even those on Gusari's list of so-called 'trouble-makers,' but rather those who'd worked there for the shortest length of time.

Take Bariux's page for example. Despite his advanced years, he had only six months of experience at the company. And while he wrote quickly in Tariek, his handwriting was terrible. Out of respect for his age, she'd reassigned him to the other task as quietly as possible, citing the urgency of completing it on time.

"Three years." Each of them worse than the last as far as working conditions went, though he kept that to himself.

"Keep up the good work." Looking around at the slowly growing stacks of completed pages, Natua knew that it was still highly unlikely that they would finish in time.

Frowning, she returned to the stack of assignments and sorted it, first by due date, then by the size of the completed job. Belatedly remembering that not all of the scribes could contribute equally, she went back through it and separated out the most difficult languages. Time would tell if the scribes copying the Tariek document were also the best at Muyin, Oik, and Yunim, but it was a start.

Finally satisfied, she put the reorganized stack away and checked the time. Nearly two hours after lunch and Gusari had yet to grace them with his presence. Should she be relieved or concerned?

Stifling a laugh at the whole situation, she took the logical next step. Rolling up her sleeves to keep from getting ink on them, Natua checked on the progress of the Tariek translation.

"You two." She indicated the two slowest scribes. "Finish the copy you're making, then start on the next project."

"And what will you do?" Kaloe spoke without looking up. He'd kept a discreet eye on her the whole time, wondering what she was up to with all her examining and rearranging. Gusari never lifted a finger unless it was to steal from their wages.

"My job." Seating herself across from him, she made sure to speak clearly for the others that were surely listening in. "We're halfway done with this project. It's also nearly time to go home."

Kaloe and the others watched in astonishment as she arranged blank paper and a pot of ink, selected a steel quill and burnished dried ink from its tip.

Catching himself still staring after she was well into the first paragraph, Kaloe cleared his throat and got back to work. The faint rustling noises that came from around him reassured him that some of his peers were also distracted—shocked might be the better word—by her actions.

Over the next hour, he kept stealing glances at her. At her work, that is. She took such care in forming her letters that he almost regretted needling her about her handwriting earlier. He'd known immediately from the document markings that the contract she questioned him about was her own translation and thought it the perfect opportunity to exact a mild revenge for the extra hour he'd spent helping his aunt the night before.

Kaloe's inner reflection was interrupted by the scribe sitting next to Natua. Tryun, one of Gusari's favorites, had an odd gleam in his eye when he reached for something. A blotter? A…

"Oh, no! Ah, I am so clumsy. So stupid!" Tryun's hands waved in dramatic apology as the ink from Natua's pot spilled across the table, ruining everything it touched.

On his feet in an instant, Kaloe dropped an old rag on the leading edge of the ink.

Natua reacted just as quickly, trying to snatch up the pages she'd laid out to dry without crumpling them.

Several of the scribes, alerted to the accident by the commotion, groaned when they saw ink dripping from the blackened sheets in her hands.

"I suppose we could trim them. Remove the edges and, um." Tryun reached for the papers and withdrew his intent almost in the same thought. "No, I suppose not." He tsked softly, then clapped his hands when the last bell rang. "I must go. My wife's mother is joining us for supper and I cannot miss a moment."

Disbelief coursed through Natua as she watched him collect his things, then whistle his way out the door. Crushing the ruined pages into the smallest ball she could, she dropped it into the nearest trash can.

Which left her staring at her soiled hands. What could she do but laugh? Well, and clean up the rest of the spilled ink. The table, already stained by who knew how many such happenings, was thankfully no worse for wear.

"Here." Kaloe, ignoring the others as they tidied up and drifted away, opened a bottle of ink remover. "This will help."

"Thank you." Natua held out her hand, expecting him to pour a little of it into her palm. Much to her surprise, cool fingers enfolded hers. "I can do it," she protested, trying to pull away.

"Hold still." Kaloe first rubbed the remover in, then wiped it off with a rag that had a few clean spots left. Above the perpetual odors of sweat, dust, and ink, he caught the faintest hint of flowers. Not the blooms of succulents he'd grown up with, but something lighter. More elusive. Distracting. "This way is more effective," he explained somewhat tardily.

"Oh?" She studied his face until she was satisfied that he spoke—and acted—in earnest.

He stopped scrubbing when she twitched violently. "Did that hurt?"

"I'm fine." Stealing her hand back, she reached for the bottle, but he was faster. Worse still, he captured her other hand! It was almost as if he'd somehow planned it.

"No, you aren't. You flinched." He made short work of her second hand, which only had the usual ink marks on the fingertips. "You should stretch your hands, too. Not just your shoulders."

"Yes, I'll, um." She flexed her fingers, then shook them out. "I'll do that." Retaking her seat, she told herself that the goosebumps on her arms were nothing more than an extension of her flinch.

Kaloe certainly had strong fingers. Well, that was only natural, she told herself as she began shuffling through the dry pages of copy to see how many more were needed. After all, scribes depended on their fingers for a living.

"What are you doing?" Kaloe, one hand wrapped in the strap of his lunch pail, observed her curiously.

"What else?" Her count completed, she glumly examined the ruined cuff on her second favorite shirt. Tomorrow she would wear another long sleeve shirt to cover the ink on her forearm; easily hidden, there was no point wasting the remover on it. "For my plan to work, this job has to be finished today."

"Plan? You have a plan?" Curious, Kaloe sat down again to be at eye level with her.

"To get the next job out on time." She quirked a smile at him, amused by his half-surprised, half-disappointed expression. "I just got here," she reminded, reaching for a quill. "And I have a lot to learn about the copy center. But some things are obvious."

He chuckled despite himself. Already he'd almost forgotten last night's misunderstanding. Besides, this was more important—a chance to help keep Gusari's hands out of their pockets for once. They were only a few copies away from completing the Tariek file. It shouldn't take long. His mind made up, he set his lunch pail aside.

"You needn't stay." Natua objected quickly when she saw him shuffling things around at his workstation.

He didn't respond, so she warned, "You won't be paid for this."

"Will you?" he demanded.

"That's not the point," she insisted.

He simply indicated the open ceiling panels. "We better hurry. Once the sun moves past the seventh evening hour, it gets hard to see in here."

Natua frowned even as she dipped her quill. "You know this from experience?"

Kaloe snorted. "Let's just say that working late without pay isn't a new experience for me." He did a double-take when she got to her feet. "Where are you going?"

"To find a runner." She folded the note to her mother so the address remained clearly visible. "You should let your wife know you'll be late tonight."

"My wife?" They stared at each other, then he burst out laughing. "I'm not married."

"Oh." Her cheeks burning, Natua scrambled to understand. If not his wife, then with whom had he been quarreling last night? His girlfriend? Or…oh, dear. Could that have been his sister? Well, whomever the young woman had been, Natua felt she'd made an understandable mistake. Both Kaloe and the young woman were of marriageable age.

"Never mind." Still chuckling, he took the note from her. "I know where to find a lad who will deliver this for you."

"Oh," she repeated. Then, "Wait!" Rushing after him—Goodness he walked quickly! Or was it just that he had longer legs?—she pressed some money into his palm. "He'll want compensation."

Kaloe hesitated a moment, jingling the coins. "It's too much, you know. You'll spoil him."

"There are two prices for everything." She shrugged and headed back to her workstation. "One for locals, and one for foreigners." She didn't like it, but she'd accepted it.

He cleared his throat, wishing he could deny it. Yet

how many times had he charged a foreigner extra at his aunt's stall because of their fancy clothes and haughty mannerisms?

"I won't be gone long." It was an easy task to find and arrange both the delivery of the note and a word to his own mother with one of the boys that hung around the marketplace. Then Kaloe hurried back, returning before she'd gotten the first page done.

They settled in to work then, the only sound between them the scratching of quill on paper. An hour later, Natua rose to stretch her back and he awkwardly followed suit.

Natua went through the motions more slowly than she usually did, to give him time to see what she was doing and position himself. Adding hourly stretches to the copy center routine might not make them work more efficiently, but his pained grunts and grimaces made her determined to try it anyway.

At the end of another hour, Kaloe wiped his quill and covered the ink pot. "Done." He grinned a little when she mimicked his finger wiggles. "Feeling alright?" He tried to take her hands again, intending to show her another technique, but she dodged his grasp. Moving quickly, he took advantage of her turned back to hastily slide two copies of the translation into a special hiding spot, just in case.

"Fine, thank you." She hurried to her desk to fetch her lunch pail. Bumping it clumsily, she jostled the lid open. "Ew." The meat sandwich was much worse for having sat in a warm, closed container for the rest of the afternoon.

"You eat that stuff?" Kaloe, who'd tagged along once the documents were secure, wrinkled his nose when he caught a rancid whiff.

Startled by his statement, she pushed the lid firmly into place. "Not when it smells like *that*."

"You ate some of it at lunch, though?" Mentioning lunch made his stomach rumble. "Sorry." He grinned boyishly. "Lunch was so long ago my stomach has forgotten about it, I guess."

Her stomach took matters in its own hands, agreeing noisily. Wrapping an arm around her middle, Natua groaned inwardly. His reaction was so matter-of-fact, though, that she didn't stay embarrassed long.

His grin grew broader and he gestured toward the door. "Come on. I know where to find some real food."

"I have to go home." She started to explain why she couldn't, then second-guessed herself. Going straight home guaranteed her a hot, heavy meal. Unless she'd already eaten? "So, I...couldn't stay long."

The food was delicious. Seasoned meat, ground and roasted, served with cool, crisp vegetables. A cup of lightly sweetened goat cheese curd, topped with tart fruit, completed the meal.

They argued briefly over who should pay for it, until she reminded him, "We both would've eaten hours ago if I hadn't decided to keep working." With that, she handed the proprietor enough money to cover both of their meals.

"And because I volunteered to stay, you're responsible?" Kaloe snorted his disdain for the idea, but dropped the matter of money. "You're sure you don't want some more food?" He eyed her trim waist curiously, wondering where she had put it all. Most kanpotarrak ate only a few bites of this or that, exclaimed about the powerful flavors, and asked for what was left to be wrapped so they could finish it later.

"Mmm, no." Natua sighed in heartfelt satisfaction. "I am so full I'm afraid I will pop!"

He burst out laughing and after a startled moment, she joined him. At least, as much as she dared. She wasn't kidding about having stuffed herself. Thankfully, Kaloe, growing young man that he was, had matched her bite for bite, so she didn't feel quite as gluttonous as she might've. He'd nearly outdone her when it came to the dessert.

"I hope I haven't kept you out too late." He wiped

his fingers one last time on the napkin, then rose to help her up from the floor cushion where she sat. "Oh!" He caught her by the elbows and supported her when she stumbled. Her hair brushed his chin and again he inhaled the subtle scent of flowers. "Are you alright?"

"I'm sorry." Embarrassed, Natua stamped her numb foot, then shook it. "I'm not used to sitting with my legs bent that way. I think my foot fell asleep."

"Let's take it for a walk." Placing both of her hands on his left arm, he invited, "You can lean on me until it wakes up."

She tried to brush his suggestion off, but found herself using him for support as they moved onto the street.

"I suppose you live in the foreign quarter?" He shrugged at her surprised expression. "Lucky guess. Now, your foot won't care which direction we're walking. However, the moons are rising and I don't want your mother worrying about you."

"That's very thoughtful of you." Seeing her lunch pail dangling beside his in his 'free' hand, she allowed him to lead her along. "Do you worry about everyone's mother?" Though she meant it as a tease, she noticed a slight sobering of his countenance.

"A little bit," he admitted. "My father died years ago. So, for a long time it has been just my mom and me."

"You worry about her." A feeling of kinship sparked within her. She, too, worried about her mother. Guilt poked her and Natua sighed softly. It was harder sometimes than others, like when they disagreed about how things should be done. Which they often did.

Oblivious to her thoughts, Kaloe lifted one shoulder. "Mostly I try not to make *her* worry about *me*."

"Does it work?" Natua bit her lip, regretting the question as soon as she'd asked it. Kaloe, *this* Kaloe, the laughing young man who spoke so gently of his mother, was nothing like the man she thought she'd encountered last night. He was kind and easy to talk with. Too easy, or she never would've voiced that thought.

"I like to think so." He blew out a breath. What was he doing, discussing his family with this…this boss? Bosses were best kept at a distance and he needed to remember that. He didn't know her and he didn't want to know her. Good thing they were already at the main turnoff into the foreign quarter. "Ah. There, see? You're almost home. How's your foot?"

"My foot?" She released his arm abruptly, shocked to find that she'd continued holding onto it even after the pins and needles tormenting her foot had stopped. What was she trying to do, give him the wrong idea? "Yes. Yes, thank you."

"Good. See you tomorrow." He turned to walk away.

"Yes." She closed her eyes briefly, annoyed that she was parroting herself, and not for the first time that day. "Wait! My pail."

"Hmm." He held it out, twitching his nose as if he could smell it despite the lid. "Don't put that where the gezi can get at it. It might make them sick."

"Oh." She huffed and marched off, equally amused and irritated by his mocking. When she reached her gate, she peeked back down the street. He was long gone, of course.

"Natua?" Her mother's strident voice came out of the tiny, shadowed courtyard. "Is that you?"

"Yes." Seriously, that word again? Natua cleared her throat and opened the gate. "I'm sorry I had to work late, Mother. An important…" She stopped when a lantern was uncovered, flooding the small enclosure with light. "You have guests."

"Isn't it nice?" Kume beamed at her daughter. "These are the Deits. They moved into the house down the street just this morning."

Chapter 5

Natua shook hands with each of them—a couple and their son—as her mother performed the introductions, hoping against hope that no one would notice her mangled right sleeve.

"It's a pleasure to finally meet you." Arru Deits' red hair, more brilliant even than his mother's flaming locks, didn't move as he bowed over her hand with all the formality of a visit to court. His eyes seemed to twinkle as he straightened. "Your mother has been telling us all about your important job."

Did the twinkle in his eyes mean that he had spotted the jagged edge where her cuff should be? Or was the dim light playing tricks on her eyes? Even with the lantern uncovered, most of the illumination in the courtyard seemed to be coming from some of the nearer stars.

"Yes, she tells us you work for a communication company." Mesym Deits smiled prettily at her. She, like her husband, stood near the lamp, and there was no question of the measuring way she was studying Natua.

Heavens, were all mothers alike? She'd barely shaken hands with this woman's precious son. Surely matrimony was months away, if on the horizon at all!

"Itzuli Communications," Natua supplied. Hoping to divert the two mothers from their probable speculations, she added smoothly, "I would've been home sooner except that I'm assisting in the copy center at present."

"You work in the copy center?" Arru stopped running a finger around his blasted starched collar and stuffed both of his hands in his pockets instead. "Not as a head translator?"

"I am a head translator." Natua, who wanted nothing more than to tumble up the stairs and go to sleep, somehow managed a smile. There was no point in embarrassing her mother, after all, who must've told them that. "However, at Itzuli Communications we have our own copy center as well."

Odiar Diets grunted and announced in his deep voice, "An unnecessary added financial burden. You should consider cutting it loose and hiring out your copies."

Natua jumped on the topic. "You have experience with copy centers, sir?"

"Over the years, I've gained a little experience on a lot of topics." Odiar stroked his graying mustache. "Copy centers always have a way of taking more than they give."

"You're speaking, I trust, of well-managed copy centers? With adequate staff and training?" Natua sensed more than saw her mother's disapproving frown. No doubt she would prefer that Natua stick to lighter topics during a first meeting. Well. That suited her. She was exhausted and just wanted to go to bed anyway. "Oh, but you must excuse my bad manners. One shouldn't talk business at a party."

"Natua." Kume's hand closed over her daughter's wrist, simultaneously discovering the butchered sleeve and jostling the lid off the lunch pail. "What in the…"

Natua hastily shoved the lid back into place. "I have an early morning tomorrow, Mother. So I'll just say goodnight." Planting a peck on her mother's check, she fled inside. Dumping her leftovers in the glass compost bin outside the rear door, she shut it firmly against gezis, and raced up the stairs to her room.

Rising with the sun the next morning, she bathed and dressed as quietly as possible, then left a carefully-prepared note on the table in the kitchen where her mother would be sure to see it.

The one thing she absolutely didn't expect to have happen occurred when a small cycle carriage slowed to a stop at the end of her walk. In deference to the slightly cooler morning temperatures, the canopy was folded back, allowing her to see inside—and the passenger to see out—far too easily.

"Miss Prezio." Arru Diets rose partway and bowed, every hair remaining neatly in place. "Are we perchance going the same direction this morning?"

Her heart sank as she realized that they probably were. Koroa had grown up around the palace in distinct sections—dwellings on one side of the marketplace, businesses on the other. Unwilling to dissemble, she forced a smile and tried to deflect the question with, "That depends entirely upon where you are heading."

"I've an appointment at the palace this morning and mustn't be late." He smiled as he settled back into his seat. "I'm sure we have time to make both stops."

Natua saw the grimace she didn't dare make reflected on the cyclist's face. Before she could think of a way to gracefully decline, however, Arru reached over and opened the door on her side.

"Thank you. I'm going to Itzuli Communications," she told the cyclist as she boarded. From the corner of her eye, she saw movement in the upstairs' window of her house. It was empty when she turned to look at it, yet the curtain was still wobbling, as if hastily dropped.

"I trust you slept well." In the bright morning light, there was no question as to the twinkle in his eye.

"Yes, quite well." She felt her cheeks pink a bit at the reminder of how abruptly she'd ducked out of last night's impromptu visit. "And you?"

"Wretchedly, I'm afraid." He gripped the side of the carriage as they rounded a corner. "I have a great deal more empathy for dried fruits after trying to sleep in that oven we've rented."

Surprised, she might've laughed if she hadn't noticed the cyclist signaling for yet another turn. "Cyclist!" Natua called out in Marroi the instant she realized what he was doing. "You'll get no extra pay for taking the long route this morning."

The man grunted and swung the carriage onto its original route.

"That was interesting." Arru's green eyes studied her keenly.

Oh, bother. He did *look* interested, and not just in learning what she'd said.

"Carriages have a way of meandering about the city," she explained quietly. "The cyclist will try to charge extra, claiming that the roads were blocked or some such excuse."

"I see." Arru smiled without giving the impression of amusement. "That's good information, thank you."

"Of course."

"Are they all like that?" He gestured at the groups of people as they passed them.

It was easy to tell the universally black-haired Marroi apart from the tourists and foreign workers. Desert dwellers and the descendants of desert dwellers, Marroi skin tones ranged from the light brown color of roasted irridu nuts to the darker shades of highly polished ergmo ore.

Natua waved at a woman she recognized from the shop where she bought her clothes, then turned to frown at Arru.

"Are all Lurrakians paragons of virtue?" Cringing inwardly at how closely her tone resembled her mother's when she was on the cusp of a lecture, Natua tried again. "I will admit, sir, that I haven't traveled a great deal. Nevertheless, it has been my experience that people are as good or as bad as they choose to be, no matter where they were born."

Arru inclined his head, yielding the point. "Well said. I hope you will forgive my rudeness in asking such an ignorant question."

Offering a smile of truce, she nodded back. "Of course. As you mentioned, you are not well rested this morning."

He frowned slightly, then sighed. "Not a good beginning, I'm afraid. And I must be in top form this trip. My company is contracted to negotiate all the travel arrangements for the Lurrakian dignitaries who will attend the wedding."

"That's a great deal of weight to carry," she acknowledged, more than a little impressed. "It's well that you arrived early. Koroa will soon be flooded with wedding guests." Goodness, she hadn't even thought of that. Where would they all stay? Despite having the honor of being Marroi's capitol city, Koroa had few permanent residences aside from the foreign quarter. The traders came in waves, supplying a handful of local businesses, but eventually returning to their lives in the wide, open deserts or rugged mountains.

"Yes." He cast a thoughtful look in her direction. "I wonder if you can help me." The carriage slowed to a stop in front of Itzuli's main building and he leaned toward her earnestly. "If the ride saved you any time at all, spare me a moment more, please."

Eager to make her getaway, and to see how things were going in the copy center, Natua remained where she was. The ride had saved her several minutes, in fact. Though the favor was unsought for, she could at least hear him out.

"I'm in great need of an interpreter," he began. "While I suppose there are many for hire here, I must insist upon better than tourist-quality. I have contracts to negotiate, cultural nuances to navigate, that sort of thing. All the better if the person I find is already familiar with Lurrakian customs." He paused, then finished, "Frankly, I can't think of a better person for the job than you. Would you be willing to take it on, please?"

Dumbfounded, Natua could only stare at him for a handful of heartbeats. "Even if my schedule permitted such an endeavor, you would find my language skills gravely lacking, sir." She rose abruptly and descended from the carriage. "I will consider my connections. If I think of anyone suitable for the job, I will surely recommend them."

Arru frowned, clearly unhappy with how the situation had turned out. "You're too kind." With a bow and a word to the cyclist, he was off.

"Who was that?" Natua choked back a yelp and glared at Pyr. Undaunted, the office messenger grinned cheekily up from his place at her elbow. "Have you got a new boyfriend?"

"Young man." He had addressed her in Lurrakian and she switched to Marroi for effect. "You march yourself right on inside and get to work."

He hooted a bit at her attempted severity, but obeyed. More or less. The soft sing-song that floated back over his shoulder as he went sounded remarkably like a childish taunt reserved for teasing those taking their first, awkward steps toward romance.

Groaning inwardly, Natua swept the incident aside and hurried toward the copy center. Entering via the open courtyard door this morning, she managed to slip in without Gusari noticing her.

Granted, he was so irate that he might not have noticed if she'd led an entire brass band in through the squeaky double doors on the other side of the building.

"Who did this?" He held aloft files taken from the assignment box beside him. "Who meddled with my system!"

System? Thinking back to the haphazard stack of files she'd organized the day before, Natua could only wonder what his shoe rack looked like.

"She did." One of the scribes pointed at Natua, outstretched arm and shoulders rigid.

Gusari's florid face paled when he saw her. "Head Translator."

"Supervisor." Natua stepped forward calmly. "I apologize for any disruption. If you have time this morning, I'd be happy to discuss your assignment system with you."

"I...I..." Gusari glared at the scribes that were still watching. "Get to work!" Pivoting with surprising agility for a man his size, he jiggled his way back to his desk.

Deciding to interpret that as an invitation, Natua

followed him. It was a good thing she'd arrived early. There was no telling what Gusari might've done otherwise.

Gusari dithered about a bit in seating himself, watching the scribes closely to make sure they were doing what he'd told them to. No more, no less.

Natua waited for him to start the conversation. When he reached for a quill instead, she spoke quickly.

"I never intended to disrupt your system, Supervisor." It got harder to call his setup a 'system' each time she had to say it. "Although I'm sure you will agree it is fortunate that I did."

He harrumphed and dipped his quill. Tapped it twice on the inkwell, then tossed it aside, scowling.

"Fortunate, you say? I put those assignments in that order for a reason!" He squirmed under the directness of her gaze—and the thought of finding a legitimate explanation for his, um, system.

"Which I will be only too happy to learn." Natua kept her arms hanging loosely at her sides despite the urge to fold them across her chest. There was no point in antagonizing the man, not when she might need to, um, *borrow* his authority again.

On the other hand, how could she back down? It was hardly good business to continue on as they had been, incurring fines and having to pay refunds to furious clients. Surely there was some way to make Gusari see the flaws in his 'system.'

From the corner of her eye, Natua saw a tall figure bend over something, then start toward her desk. Kaloe? What was he…?

"Head translator." Gusari frowned. "Are you listening?"

"I was just going to get my chair." She managed a bright smile to cover the surge of annoyance with herself. "One moment, please."

They spent most of the morning discussing the options until Gusari threw up his hands.

"Very well, very well. Have it your own way!"

Drumming his fingers on his desk, he barely disciplined a scowl. "I warned Mirko you would be trouble."

"What?" Natua couldn't believe her ears. "You told Manager Mirko that I…"

"A thousand pardons." Gusari jumped to his feet, pudgy hands flapping at the ends of his wrists as if to shoo away what had slipped past his lips. Bah, this woman! Meddling didn't begin to describe her! "What I meant to say is that I expressed certain…concerns to the manager. Yes." He nodded rapidly, making his flabby cheeks dance. "You are an expert translator, a gift to Itzuli Communications in your role. Yet here." He sighed and clasped his hands together at chest level. "We are besieged each day by work."

Natua took the time to consider her answer carefully. If she chose to be insulted by Gusari's stated perspective, sooner or later she would have to defend herself. Or, she could simply accept it as his opinion and get back to her assigned task of improving the copy center. Somehow and, apparently, without Gusari's help.

"I understand your concerns. Indeed, if our roles were reversed and you were assigned to assist with translations, I should be hard-pressed to find the merit in that plan." She got to her feet as well, smoothing her bata and straightening the gerri out of habit. "Since Manager Mirko has assigned us to work together, I am sure that, as professionals, we will find a way to do so."

Gusari smiled, but his eyes took on a less-than-friendly gleam.

"Let us try my system for the next two weeks," she continued smoothly. "If there are no fines or refunds to be paid out by then, we can consider that it is in fact a successful change in how things are done here at the copy center."

"Of course. As you say, it is Manager Mirko's wish that we work together." Gusari lowered his hands to his sides and hid his clenched fists in the flowing folds of his bata.

"Excellent." She bowed slightly. "With your permission, I will review some of the work being done." Before she could leave, one of the scribes approached Gusari's desk. It was none other than Tryun, the fellow who spilled the ink.

"What is it?" Gusari growled at him.

"It's this document, Supervisor." Tryun shot Natua a disdainful look and passed a stack of papers to Gusari. "The runner is here to pick up our deliveries and this'n ain't done."

"Not done?" Natua squinted at the package in Gusari's hands. "That can't be right. I personally…"

"You personally?" Gusari's eyebrows inched upward. "What?"

"She told us to move on to the next—"

Gusari flung up a hand, stopping Tryun's whine mid-sentence. "What is it that you personally did?"

This was not the time to back down, not after her hard-won victory with the 'system.' Lifting her chin, she answered, "I personally saw to it that the required number of copies were completed."

"Is that so?" Gusari fairly crowed, delighted to be the one to deliver the bad news. "How is it, then, that we are two copies short?" He shoved the papers at her.

Accepting them as gracefully as she could, Natua flipped through the stack, counting rapidly. Fifteen copies, sixteen, seventeen, eighteen. Only eighteen? There should be twenty. She started to turn toward Kaloe, intending to ask him to confirm that there were twenty copies when they left.

But he wasn't at his place at the copy table. He wasn't at the copy tables at all. Expanding her visual search, she looked toward the open store room door. And spotted something on her desk that didn't belong there.

"We all make mistakes, Head Translator." Gusari began to half-sooth, half-mock.

"One moment." Walking away in the middle of his

gloating, Natua strode over to her desk and picked up the two missing copies. It didn't make any sense, but she tucked them into the pile just as if she'd planned the whole thing. Setting the package on her desk, she folded the protective cover into place, then returned the whole thing to a slack-jawed Tryun. "Hurry," she prodded when he kept staring at her. "The runner is waiting."

Bowing to Gusari once more, she took herself off to the relative safety of the copy tables. Collecting the dried, completed copies, she checked for errors here and there, waiting for things to settle down. Slowly, she edged her way closer to Kaloe.

The 'missing' copies had to have come from him. When had he hidden them? And why?

Slanting a gaze at Tryun, she wondered uneasily if she didn't already know the why of it. Tryun had spilled the ink deliberately last night, that much she was sure of. If he'd found all twenty copies in the packet this morning, would two have still somehow gone missing? *Permanently* missing?

Natua was so absorbed in her thoughts that she almost didn't hear the bell when it rang.

"Sorry!" A younger translator, eager for lunch, apologized when he nearly knocked her over on his way past.

"Of course." She remembered with a twinge of her stomach that she hadn't packed a lunch, intending to eat at a food cart instead. Goodness, she'd better start looking for one. Did they have daily routes or wander the city at random? Pivoting toward the door, she walked right into—

"Translator." Kaloe caught Natua by one arm to steady her. If she'd been an inch taller, he would've taken the top of her head on his chin when she turned so suddenly. "You aren't hurrying out to eat another of those sand things, are you?"

Surprised, she chuckled. "You mean a sandwich? No, not today."

"Sand-wich." He repeated the odd word and fell in beside her. All night long he'd tried to decide if he trusted her. Even now, after how smoothly she'd handled Gusari and Tryun, he couldn't make up his mind.

"I'm afraid you've gotten the wrong impression about sandwiches." She paused at the gate of the small courtyard. The street was empty in both directions. Blast. "When they're freshly made, most of them are quite good."

"Ah, well." Kaloe suddenly realized she wasn't carrying her pail. They couldn't talk freely at work, there were far too many ears. However… "I'll, um, I'll have to try one sometime. Not today, though. I only have time for a quick food cart lunch today." Excellent. He had her full attention. "Thankfully, one of my mother's cousins runs a food cart not far from here." A casual nod to his left indicated the direction.

"Does this same cousin also own a restaurant?" Natua observed his elaborate shrug with mild amusement. Why was she so surprised?

"If she did, it would be the same good food I ate last night." He discreetly avoided coming right out and stating that they'd eaten together, for both of their sakes.

"That sounds like a recommendation to me. Perhaps you'd be willing to introduce a new customer?" She still wanted to ask him about the extra copies and this sounded like the perfect opportunity.

Chapter 6

Just over a week later, Gusari sat at his desk, glaring at the dwindling stack of assignments. He hadn't been able to pocket any extra—um, dock anyone's pay—for days! Some of his creditors were getting anxious. Their frequent visits made his wife anxious. She, in turn, made his life miserable. And it was all Head Translator Prezio's fault.

The woman was a magician! He had secretly rearranged the assignment box twice, with an eye to profiting from private, mmm, incentives offered to him for early delivery of certain projects, yet somehow Prezio went straight to the next one coming due each time. A handful of times he'd gleefully counted the number of copies produced, knowing they'd never be able to complete the task in the remaining time. At the last moment, Prezio had calmly produced the needed extra copies with the explanation that she'd taken them to proof them or some such rot.

In short, Gusari was growing weary of her. Yet in his last meeting with Manager Mirko, things hadn't gone so well. Oh, Mirko wanted her gone even more than he did, but held firmly to the point that the copy center needed to support itself.

She is gall in the water, Mirko growled. *However, even galled water tastes better when served in a golden cup.*

Gusari could still hear the tap of Mirko's long quill on the ledger that marked the copy center's first time in the black in far too long.

"Supervisor?" A faintly whiny voice at his elbow made him jump.

"What is it?" Gusari growled at Tryun, the scribe who acted as his eyes, ears. And, perhaps, hands? That was an interesting idea. Exactly how far could he trust Tryun? More importantly, how much would it cost to have the man sabotage a few projects? They would have to go beyond destroying a few copies here and there.

"Apologies for interrupting your contemplation, Supervisor." Tryun bowed and offered the paperwork he'd brought as an excuse to consult with Gusari during working hours. "Is everything well?"

"Everything is very definitely *not* well." Gusari snatched the papers from him, but his focus remained on the problem Head Translator Prezio presented.

"Ah, I am sorry to hear that." Tryun glanced surreptitiously around the room. "How can I help, Supervisor?"

The pages Gusari was rustling through stilled. "It sounds to me as if you already have an idea in mind."

Tryun sidled closer, but not too close. He walked a narrow ledge with his fellow scribes as it was. If he was seen to be openly friendly with Gusari, it would destroy his usefulness as a spy. Bending as if to examine something in the papers, he suggested slyly, "Dilute the ink."

A slow smile spread across Gusari's face as he considered the suggestion. "An interesting thought." Thrusting the papers at Tryun, Gusari dismissed him with a flick of his fingers. Leaning back in his chair, which squeaked loudly in protest, he knitted fingers together while he studied on Tryun's idea.

It was so simple it was almost brilliant. Better yet, it was so simple, he didn't need Tryun's help. Various solvents were stored in the supply closet on the shelf below the bottles of ink. A few moments of privacy would solve his problems. And best of all, Tryun had volunteered it. Free of charge.

As the day wore on, Natua noticed a worrisome change in Gusari. The better the copy center did, the more uncooperative he'd become. Today, however, he was positively affable when she approached him to ask about making another change.

"Now, let me see if I understand." Gusari leaned both forearms on his desk and frowned just enough to look thoughtful. "You want to tutor a few scribes so that their handwriting will improve." He paused until

Natua nodded. "Then, if that does improve efficiency, you would like to begin a rotation of tutoring in the more difficult languages."

"That's right." Natua stood her ground, waiting for him to give his answer. She'd already begun discreetly tutoring a few of them, having rearranged the seating so that she could watch those that struggled the most.

"I am concerned." Delighted was more like it. Between her idea and Tryun's, they would fall further behind than ever! "For the first time in many months we are almost on schedule. Manager Mirko will not be pleased if we resume our former tardiness." He expected her to hesitate, perhaps even to reconsider. Instead, he watched in amazement as her shoulders squared and her chin lifted. Was this woman afraid of nothing? Not even losing her livelihood? For that, he could almost envy her.

"I am prepared to take full responsibility for this experiment." Natua nearly shuddered at the hope that flickered in Gusari's eyes.

"How can I refuse such a generous offer?" Gusari gestured toward the scribes. "Please, proceed."

The uneasy feeling that Gusari expected her to fail rode on Natua's shoulders while she organized the four scribes she'd identified as needing the most help.

"This isn't fair," one of them muttered, tossing her shoulder-length hair. "We're needed to complete assignments on time!"

"You don't have to participate." Natua put it to them bluntly to save herself the hassle of fighting them every inch of the way. "Only know this." She looked each of them in the eyes as she spoke. "You were chosen for this training because you make so many mistakes that the copies you manage to complete are usually discarded." Shoulders stiffened and the eyes looking back at her hardened. "It was a choice between replacing you with more adept scribes—or helping *you* become more adept scribes. I have made my choice.

Now you must make yours."

It was just that simple. She handed out their assignments without another word, turned her back, and went about her routine of spot-checking the others.

Even as she scanned pages and hung them to dry, Natua kept an ear open in case one or all of the scribes-in-training decided to get up and leave. Bariux, the oldest of them, was the most likely to take umbrage and leave in her opinion. On the other hand, he wore a carved stone band on his hand and spoke of his family with pride. She was banking on his need to support that family to help him look past any vanity long enough to complete the short training.

"Translator." Kaloe cleared his throat and held up his freshly completed page. As she took his paper, he nodded toward the four scribes clustered in the far corner. "Is there a new assignment?" He hadn't encouraged her when she'd brought up the idea of singling out the worst scribes, but apparently she'd gone ahead and done it anyway.

Natua flicked a glance at the training group, then returned her attention to his copy. "Of a sort." Finding no errors in his work, she nodded briskly. "Good work, Tetsu. Keep it up."

Kaloe stifled a chuckle as she walked away. She'd begun calling him by his last name the third time they ended up eating lunch at the same food cart. She also used it when they coincidentally walked the same way at the same time after work. They might be off the clock, but she seemed determined to keep them firmly fixed in their professional positions. And that was alright with him.

"Kaloe." The older woman sitting across from him kicked him gently. "Get back to work."

Natua took her seat and exhaled slowly. Before she'd gone to speak with Gusari, she'd whittled down the stack of translations he still expected her to review. The few remaining were either in the simplest languages or translated by the best of the best. Some were both. None actually needed proofreading.

Rearranging her desk so that a casual observer would think she was working hard to complete the stack before the end of the day, she laid out the pages of the current project that she'd quietly collected during her rounds just now. Though she was firmly convinced that her experiment would be effective in the long run, she had no intention of letting efficiency suffer in the meantime.

Picking up a quill, she set to work. Time flew by more swiftly than she could write, and it was with some dismay that she heard the last bell of the day begin to ring.

Kaloe rose with the others and smiled at the soft chatter that went on around him. It was a pleasant change from the surly silence he'd grown accustomed to during his years there; and in such a short time. He didn't allow himself to dwell on the question of how long it would last after Prezio went back to her work as a translator.

"Kaloe. You coming?" A younger scribe stood in the doorway, eagerly tossing a ball back and forth between his hands. A fast game of pilota would work out the kinks that came with spending a day hunched over, pushing papers around. "My cousin said you could borrow his dragon."

"Can't." Kaloe shook his head a bit sadly. "I have to help my aunt."

"Again? I thought you said your uncle was better!" The lad let the ball run down his bicep and popped it from his inner elbow to his other hand.

"It's been five weeks. How long does it take a broken bone to heal?" Another scribe interjected as he passed, without actually stopping to hear the answer.

"He's well enough to sit at the stall with my aunt now." Kaloe shrugged. "But one misstep and he's back in bed."

"Hey, c'mon!"

"Let's go!"

"Sorry, Kaloe." The ball handler looked over his shoulder at the voices calling him from outside. "Alright, alright!"

Kaloe was just about to hurry off himself when he glanced over his shoulder and saw that the translator was still at her desk. And…Gusari was still at his? When was the last time *that* had happened?

His gut twisted into a knot, warning him that something was decidedly wrong. *Always trust your senses, son.* His father's voice echoed in his mind as he made his way over to the translator's desk.

"It's time to go," he told her without preamble. He couldn't think of a way to stop Gusari from doing whatever he had planned, but the thought of leaving Natua alone with him made Kaloe's skin crawl.

"What?" Natua blinked at him. She'd estimated how many copies they would run short based on the productivity of the scribes she'd placed in training earlier and, a bit overconfidently, set herself the task of making sure they were completed. "Oh. Not yet. I have to…" She stopped talking when his hand settled lightly on hers.

"Translator. It's time to go."

Easing her hand out from under his, Natua angled her gaze in the direction that Kaloe *wasn't* looking. A cold chill crept up her spine when she saw Gusari's face. She'd never seen him look so happy.

"I think you're right." Swiftly, she tidied her desk, including stashing the copies she'd made. She still wasn't sure where Kaloe hid things, but she'd quickly learned to follow his example. When she didn't, they had a way of vanishing overnight.

Kaloe waited impatiently, unwilling to leave her alone with Gusari. Somehow, warning her just wasn't enough. His protective instincts aroused, he even went so far as to silently insist that she precede him out of the building.

Natua's heart warred with her mind as she led the

way out of the building, but she didn't say a word until they were safely outside of the courtyard.

"What's going on?" she hissed, pulling him over to stand beside the nearest building.

"I don't know." Kaloe shot a grim look back at the copy center. If Gusari was up to something—and he was, as sure as Jatorri had two moons—he'd be watching the door they'd just left through. Likewise, it would be impossible to sneak in via the squeaky double doors. Which only left him one option. "Wait here."

"What?" Before she could stop him, Kaloe was gone, dashing across the narrow road and hopping onto the short wall that surrounded the courtyard. She watched in disbelief as he ran along the wall, then leapt at the last moment, catching the edge of the roof with his fingertips. *What was he doing?*

In an instant, he had pulled himself up and vanished.

Natua stared at the spot where she'd last seen him, willing him to reappear. This was ridiculous. They could've just waited for Gusari to leave and then gone back into the building. Honestly, was Kaloe crazy? Or did he just want to show off? The effortless way he had pulled himself up onto the roof *was* rather impressive. He must be very strong. And yet he'd been so gentle in his support of her the night her foot fell asleep.

She gave herself a firm shake and sternly redirected her thoughts. This was about work. It might be naïve of her to think that one should give their best efforts to whatever job they took, but it was becoming increasingly clear that Gusari did not have the best interests of the company at heart.

Which raised the question of why he still worked there. Did Mirko simply lack hard evidence that Gusari was the copy center's primary hindrance? And, with enough evidence, could she go to Mirko and ask to have Gusari replaced? And…what would she do if Mirko refused her request?

A horrid squeak rent the silence, followed by a softer squeak and the slam of a door. Gusari! He must've left via the double doors!

She looked to the rooftop and was startled to see Kaloe emerge at the peak instead of the lower corner where he'd ascended. Her lungs seized up when he lowered himself over the edge, dangling there like a bit of dragon bait. He could break a leg falling from that height!

Abruptly he released his hold and fell—but rather than falling straight down to the ground, he waited a moment then used his feet to push off the wall. With impeccable timing, he performed a mid-air twist that altered his trajectory from plowing into the gravel and sand head-first to a soft, bent-knee landing.

Stunned, Natua was still staring at him when he rejoined her.

"Come on." Grabbing her hand, he pulled her along with him until they were several streets away.

"Alright, alright." She pulled him to a halt. "This is far enough." They stared at each other for a moment, each trying to catch their breath. "What just happened?"

"Gusari." Kaloe scowled, irritated with himself. "I was too late to see exactly what he did, just that he came out of the supply room."

"See?" Natua frowned, then nodded sharply. "The skylights. I didn't even think about those."

"I'd give a week's pay to know what he did in there," Kaloe grumbled, barely hearing her.

That stopped her. A scribe didn't make much, and those supporting more than just themselves needed all of it to get by. She took a good, long look at him before asking gently, "You're sure he did something wrong?"

"What else?" He cocked an eyebrow at her. "It's Gusari."

"That's true, but he might've been preparing the inventory." That didn't seem likely even to her, so she bit her lip and tried to think of any legitimate reason for a man of Gusari's bent to stay an instant longer at work than he had to.

"I'll get there early tomorrow." Kaloe announced his decision as he made it. "Poke around and see what I can find."

"You won't even know what to look for," she protested. "And if you're seen, someone will tell Gusari. It won't work, Kaloe." Her effort at vetoing his stated intent had the opposite effect, for his jaw set in that stubborn way he had. Desperate, she blurted, "Besides, I have a better idea."

"Really. A better idea." He folded his arms across his chest. "Let's hear it."

"Natua!"

She turned to see who was calling her. And to escape Kaloe's intense gaze. Any relief she might've felt at the delay in having to answer evaporated when she spotted Arru Deits striding toward them, grinning broadly.

"There you are." Arru spared the lad beside her a brief inspection, then dismissed him to give Natua his full attention. "I've been looking for you all week."

"Looking for me?" She didn't have to feign confusion. "Did we have an appointment?"

"Appointment?" He laughed and touched her arm. "Unofficially, I suppose we did. You promised to help me, after all." When she still hesitated, he looked back at where he'd been when he spotted Natua and waved. The area around the nearby stalls was nearly deserted, with the exception of two men and one plainly dressed woman. "Come, there's someone I'd like you to meet."

Kaloe leaned forward and quietly spoke to her in Marroi. "Palace guard."

Arru noted the lad's action and offered sardonically, "Perhaps you would care to join us?"

"Do you have the time?" Natua, who'd turned to face Arru, now looked up over her shoulder at Kaloe.

"I know you have somewhere to be."

Something in her eyes compelled him to respond, "I have time." He wasn't sure what he was protecting her from this time, but the message in her eyes came through as clearly as if she'd shouted it in Marroi. Then again—he eyed the Lurrakian man curiously— maybe he was protecting her from a *whom* rather than a *what*.

Arru frowned, but recovered quickly. "Come along, then." He would've offered his arm to Natua if she hadn't stepped to one side, putting Kaloe more or less between them for the short walk.

"Permit me to introduce my friend." He bowed to the woman perusing the rather primitive wares. Blasted waste of time in his estimation. She was shopping for a wedding present, not a trinket! "Leuna Oneko, meet Natua Prezio. She's the woman I've been telling you about."

Natua didn't care for the smug, you-can-thank-me-later look on Arru's face, but politely reached out to shake the other woman's hand. Overriding her irritation with Arru was the growing sense that all was not as simple as it seemed.

First of all, palace guards did not accompany random Lurrakian tourists on visits to the marketplace. Secondly, there was the small, worn box hanging from Leuna's shoulder. It seemed to be almost a part of her, judging by the way her hand rested on it, keeping it close to her side. Lastly, there was something familiar about her face. Natua didn't believe they'd ever met; yet she'd not only seen Leuna's face before, she remembered it.

"Doctor Oneko." Natua nearly gasped as it hit her. "I am honored to meet you."

<h1 style="text-align:center">Chapter 7</h1>

"Please, call me Leuna." The future queen of Marroi added a smile to her petition.

"As you wish, Leuna." Natua repeated her name and returned the smile. She heard Arru inhale, as if about to speak, and hastily introduced, "If I may, this is my confrere, Kaloe Tetsu."

"Agurrak." Leuna offered an informal Marroi greeting along with her hand to shake.

Kaloe hesitated, torn between propriety and, well, propriety. One was not supposed to shake hands with royalty, or even someone who was going to be royalty. Yet he could think of no way to ignore her outstretched hand that wasn't rude.

"Azoka eguna, Zure Tasuna." Kaloe took her hand and bowed deeply over it as he wished her a fair day.

"May you have many of them." Leuna returned, her tone a tad wistful.

"I'm sorry we interrupted your shopping." Natua apologized, looking for a way to excuse herself and Kaloe before Arru could maneuver her into something else.

"No, not at all." Leuna gave a self-deprecating laugh and gestured at the stalls. "I'm not even sure what I'm looking for."

"A wedding present, I believe you said." Arru flashed his most charming smile at her. "Personally, I recommend a visit to the import shops. Why, my parents visited that district only yesterday and spoke highly of the quality of the goods they encountered." His focus fixed on Leuna's carefully schooled features, Arru completely missed seeing Natua frown and Kaloe stiffen.

Before Kaloe could ask what was wrong with Marroi goods, Natua cleared her throat. "A wedding present. That's no easy task."

"Nothing to worry about." Leuna smiled wryly.

"I've got a few more weeks to figure it out. Plenty of time."

"I'm sure Natua will be happy to help you with that." Arru volunteered her services without so much as blinking at his own audacity. "Her language skills will come in quite handy, of course."

"I'm afraid my language skills," Natua seized the weakest point of the suggestion, "are limited to the written word. Furthermore, I've never met King Txoko. I would never presume to offer advice as to what would please him."

Arru's face flushed nearly as red as his hair, but Leuna spoke before he could.

"The written word?" Leuna graciously ignored the rest of Arru's impertinent suggestion. "Oh, yes, I remember. You work as a translator." Turning a smile on Kaloe, she guessed, "I suppose you do as well?"

"Nothing so grand, Zure Tasuna." Kaloe shook his head slowly.

"No, please." Leuna interrupted gently. "If you insist upon calling me by a title, couldn't it be doctor? I'm not queen yet."

A tiny smile worked its way through Kaloe's determined formality. "Very well, Doctor."

The moment was ruined by the sound of the stall keepers calling to each other. A cart rattled up to one of the stalls a row over, setting rumble of them streaming in from somewhere.

"Oh, dear." Leuna's shoulders hunched guiltily. "I think they must be getting ready to close up." It wasn't exactly her fault that the palace guards insisted on clearing a row before letting her browse, but clearly no business had been transacted since she'd arrived.

"Doctor." A middle-aged woman approached and gave a half bow to the group in general. "Forgive me for interrupting."

"It's fine, Fiantza." Leuna smiled at her mirabe, a combination maid and cultural guide who had kept her out of so much trouble since her arrival in Marroi. "I know it's time to go. Only…"

"We must go," Fiantza insisted gently. "Otherwise we'll have to hire a cart to carry everything I am buying."

"Everything?" Leuna swung around to find that the guards were being trailed by a bored-looking boy. "You've been buying things?"

"Something from every stall on this row, just like I said I would." Fiantza smiled fondly at her lady. They'd spent too many hours discussing the problem of what to buy for the king for her to be upset if Leuna forgot little things. On the other hand, it was a good thing they needed so many souvenir gifts for the wedding guests. "Shall we?"

"I'm afraid we have to go now."

Natua was quick to join Kaloe in bowing, though she didn't bend quite so low. "Oh!" Startled, she gasped and jumped backward when three dragons landed in the middle of the row with a rattle of scales and subdued roars.

When Natua ventured to peek at them again, a sleek, white dragon pranced in the sunlight. The other two dragons looked boxy, almost clumsy compared to her. In that way, the dragons were uncannily similar to their riders.

"It's alright." Leuna stepped between the dragons and her countrywoman. "Believe me, I know dragons take some getting used to, but I promise. These mean us no harm. They are only here to carry myself and the others back to the palace." Behind her, the guards swung aboard their mounts, patting their neck scales and speaking soothingly to them.

"It's true." Kaloe's voice was barely above a whisper. "You ride a distira! Is she the one you rescued at the festival?" The story was known far and wide throughout Marroi, of how poachers had slain several wild distira before Leuna found one, ill and captive in a hidden cave.

"Yes, well. We sort of saved each other." Leuna

ducked her head a bit shyly and Fiantza stifled a snort. "She gets upset if she sees me riding another dragon."

Natua stared at the dragons, working hard to control her breathing. Chasing off a gezi was one thing. These dragons were large enough to eat their whole group, then go looking for the main course.

"Truly, Marroi will have an extraordinary queen." Kaloe bowed so deeply his head went below his waist.

"Thank you." Leuna sent a worried glance toward Natua. "We'd better go. I hope we'll see you again."

Natua managed a shaky half bow, and was grateful for Kaloe's gentle hand on her arm as she straightened.

"Don't worry. I will see her safely home." Kaloe promised with a huge smile.

"No need to trouble yourself." Arru waved goodbye to Leuna with one hand while he reached for Natua's arm with the other. "I'm going that way. I'll see her home."

Natua turned instinctively toward Kaloe as the dragons took off, hiding her face from the dust and grit their wings stirred up. Arru, taken unawares, buried his nose in the elbow of his outstretched arm and shut his eyes tightly against the airborne onslaught.

The feeling of Natua leaning against him cemented Kaloe's resolve. "A thousand pardons, zahar." He bowed as if the term was respectful and ignored Natua's quickly hidden amusement. "We first have some stops to make and do not wish to delay you."

"You're very thoughtful." Arru slowly lowered his arm, acutely aware that Natua was making no effort to come to him. "Shall I tell your mother you'll be late?"

"Thank you, but that won't be necessary." Natua demurred from where she stood at Kaloe's side. Odd. The dragons were gone, why were her knees still so wobbly?

"Good night, sir." Kaloe tipped his head in the barest salute, then whisked Natua away through the rows of stalls.

"Wait!" Natua whisper-yelled. She didn't want to take the chance of Arru hearing her. "Where are we going?"

"My aunt's stall. Hurry, I'm late!" He released her arm to take her by the hand instead, tugging her along until they reached his destination. "Osaba." He bowed hastily to his uncle and addressed him in Marroi. "I'm sorry I'm late."

"You need a new job, boy." Osaba grunted without looking up from where he was packing a crate with gerris and shawls. "Come work with me. We close shop at the same time every night."

Natua bit the inside of her cheek to keep from laughing at it all. How in the world had she started for home to end up here? And what was she going to do about it?

"Ah, well, yes." Kaloe threw Natua an apologetic glance as he swung a stack of crates onto the waiting cart. "But the kanpotarrak at Itzuli are much nicer than the ones that come to the stalls to buy trinkets."

"Ha." Osaba finally lifted his head—and saw Natua. Gesturing to the half-dismantled stall, he switched to his limited Lurrakian to tell her, "Apologies. We are closed."

"Yes, I see that." She responded in Marroi to Kaloe's 'osaba' or uncle, lest he go on to 'divulge' something embarrassing to Kaloe.

"Osaba, this is my boss." Kaloe lidded the long display case of carved bone ornaments and nestled it at the front of the cart where it wouldn't get jostled as badly. "Head Translator Prezio."

"Your boss." Reaching for his cane, Osaba tried to get to his feet.

"No, no, good father." Natua held up her hands, palms forward, and advanced a step. "You mustn't get up on my account. Think of your leg!"

"My leg?" He blinked at her, one hand dropping to the injured limb. "You know about my leg?"

"The whole town knows about your leg, Father."

Natua looked to her left in time to see a young woman come around the corner of the stall. The same young woman she'd originally seen struggling with Kaloe!

Either the girl didn't see Natua or had decided to ignore her, for she turned accusatory eyes toward Kaloe. "You took your time getting here. What did you do, stop to chat with the king?"

"The future queen, actually." He spoke so casually that his words didn't register immediately.

"The queen?" An older copy of the girl sent him a doubtful look. "You've no need of an excuse, Kaloe, not after helping us for so…"

"No, it's true." Kaloe interrupted before she could thank him again. He nodded at Natua. "Ask her."

Natua laughed lightly as they all turned skeptical eyes her way. "The queen was shopping at the edge of the marketplace." She pointed. None of them looked away and she felt the heat begin to rise in her cheeks. "Tell them about the distira," she prompted Kaloe.

That did it. The three of them erupted in questions, all of their attention on Kaloe again.

Natua waved goodbye to him and slipped away. Stopping at the first group of playing adolescents that she found, she hired one to take a message to her mother, then headed back to the copy center. It was still too risky to let Kaloe go prowling around before work started tomorrow. But no one would be there right now. She could poke and pry to her heart's content.

Luckily, Gusari had given her a key, and now she silently let herself in. Moonlight wavered through the dragonglass skylights, casting weird shadows in the usually well-lit room.

Stifling a shiver, Natua eased her way around the sunken area where the scribes' tables and benches sat empty. Somehow she arrived at the storage room with only one bruised shin and pushed through the heavy drapes that separated it from the rest of the space.

The skylights didn't extend this far along the

ceiling, being naturally concentrated over where the actual work was done, so she scrabbled about in the semi-darkness for a lantern and a striker. Three tries and a singed forefinger later, she exhaled in weary triumph when the lantern sputtered to life.

"Adventures are something you laugh about later," she muttered, quoting her father as she scanned the shelves for anything amiss. "Assuming you live long enough."

The area where the more expensive paper was kept had a layer of dust so thick she could've written her name in it, so it was unlikely those stacks had been tampered with. The shelves for the regular papers were wiped clean by daily use, but still she didn't see any damage or reduction in the typical amount. Quills. Blotters. The measuring tools used for complicated designs on special documents. Everything looked fine.

Hungry, and a little bit frustrated to find herself on a fool's errand, she lifted the lantern, ready to blow it out. Except... Shifting the angle of the light set it to reflecting off something. A small, basically round spot on the shelf to her right. Was that liquid?

Curious, she reached out and tapped it with one fingertip. Ink. The damp spot was ink.

Raising the lantern again, she moved it slowly along the shelf, looking for more clues. Then the shelf above it. Here and there, she spotted a bottle of ink that wasn't quite right. Two were damp around the edge of the cap. There were a few more scattered throughout the next row of bottles that would've been taken to the floor for use.

Natua bit her lip and studied them. It couldn't be a coincidence that five bottles appeared to have been tampered with since leaving the factory. Since tonight, actually, given how quickly things dried in this climate.

Something heavy squeaked in protest in the main room. A soft thud followed the sound almost instantly.

Her heart pounding in her throat, Natua seized the five bottles and moved to the far corner of the little room. There was literally nowhere for her to hide, so she did the next best thing. She blew out the lantern and jammed herself as far into one corner as she possibly could.

Just when she had almost convinced herself it was just a very lost gezi dragon hunting for a snack, a soft swish of sound reached her ears. Then, breathing. Someone was in the store room with her!

Light flickered, flared into a bright ball inside another lantern.

"Kaloe!" She jumped indignantly to her feet. "What are you doing here?"

He jerked back against the drapes so hard that he stumbled backward right through them! Another, much louder thud preceded a *crash*.

"Kaloe?" Leaving her lantern. Natua raced out through the drapes and nearly tripped over the broken stool that Kaloe had accidentally knocked over mere moments before.

Only he hadn't just fallen, he'd dropped the lit lantern on the stone floor! Tiny rivers of fire were spreading across the floor as the fuel escaped its broken canister.

"Fire." Natua started to reach for the drapes, but stopped herself. Gusari might overlook a broken lantern, but even he would question soiled and fire-damaged drapes. Grabbing the broken stool instead, she flipped it upside down and used its seat to mercilessly stamp out the flames.

Kaloe likewise, once he'd reoriented himself, snatched a crate of old rags and used them to first smother the fire near the canister, then soak up the rest of the fuel.

"Well." Natua leaned against the stool's two good legs and tried to catch her breath. "That was…an adventure."

"What are you doing here?" Kaloe ran his fingers through his hair. "Better yet, what were you doing in there, popping out of dark corners? You scared me out of a year's growth!"

Natua was surprised to hear herself laugh. So surprised that she gave the first answer that came to mind. "Good. You're tall enough as it is."

Kaloe scrubbed a hand over his face, but his shoulders were already shaking. Soon they were laughing so hard, their sides ached. Their merriment transpired silently, though, for they were still somewhere they weren't technically supposed to be.

Natua felt her way back to the corner where she'd left her lantern and relit it. Placing it on the floor where it wouldn't easily be seen from outside, she gestured to Kaloe that they should clean up their mess.

"I thought you were going home," he whispered as he used a broom to swish one of the cleaner rags across the former-fire trails.

"What about you?" She shot back. "I left you tending your uncle!"

"You don't have to worry about him." Kaloe put the broom away and returned the crate of rags to its place. "One of his neighbors has a son only a few years older than Anella. He volunteered to help tonight."

"Wait. Who is Anella?" Natua balanced the stool carefully back on the stack it had come from and made a mental note to ask Gusari why they were storing broken furniture.

"My cousin, of course." He chuckled. "You saw her less than an hour ago."

"Oh." Had it only been an hour? The sandglass was shut down for the night, so there was no way for her to be sure. "Yes, I remember." She blushed as her thoughts wandered back to their very first encounter.

"That's good enough." Kaloe blew out a breath. "Now, tell me what you found in there." He jerked a thumb toward the store room.

"See for yourself." She led the way to the small stash of bottles.

"This is it?" He picked one up and examined it in the light of the lantern. "I don't see anything wrong with it."

"It's dried now, but," she pointed at the cap, "there was a damp spot. When I got here, none of these looked quite right."

"Hmm." Frowning, Kaloe picked up two more and began juggling them.

"What are you doing?" Natua sputtered. "Put those down!"

"I'm thinking." Instead of putting them down as she'd asked, he swiped the other bottles and began juggling five. "We have to have ink to do our jobs."

Relaxing a little when she realized none of the bottles were smashed on the stone floor, Natua took a deep breath. "Not just any ink, either. Itzuli uses high-quality ink. It won't run, smear, or fade. That's just one way we…" She interrupted her spiel with a yelp and a dive for one of the bottles as Kaloe suddenly stopped moving.

"Won't run, smear, or fade," he repeated. Pointing to the bottle she'd rescued he added, "Good catch." Turning to where the lantern waited for them on a shelf, he held a bottle up to it. "Bubbles." That was to be expected given that he'd just been juggling with it. "Hold these."

Natua accepted the bottles and watched, bewildered, as he took a regular bottle from the shelf, shook it, then held it up to the lantern next to the one he'd been juggling.

"Look." He shifted so she could see.

"Aren't they the same?" She asked after studying them.

"Not quite. This one." He tapped the bottle he'd taken from the shelf. "It's darker."

"Darker? You mean." She lifted another of the suspicious bottles and confirmed that the light passed through it more easily. "These are diluted?"

"Clever. Simple. Fast. No wonder he was already done by the time I reached the skylight." Kaloe scowled in disgust. Putting the good bottle back, he rearranged things so that the shelf looked normal. "Here, let me have those. I'll empty them out and put the empties out to be returned to the factory."

"That's one idea. Except." Natua blew out a breath. "Gusari will be watching for the results of this sabotage. If it never shows, what will he do?"

"I know exactly what he'll do if it *does* show. He'll dock our pay again," Kaloe muttered.

"We're not letting that happen." She asserted firmly. "Gusari isn't fit to be a supervisor."

Kaloe's eyes widened. "Can you do that?" When she frowned in confusion, he clarified, "Can you terminate him?"

"Ah. Um, no. Even I, a head translator, would need considerable evidence before I went to Manager Mirko to make that sort of an accusation." She paused, eyeing the bottles with fresh interest. "Evidence we can start gathering now. But we can't empty out the bottles."

"We can't because…" Kaloe let the thought hang there, waiting for her to fill in the answer.

"Because if we wanted Gusari to know we were onto him, we could've just stayed and caught him in the act this afternoon. And if he doesn't know we're building a case for his dismissal, he'll keep creating evidence for us to use against him."

"How much evidence will it take?" Kaloe didn't bother trying to hide his eagerness.

"That depends. On Manager Mirko, mostly." Natua pocketed one of the bottles as their first solid piece of proof. "We'll know when we have enough, I think. Come on."

Chapter 8

Natua stumbled down the stairs the next day, her eyes more closed than open. *Ouch!* Hopping on one foot, she nursed the toes she'd just bruised on the ridiculous wall trim. If not for the truly delicious smell of breakfast, she might've collapsed right there on the lounge chair in the front room, and gone back to sleep.

When she finally reached the kitchen, she found her mother waiting for her, arms folded across her chest.

"Good morning, Mother." When her mother didn't respond, Natua took a big drink of chilled juice before trying again. "Did you sleep well?" Her stomach growled, warning her that juice wasn't enough. Pulling her chair out, she sat and waited for her mother to join her.

"Sleep?" Kume scoffed. "How am I supposed to sleep when I don't have any idea of where you are?"

"No idea…" Natua's brain wasn't functioning at its normal speed, because she couldn't fathom how that was possible. "Didn't you get the message I sent?"

"Message?" Kume jerked her chair out. "A street urchin came wandering by late last night and said you sent him. Told me I shouldn't wait up for you." She sat with such emphasis that the utensils on the table shivered in fright. "Is that your idea of a message?"

"He was hardly an urchin, Mother." Too late, Natua recognized that she'd addressed the wrong question first. No, wait. That was actually never in question. Her mother said he was an urchin; therefore, in Kume's mind at least, he was and ever would be an urchin. "I mean, he did deliver the message. It's not his fault I was busy with work and didn't send more information." That still wasn't right, but she hoped it was at least better. Her eyes more open now, she finally got a good look at how she was dressed. Oh, bother. She thought she'd managed to 'lose' the loud yellow gerri someone had given her as a gift for her last promotion.

"Work, is it?" Kume huffed and spread her napkin daintily across her lap. "If you don't want to tell me what's going on, at least have the decency not to lie to me!"

"Lie?" Dumbfounded, Natua set down the knife and fork she'd just picked up. "Mother, I'm not lying. Something came up at the copy center and I stayed late." She wasn't sure she wanted to know *how* late, in fact. Even with Kaloe's help, it had taken easily an hour to make copies to replace what they were going to allow to be ruined today.

"And I suppose your jaunt to the marketplace was for work, too." Kume's fear of being left out of Natua's life made her unnecessarily harsh. "You were seen, Natua. With a man!"

Natua was halfway out of her chair before she comprehended *what* her mother said, and not just the accusatory *way* she had said it. Confused and hurt, she finished getting to her feet.

"I haven't done anything wrong, Mother." There. That was the root question. Her brain finally connected 'a man' with Kaloe and she almost laughed. "My confrere had to take care of family business at the marketplace, but after that we went back to the copy center and finished our work. Then, because it was so late, he was kind enough to walk me home."

Her appetite severely dampened, Natua looked at the food her mother had prepared and shook her head. "I have to go."

Kume remained in her seat, frozen in place like a statue. The statue jumped when the front door closed firmly behind Natua, and a tear trickled down its cheek. Then another. Breaking free of her shock with a sob, she buried her face in her napkin.

"She doesn't want me." Kume moaned. "She'd never leave me behind…but she doesn't want me."

Outside, Natua wiped away a few tears of her own.

It didn't make sense. Her mother should've known her better than anyone in Marroi and still Kume had accused her of…of lying. Seeing a man on the sly.

"Me, dating Kaloe." Natua sniffled and dabbed at her eyes. "What an idea."

She was working with him, though. And today was their most important task thus far. If breakfast at her own table was out of the question, she had better pick up some rolls and fruit on her way to the office.

It was odd, really. With as often as she'd been eating out lately, their food bill should've increased significantly. Instead, she was beginning to see buying food imported from Lurrak as an unnecessary expense. For herself, at least.

Natua walked faster and faster until she was almost running, but every thought out-ran her, circling back to her mother.

After six years in Marroi, her mother had eaten local food less than a handful of times. Even for the sake of reducing expenses, would she consider making the change now?

Also, what good was sending messages if they weren't believed? Not to mention the subject of dating.

Natua paused at a corner to get her bearings. Spotting a food stall, she purchased a few things to nibble on, though by now her stomach was knotted so tightly she wasn't sure she'd be able to eat at all.

Dating. How long had it been since she'd even thought of that? The fact that she couldn't remember did nothing to lift her spirits. Oh, she'd met some nice men when they first moved to Marroi, but none of them ever expressed more than a casual interest in her.

So. Was that it? No one pursued her, so she'd just…buried herself so deep in her work that she'd forgotten about it? Gracious, at this rate she'd be able to proudly proclaim she'd well and truly earned the title of 'spinster.'

The more she thought about it, the more something within her rebelled at the thought of running up the white flag so cavalierly. Surely she could dredge up the initiative to change her situation? Well, perhaps initiative wasn't quite the right word. Women weren't exactly allowed to take the initiative in this sort of thing. It was acceptable to encourage a desired suitor in his pursuit; but decidedly *un*acceptable to trade hats and become the pursuer.

"Morning." Kaloe stepped out of the crowd to walk beside her.

"What?" Startled, she mumbled around the bite she'd chewed and forgotten about. Swallowing quickly, she offered him a half-smile. "Mm. Hi. Sorry. Eating on the run this morning."

"So I see." He frowned slightly. Was it his imagination or was she losing weight? It didn't seem possible given how much he knew she could eat in a sitting. Maybe she only ate that much because she wasn't eating regularly the rest of the time? "Hey, slow down." He touched her arm lightly.

"Sorry," she said again, matching his less-frantic speed. "I'm…" What could she say? That she was upset? No, she wasn't ready to discuss the why of it. Especially not the part about how her mother thought they were romantically involved.

"Tense?" He let his hand settle on her elbow so that he could more easily guide her through the crowd. "Don't be. Everything is in order."

"I hope it goes as planned." She tossed the last of the roll to a circling gezi and tried a bite of the fruit. It went down a little easier, so she ate some more. "Gusari gets his ruined work and we get the project done on time."

"I think it's good that we decided to do it this way." He stopped them across the street from the copy center's courtyard so they could finish their conversation in peace. They were plenty early, anyway. "I'd rather get it right the first time. There probably won't be a second." He paraphrased one of his father's sayings.

"That's not the only thing we have to consider." Natua wiped sticky fingers on the paper her food had come wrapped in. "I'm worried about you, Kaloe." She looked up as he looked down and her heart stumbled.

"Me?" He clasped his hands behind his back to keep from smoothing her hair, touching her cheek. Somehow he couldn't help shifting an inch closer to her anyway. "I haven't done anything special." That reminded him, though. He still needed to enlist a few of the other scribes to claim some of the spare copies they'd made last night as their own work. That would be a lot less noticeable than if he tried claiming he'd doubled his own productivity, for one day only.

As the distance between them closed fractionally, Natua jerked back. Took a deep breath of clear, warm air. *It's the Marroi way*, she reminded herself. *They stand close together when they talk.*

"What? What is it?" Kaloe asked, alarmed. He'd sort out the emotions rioting through his veins later, after he was sure she was alright.

"Nothing." She shook her head. "We should, um. We should go inside." To distract them both from her embarrassment, she paused long enough to add, "I've decided to have one of the other translators approach Mirko when the time comes. I'm hardly his favorite and as you say, we'll only get one chance to be heard."

"No." He interrupted unapologetically. "None of the other translators have spent time at the copy center. No one else has witnessed how Gusari abuses his power, how it harms the company. How it harms us." Kaloe spoke with such conviction that Natua felt it down to the soles of her feet. "You are our best champion."

He stepped aside then, bowing as his arm moved in a sweeping invitation for her to precede him.

His words rattled around inside her head all that morning. 'No one else has witnessed...'

Not even Manager Mirko? her subconscious whispered. It nagged at her as she worked through her morning routine. Gusari met with Mirko almost weekly. Sometimes he took his ledger with him. Mirko must've seen dozens of entries about docking the scribes' pay. Dozens upon dozens, from what she'd heard. And witnessed.

Yet try as she did, she couldn't recall the slightest intimation that she'd been sent to the copy center to investigate Gusari for unethical practices. There was nothing about it in the complaint reports Mirko gave her. As for their tense conversation in his office, well. In retrospect, she saw it clearly as a power struggle. A one-sided power struggle, at that. She just wanted to do her job in peace.

The main point, though, was that all of the facts boiled down to one thing—Mirko knew about Gusari. *He already knew!* Puzzle pieces began slamming into place for her with such force that she had to go sit down at her desk to process it all.

Kaloe watched furtively as Natua's face went from kanpotarrak pale to an unhealthy ashen color. He racked his brain for a reason, but nothing he came up with made sense. Was she ill?

Suddenly she looked up, making eye contact with him. Offered a tiny smile, then began shuffling through her stacks.

Kaloe was far from satisfied with that ghost of a smile, yet there was nothing he could do in the here and now. Frustrated, he explosively exhaled the lungful of air he'd been holding in.

"Hey!" The scribes near him glared as they straightened the copies they were working from.

"Watch it, will you?"

"What happened, Tetsu? You forget how to breathe like a normal person?"

Kaloe apologized until things settled down again and did his best to work as usual. However when he pushed aside worries about Natua, thoughts of Gusari crowded in. It was already mid-morning by then. Several pages made with the adulterated ink were drying. Soon everyone would be able to see that something was wrong with those pages.

Soon. How long would that take, anyway?

Kaloe nearly tore the page with his quill when a strange sound reached his ears.

"No, no, no!" Gusari cried out in dismay as he shuffled through the pages Tryun brought to him. "How could such a thing happen!"

"Supervisor! What's wrong?" Natua roused herself to hurry over, though she was careful to feign ignorance.

"See here! Tryun was organizing the dried papers when he found these." Gusari slapped the pages onto his desk and spread them out for her. "Can we send this to our customers? Is this quality work? Can you even *read* it? Hmm?"

The urge to roll her eyes at Gusari's 'poor Tryun' tone was strong, but Natua managed to resist. Besides, from the way Tryun was frowning, she would've guessed he was truly upset. By the damaged copies? That didn't make sense. Lately when she had to pitch in and complete a few copies herself it was because Tryun was moving as slowly as a basking sand lizard.

"I don't understand. I've never seen anything like this." Natua didn't have to pretend now. The ink hadn't run, exactly; neither would she call it smeared. Here and there she could make out a letter, but for the most part, it looked like someone had brushed ink across an already damp page. "Thank goodness most of these were just training copies. We didn't lose much actual work, only four or five copies."

"What?" Gusari leaned forward sharply. "Are you sure?"

"Yes, of course. See? I have them initial their pages." She tapped the blobs in the upper corners of some of the sheets. She made the observation innocently, then clamped her mouth shut to stifle a yawn. They'd grossly overestimated how many copies would get ruined, representing lost sleep, but she supposed it was better to have more than they needed.

"Ah. Yes." Gusari visibly deflated. He'd been counting on a lot more damage.

"Bariux." Natua turned catch the scribe's eye. "Will you and the other trainees please cap your ink bottle and bring it here? Also the ink bottle being used by table number," she squinted at one of the pages as if trying to make out the handwriting, "three. Thank you."

"Head Translator, what are you doing? They must have ink to work." Gusari's usually imperious voice had the faintest tremble as he spoke.

"Gathering evidence." She reflexively wiped her palms on her trousers when Gusari's normally damp face broke out in a fresh layer of perspiration. "Naturally, I'm very worried. Table three got a fresh bottle of ink from the store room this morning, as did my trainees." Natua paused to thank Bariux with a smile and whispered some additional instructions. "There are likely more copies made with this ink drying, and more were being written until just now, when the problem was reported. I'm afraid the ink must've been tampered with. Supervisor, I'm sorry, but I think we should take this to Manager Mirko and see what he wants to do about it." She made the suggestion partly because it felt natural—and partly to see how he would respond.

"Mirko? Do about it?" Gusari echoed her numbly. He couldn't have her going to Mirko. It was one thing for Mirko to blink at, um, goings-on when only they two were aware of them; and quite another for Mirko to risk his own reputation for Gusari's sake. "Why, what is there to do? We lock the doors every night. In fact, last night I locked the doors myself." This woman! She ruined all his plans. How could he risk docking the scribes with the threat of a visit to Mirko hanging over his head?

"The ink didn't adulterate itself." She lifted troubled eyes to his. "I think we're being deliberately sabotaged."

"The ink!" He slapped the desk so hard his palm stung. "I mean, the business we buy it from. Of course. That explains it all."

Jumping clumsily to his feet, he plucked the bottles out of her hands. Two. Lucky he'd spread the five bottles out. True, he'd hoped to reap the rewards of this idea for some time to come, but now he just wanted to retrieve them and be done with it. Served him right for listening to *Tryun*, of all people. He should've known better.

Wait. Aha, now there was an idea! A way to get all of the bottles back at once.

"You are right to be concerned, of course." He set the bottles on his desk and smoothed his tunic. "You there!" He pointed at Bariux, who was walking toward them anyway. "Fetch all of the ink bottles from the store room that are marked with a…" He squinted at the two bottle caps as if he know perfectly well which ones he'd diluted. "With a twelve. They're suspect." That was better. He was in command here, not her.

"I have them here." Bariux showed him the bag he was carrying. "The head translator wants us to write a few lines with each bottle, to test the ink."

"Oh." Gusari cleared his throat. "Exactly what I was going to have you do. Bring the, *ahem*. I mean. If you find that any more of them have bad ink, bring those bottles to me." Retaking his seat, he waved dismissively at Natua. "Don't worry, Head Translator. I'll investigate this myself."

"Then you agree there is something to investigate." She cornered him with his own words. Defeating him when he obviously had Mirko on his side would be no easy task, but she wasn't going to let him relax in the meantime. Easy task? It was veritably impossible. Now that Mirko was no longer an option, that left…the authorities and Director Rysl.

Not necessarily in that order.

"Ah, I…" Gusari gathered the spoiled papers into a haphazard stack and held it out to her. "I think it's high time I reminded our current ink supplier that there are *other* ink suppliers. Don't worry, Prezio. I'll make sure they know they can't sell us inferior goods and get away with it." Pfft. Nobody could get away with *anything* with Prezio around. How many more weeks was it until he could expect to be rid of her for good?

Well now. Another idea. Why wait to be rid of her? He, Supervisor Gusari, was a clever man. His recent defeats merely demonstrated that he was going about this the wrong way. If he wanted his copy center back, firmly under his control, he needed to take it.

Kaloe, watching as closely as he dared, sat up straight when Natua and Gusari made eye contact with each other. If they'd shouted their challenge at each other from opposite ends of an arena, it couldn't have been plainer. The minor skirmishes were over. They would do battle in earnest now.

Natua stretched her arm out over the waste paper bin beside Gusari's desk—one he could easily have reached himself—and dropped the pages he'd just handed her.

Chapter 9

Kaloe left the copy center alone at the lunch hour that day. He'd watched hopefully, but Natua hadn't even looked up from her work when the bell rang. Since he wasn't all that hungry, he started to walk instead. Walking would help him think. Walking would…take him directly to the tailor shop his mother ran?

Shaking his head and chuckling at himself, Kaloe ducked through the doorway and looked around.

"Oh, hello, Kaloe." A young Marroi woman straightened the tunic she'd just finished repairing, then gave him her full attention. The sheer, turquoise veil she wore over the lower half of her face was a token homage to her eastern ancestors' custom of hiding as much skin as possible from the scorching sun. "Can I help you?"

"Anicha, hi." He rubbed the back of his neck and hoped he was imagining the interest in her eyes. "Is my mother available?"

"Kaloe?" Patare Tetsu's voice floated through the thin curtain that separated the shop floor from the working area. "Is that you?"

Kaloe grinned, nodded to Anicha, and parted the curtain. "Are you well, Mother?" Stopping, he kissed her weathered cheek.

"You didn't walk halfway across the business sector to ask how I am doing." She pointed at the chair beside her. "Sit, and tell me what's wrong. Is it work?"

Sobering a bit, he took the chair she indicated. Partially out of habit, but mostly to keep his hands busy while they talked, he reached for the cushion they reserved for dull pins and needles.

"It's not work. Not exactly." Kaloe sprinkled a little oil on the old dragon scale clamped to the table by him and began deftly sharpening the dull points one by one. "It's more about Dad." He shouldn't have come.

~84~

His mother had three assistants, and two of them were in earshot.

Patare's hands stilled, then resumed their embroidering. "Go ahead." She would've preferred to wait until they were both home from work and could talk privately. Yet she knew her son and didn't believe he was there for idle conversation.

"He taught me a lot." Kaloe kept his eyes, which were growing damp, on his work as he spoke. Though more than ten years were passed since his father's death, he knew his mother still missed him. "And you've taught me most of the things he didn't get the chance to."

Patare waited a moment when he paused, then gently prodded, "Go on, son. What's troubling you?"

"I think…" He dried a needle on a scrap of cloth. "I might like someone."

Patare added several stitches to her pattern before weaving the needle partway into the fabric and setting the project aside. "It's getting late and I know how strict your supervisor is. Come, we can talk on the way to the copy center."

Bemused, he returned the pin cushion to its place and followed his mother to the back door, where she adjusted her gerri to shield her head from the sun.

"Now, then." Patare linked her arm through his and practically pulled him out onto the street. "Tell me all about her!"

She sounded so excited that Kaloe had to stifle a chuckle. "The first thing you should know is that she *doesn't* know." He shrugged in answer to her startled expression. "I said I *think* I might like her. I don't know for sure. That's why I wanted to talk to you."

"To me?" Patare shook her head emphatically. "Only you can decide if you are in love, my son."

"Of course, but…" He hesitated, then raked his free hand through his hair. "It's complicated. I mean, I just started to wonder this morning."

"You started to wonder." Patare chuckled and

patted his arm. "Kaloe, you are so much like your father. Yes, really." She sighed and side-stepped a ball that had gotten away from some children. "He was a dragon wrangler when I met him, you know. I, well, I was just a caravanner's daughter. We sometimes spent a whole week in one city, though that wasn't often. The closer I got to marrying age, the more worried I became. To me, everyone outside of my family was a stranger. Even when I recognized someone because we'd been to the town before, they were taller, older, had done new and different things."

Kaloe squeezed her arm gently, appreciating the sadness he heard in her voice.

"It wasn't all bad." She gave him a smile, then swallowed hard and continued. "Your father was footloose and fancy-free when we met. He brought me some torn shirts to repair, and I asked how they came to be so damaged. I'd never known anyone so easy to talk to. Later, he tried to convince me that was when we started courting." A warm chuckle bubbled up out of her.

Kaloe knew he had heard the stories before, but this time he seemed to be hearing different things. "So you fell in love with him because…you liked him?" Natua seemed to like him. Maybe he dared to hope after all.

"That helped. But also, I decided to fall in love with him." She nodded very seriously. "It was a big risk at the time. He couldn't stay with our caravan all the time, though he visited us as often as he could. So, marrying him meant I would leave behind my family, our way of life. And loving him, well. Much of the time, caravan women treated marriage as a business arrangement. They would be partners, in all aspects of life, but love? It cannot be bargained for, only cultivated over time. To say that I wanted to marry a man I was already in love with made me something of an oddity."

"I didn't realize." His steps slowed as the copy

center came into view. "She's amazing, Mother. In just the few weeks since she started working at the copy center, everything has changed."

"Aha, so she's a scribe." Patare deduced.

"What?" He blinked. "No, actually. She's a translator. A *head* translator."

"But…" Patare's hands lifted questioningly. "Why would a translator be at the copy center? I thought they all worked in that fancy building, over there." She flicked her fingers at the stone building that towered over the squat copy center.

"Usually they do. She's a sort of a special assignment. I think Gusari complained about some of the bad translations we were getting." Used them as an excuse, more likely. The man had more excuses up his sleeves than some of the perpetually tardy scribes. "Anyway, she's here for now and I…"

"And you like her." Patare's voice was soft with pity. "Son, please understand me. Any woman would be lucky to have you. But this one. She's a boss. Will she even remember you when she goes back to her big stone building?" Patare knew how it was to be busy. How many times, despite her best intentions, had she failed to cross the narrow alley to share a simple beverage with the shopkeeper next door?

"As I said. It is complicated." His chest constricted painfully at the thought of Natua leaving him. It was true that the copy center shared the same property as the large, stone building where the translators worked. Nevertheless, as a child he'd traveled with his parents a good deal for his father's work, and the sting of finding he'd been forgotten by his 'friends' each time they returned to a location clung to him like the barbed spine of a succulent plant embedded in his heart.

"Do I know her family?" Seeing the sadness in his eyes, Patare offered the only crumb of hope she had. "If they are customers at the shop, perhaps I could befriend them and…"

"Thank you, Mother, but," he sighed heavily, "I imagine they use the same shops and services as everyone else in the foreign quarter."

"Everyone else?" Patare's eyes widened as she took in his meaning. "This girl of yours. She is a…"

"Kaloe! There you are! I missed you at the food cart." Natua halted her approach abruptly when she saw that Kaloe wasn't standing in the shade alone. "Oh. A thousand pardons." She bowed to the older woman and started to retreat.

"Head Translator Prezio." Kaloe straightened, determined to take advantage of the coincidence. "I would like to introduce you to my mother, Patare Tetsu."

Natua felt the air leave her lungs in a rush. This tall, distinguished-looking woman was Kaloe's mother? Somehow she'd translated the love in Kaloe's voice when he spoke of his mother into a mental image of a small, sort of round woman, whose face crinkled when she laughed.

"I am twice honored today." Patare's tone was politely neutral when she spoke. It was beyond the limits of credulity to believe this could be any other than the woman her son cared for. "My son comes to visit me on his lunch. And now I get to meet the boss he speaks so highly of."

"The honor is mine." Natua bowed again, though not quite so low as for the introduction. "Your son never speaks of you to me, Ma'am. Rather, he sings your praises."

Patare's face softened at the artful turn of phrase. "You speak Marroi like a native," she complimented. More than that, she detected a straightforward sincerity about this boss-woman that she liked.

"You are far too kind." Natua knew her own limits too well to take the flattery to heart. But it was awfully nice of her to say.

As Kaloe looked down at them smiling at each other, his heart flipped in his chest, shivered happily, then settled back into place.

Natua turned to Kaloe, intending to excuse herself, only to have all thought driven from her mind by the intensity of the expression in his eyes. She blinked, and it was gone.

"Thanks for walking me back, Mother." Kaloe bent to kiss her cheek, then whistled to hail the empty cycle carriage he saw going past. He grinned when it stopped. "You can return to the shop in style."

"No, no, no. I will not waste your money on…"

Natua stayed where she was, both to give them a moment and because her knees were still a little watery. It was tempting to congratulate herself on having such a vivid imagination, for clearly Kaloe was unaffected by the…the…whatever it was. Or wasn't. Except that she was his boss—and much older than he was. Thinking she saw *any*, um, emotion in his eyes aside from respect was inappropriate.

"Hey." Kaloe stopped a few feet from her. He hadn't meant to get caught gazing at her with his heart in his eyes, and wasn't sure whether or not he hoped she'd noticed. "Sorry about lunch."

"That's okay. I ate at the, um. The food cart." Her heart did an odd pirouette when she heard his voice and she sternly ordered it back to work. "I brought leftovers, though. If you're hungry, I mean." She lifted the bag, then nearly dropped it when his fingers grazed hers. "We don't have to have lunch together." The words came out more sharply than she'd intended and she took a deep breath, fighting for control of her brain, her voice, her heart. Everything seemed to be rebelling at the same time and for no good reason!

"I enjoy it, though." His eyes met hers. "I like talking with you."

"Oh." She pulled her hand away to smooth her hair. "Um, that's good. Because we have a lot to talk about. Yes, Gusari has something up his sleeves."

Kaloe pushed aside his disappointment at her chosen topic and scrounged up a grin from somewhere. "*Both* sleeves? That sounds ominous."

"Hilarious." Amused despite the very real threat Gusari posed, Natua smiled and the strangest thing happened. Her heart settled down to its normal rhythm. Whatever had been disturbing it must've passed.

"If I were being serious." He looked past her to where a stream of scribes was trickling into the copy center. "I'd say Gusari sees himself as a goraka, a sandstorm that rages big enough to blot out the sun for an entire town. In reality, he's just a swirl of dust."

"And…how do you see yourself?" She gave him a quick once-over, deliberately challenging him. Whatever Gusari was planning, the soon they figured it out the better. Could she count on Kaloe to keep his eyes open if he thought they'd already won? "As a tamer of dust swirls?"

"Not exactly." He reached out and lifted the strand of her hair that had come loose again. It curled around his finger even as he tried to hand the end to her. "But I think I know someone who is." All he was sure of at that moment was that he wanted more time with her. To get to know her better, learn if she shared his growing feelings. Helping her to defeat Gusari probably meant shortening her time at the copy center. But he would do it anyway, because he could tell that defeating Gusari was important to her.

"Hey, Tetsu!" A shrill whistle accompanied the call. "Get over here or you'll be late!"

Kaloe chuckled. "Come." Taking her by the elbow, he turned her toward the copy center. "Our dust swirl awaits!"

Except Gusari wasn't there. Natua kept an eye on Tryun throughout the day, having detected him as Gusari's man, and was unsettled to find him more cooperative than usual. What were they up to?

"Head Translator!" A youthful voice called out to her. "New assignments for you!"

"For me?" Natua gave Pyr a confused smile as she

moved a stack of un-reviewed translations so he could set the new stack down. "What do you mean?"

"Manager Mirko's orders." Pyr mock saluted her once his arms were free. "Something about congratulating you on all of your progress here." Some gift. Over a dozen new documents for her to translate. Leaning closer, he added in a low tone, "Truth is, we're falling behind without you."

"Flattery will get you nowhere." She winked and tapped him lightly on the nose. Matching his softer tone, she asked, "Is Head Translator Japoni doing alright?"

"He's doing his best." Pyr shook his head. "Has to use his dictionaries a lot, though."

Natua nodded and flipped quickly through the files he'd brought her. Oddly, none of them bore the usual tags that would've marking them as assigned to her for translation. What did that mean, exactly? She bit her lip, glanced around the copy center, and made up her mind.

"Let's see if we can help him, alright? Take these." She handed him four of the moderately-difficult assignments, all in languages Japoni knew as well as his own name. "And skim a couple of the harder ones out of his box. Can you do that?"

"Easy as falling off a dragon." Pyr returned her earlier wink and vanished the way he had come.

Natua winced as the doors screeched shut and eyed the new documents. Manager Mirko sent them himself, did he? Perhaps at Gusari's suggestion? Or was she just a little bit paranoid?

Either way, these weren't going to translate themselves. After confirming what time it was, she picked an easier file to start with, hoping to finish it before the last bell.

Time spun on at its usual pace and the scribes were quick to gather their things when it was time to leave.

"Hey, Kaloe. Ready for that game?" The younger scribe smiled, a tad cockily.

"Going to show us how the caravanners play?" snickered another.

Kaloe shrugged off the attempted insult, but the first fellow didn't.

"What's wrong with caravanners?" Bracing fists against his hips, the fellow stared the snickerer down. "Weren't we all caravanners once, before the oases were mapped and the great cities built?"

Kaloe left them to the old argument while he went to check on Natua. "Translator." He waited a moment, then tried again. "Natua."

Blinking, she looked up. "Hmm? What? Is something wrong?" She set her quill down with a wince.

"Nothing's wrong." He swiftly caught hold of her writing hand, pressing it between both of his own. "Hold still," he warned when she tried to retrieve it. "The last bell has rung. Didn't you hear it?"

She blinked again and reached up to rub her eyes. "Oh, now really." Indignant, she glared at him when he captured her second hand, too.

Amused, he turned both of her hands so that she could see her inky fingertips. "You should be thanking me, Translator." It was one thing to get a little more ink on his own hands, and quite another to see it smeared across her face. She already had a small smudge on her chin, which he found adorable.

"Oh my. Thank you. I must be more tired than I thought." She grimaced to cover a flinch, but he must've noticed anyway because his touch became even gentler.

"Did I hurt you?" His fingers happened to be on her pulse when he paused to ask, and he felt her heart leap as their eyes met. So. He was not alone in his attraction after all.

"No. I… Thank you." Pulling her hands free of his touch, Natua flexed them to demonstrate how much better they felt. "I should get going. I have to pick up a few things for supper." *And be home to eat it for a change.*

"Ah." Kaloe, noticing the pile of untranslated files for the first time, couldn't help frowning. "A gift from Gusari?" He tapped the stack.

"These? Hardly." She tossed her head in mock pride. "These were sent to me by Manager Mirko himself, in recognition of my fine work here."

"Manager Mirko?" Kaloe half-nodded, allowing the corners of his lips to curve down for the duration of the motion. "What an honor. Do you suppose, if you work extra hard here, he will allow you to do all of the translating as well as overseeing the copies?"

Natua barely stifled a groan at the thought. And yet. "That's what they're doing, isn't it? They want me to have to choose between translating and," she gestured at the room in general, "everything I'm supposed to be doing here."

Kaloe's heart twisted within him at the disheartened note in her voice. "Why not do both?"

"Tetsu!" Roared the scribe with the ball. "Are you coming or not?"

"Will you come?" Kaloe grinned at Natua hopefully.

"What? Come where?" She looked around at the small huddle of scribes by the door.

"We're going to play a game of pilota. It won't take long," he added, remembering that she had things to do. "You can watch us win."

"A pilota game?" She stifled a chuckle and twisted to pop her back. "I'm too old for such things." At the moment, she felt closer to sixty-three than thirty-three.

"Too old to watch a game?" Kaloe didn't believe her. But if he delayed any longer, they'd leave without him. "You can come watch the next one. It'll be fun, I promise." To the others he called back as he moved to join them, "Are you sure you're ready for this? Because I know I am!"

Natua watched them leave, enjoying the friendly jostling and harmless back and forth as they crowded their way out through the courtyard door.

Why not do both? She rolled her shoulders to loosen tight muscles. Easy for him to say. And at the same time…what an interesting idea.

Chapter 10

Natua let herself in the front door at home and braced for a continuation of that morning's confrontation. She'd come prepared, though. Armed with a jar of her mother's favorite fruit jelly and a fresh loaf of bread, she took a deep breath and…

Wait. She didn't smell anything cooking. Or hear anything from the kitchen. Neither were there any footsteps or humming or even the squeak of the old rocking chair her mother had insisted on bringing from Lurrak.

Peeking into the kitchen, Natua confirmed that it was empty. Except for a note on the table.

"Gone out with the Deits," she read.

Perplexed, Natua set the jar of fruit on the table beside the note. Now what? Go back to the copy center and try to clear out a few more translations? She could leave a note on top of her mother's. But who would walk her home? Who would make her laugh, no matter how difficult the day—and Gusari—had been? Just thinking about Kaloe made her smile.

Ah, but this time was too precious to spend daydreaming about…someone she worked with.

"It could be worse, I suppose." Picking a ripe truip from the bowl, she bit into the dark orange fruit. "I might've been home when the invitation came!"

Chuckling, she bounced up the stairs, feeling lighter than she had for days. With any luck at all, her mother would be gone for another hour or more. That would give her plenty of time.

Dropping to her knees at the side of her bed, Natua reached up under the head and pulled out a long case. Ah, but she didn't want to get it sticky. Finishing off the fruit, she carefully rinsed her hands, then wiped the wooden carrycase.

"Hello, Papa." She whispered the greeting as she opened the latch and raised the lid. Military awards jingled in their places hanging from the lining. Tenderly, she lifted out an old shirt and slipped it on, leaving it unbuttoned and hanging loose around her shoulders. "Looks like I'm never going to grow into your hugs."

Wiping away a tear, she propped a picture of her father up against her bed. "Sorry it's been so long, Papa. Things just got so busy. We're in a new place now. It's a little bigger than the last one, and Mama can't decide whether to complain about more space to clean or rejoice because our neighbors are quieter."

More tears fell as she recounted other things that had changed over the missed months. After a while, her throat sore from so much talking, she recounted, "You should've seen him move, Papa. The way he scaled that wall. I had no idea Kaloe was so nimble!"

Then, with a sigh, "I wish you were here, Papa. You'd know what to do about Gusari and Mirko. They twist every situation to their own advantage, leaving the workers and the company scrape by as best as they can. I could go to Director Rysl, but I keep asking myself if he retired to spend more time with his family? Or because he was done with the business and doesn't actually care anymore?" She tapped one of her father's medals and watched the thumbnail-sized teardrop crystal spin in the dwindling light. "Rysl was always kind to me. I think he cares."

Cocking her head to one side as her whisper faded away, Natua tried to estimate how long she might have until her mother arrived home. Rising, she removed her father's shirt, folded it carefully, and returned it to its place in the case.

Unfastening two clasps, she released her father's field sword. Setting aside the hardened, polished wooden scabbard, Natua set herself to a simple drill.

"Ouch!" Not simple enough, apparently. She really did spend too much time hunched over a desk. Pausing to stretch, something she never used to need to do, she tried again.

Step, turn, block, lunge. The razor-sharp blade sang through the evening air as she shifted to another drill, then another. Each was easier than the last as her muscles warmed to the once-familiar motions.

The sound of laughter from downstairs froze her in a half-crouch, sword over her head in a defensive position.

"She's home!" Swiftly, Natua replaced everything, snapped the case's latch closed, and slid it back into its hiding place.

"Ah, that girl." Kume's exasperated voice floated up the stairs. "I can already tell she's not home. She stays out until all hours of the night, working."

"Working?" Arru's deep voice echoed the word lazily, laced with the barest hint of amusement. Had he walked her mother home? "Yes. I'm sure she is."

His laugh set Natua's teeth on edge. It had a nasty tone to it, as if he knew something about her and not to her credit. How dare he?

Not in her own house, he didn't!

Marching out onto the landing at the top of the stairs, Natua was about to speak when her mother beat her to it.

"Now you listen to me, young man. I know you've done a lot of traveling and seen a lot of things, enough to keep me listening to your tales until the moons have risen." Kume faced him squarely, one forefinger extended warningly. "But if you think you're going to come into *my* house and insult *my* daughter, you have drastically miscalculated."

"Well said, Mother." Natua descended the stairs slowly, attempting to exude a calmness in defiance of the joyous way that hearing her mother defend her made her feel. "As for you, Arru Deits. When you were telling my mother that you saw me meeting with a man in the marketplace, did you also mention you introduced that man and me to the future queen of Marroi?"

Arru's slightly sunburned cheeks flushed, making

his freckles stand out like tiny brown islands in a sea of unsightly red. "How did you…?"

"How did I know you were the one that told her?" Natua folded her arms across her chest, thoroughly vexed with him for all the chaos he'd caused them. "Does it really matter?"

Kume stared back and forth between them, then faced Arru again, her lips compressed so tightly that they were white against her pale face. "You may go."

Finding that he was summarily dismissed, Arru thrust out his lower lip and stormed through the door.

Closing and locking it behind him, Kume turned to her daughter. "You met Doctor Oneko?" The words were simple, but her tone conveyed her complete surprise.

"For a moment." Natua didn't hesitate to be fully transparent. "Of course, she was shopping for a wedding gift at the time. It's quite possible she wouldn't even remember me if we chanced to meet again."

"I see." Kume dropped her eyes. "I must apologize for my, um. For what I said this morning. He never mentioned that he spoke to you. I didn't realize that…"

Natua closed the distance between them, gathering her mother in a hug. "It's okay, Mama." She held on until her mother's arms inched around her waist and hugged her back. "We don't talk enough anymore, Mama. I'm gone all day for work, and I can't imagine how awful it must've been to hear about my life from someone else." Drawing back, she looked into her mother's eyes. "Especially given how he chose to portray things."

"I should've known better." Kume sniffled, then took a deep breath. She could cry later. Right now she wanted to talk with her daughter. The time she'd spent with the Deits that evening had shown her just how fortunate she was. Arru, whom she'd believed to be a model man of Lurrak, arrogantly dominated the conversation until she felt embarrassed for his parents. His blatant discourtesy in talking over them aside, his chosen topics of conversation and turn of phrase had revealed a boorish side of himself that she never would've guessed at otherwise. "Will you tell me what actually happened?"

"I'd like that." Smiling, Natua gave her mother another squeeze and released her.

They talked for an hour over a late-night snack of sweet lurst jelly and bread, pushing past moments of awkwardness in their determination to become reacquainted.

"I hardly remember deciding to come here," Kume admitted. "One moment we were stressing over your exams and graduation, and the next we were riding those awful dragons."

"Mhmm." Natua shuddered at the memory of riding in the howrah, a partial enclosure strapped to the back of a massive zaldiz draft dragon. Looking *out* over the side was one thing; looking *down* had proven quite another! "I'll never forget that. I wasn't afraid of dragons until I had to actually ride one."

"Yes, exactly!" Kume nodded fervently. "I…" She hesitated, then became absorbed in tracing random figures on the tabletop with her finger. "I'd ride a dragon again if it meant going home."

Natua's heart dropped so hard it set off shock waves of distress when it struck the pit of her stomach. "You want to go back to Lurrak?" This time her mother's answering nod was slow and serious. "Mama, I didn't know that." She bit her lip, wishing she'd taken the time early on to help her mother get acquainted with the country they were living in. Any effort she made now would be a drop of sweet in the bucket of sour discontent her mother had accumulated. "Don't you like anything about Marroi?"

"What is there to like?" Kume spread her fingers, palms up, in a gesture of true uncertainty. "I don't miss the cold, mind, but here it is permanently hot enough to melt my sanity. Why, I used to love keeping house when your father was alive. Now every chore is pure misery."

"Pure misery." Natua couldn't believe her ears. "And you're only telling me this now?"

Kume sighed sadly. "Why should I burden you, child? Weren't you going out every day to earn the money that kept us housed and fed? Didn't you have enough on your mind without my asking you to help with the cooking and cleaning, too?"

Tears sprang to Natua's eyes and she reached across the table to grasp her mother's hand. In her open-eyed retrospect, she now saw every clean dish and dusted surface as a gift of love from her mother. Even the—no, *especially* the hot meals!

"Mama, I've made a decision. Starting tomorrow, we're going to look for someone to take over the housework." Natua squeezed her mother's hand when Kume opened her mouth to protest. "And, since you're going to need something to do with all of your free time, I think we should have a party. It's about time I introduced you to some of the friends I've made over the years." Already names were popping onto her mental guest list. Her young friend Pyr, of course. Japoni and his wife, and their adorable baby. Kaloe.

"A party?" Kume gaped at her in shock. "Here? In this little home?"

"Why not?" Thoroughly enjoying herself, Natua pressed ahead. "It doesn't have to be a big party. Goodness, if we can't fit everyone in the house at one time, we can just have two parties. Or four. Or ten, for that matter!"

"But the expense!" Kume raised her hands and tilted her head to one side, eyes wide. "Shall I stay home and plan parties while you work extra hours to pay for them?"

"Mama, listen." Natua waited until Kume was looking her in the eyes. "You're right. We can't afford to throw three or four parties in a week. Maybe not in a month. And that's alright. If we get a housekeeper and throw the first party, and you still hate Marroi, we'll find a way to go back to Lurrak. I can get a job there and be just as happy as I am here." Her heart twisted as she said the words, warning her that she wasn't being honest. "But let's give this a try. Let's visit the marketplace and…and tour the palace. You can't truly judge Marroi by the foreign quarter and our pocket-sized kitchen, now can you?"

Kume shifted uneasily in her seat, wondering what she was getting herself into. "Alright." Hope surged in her chest. "If we can do all those things *together*, I'm willing to try."

"Marvelous!" Natua glanced at their sandglass and nearly yelped. "Goodness, how did it get so late? I'm not a bit tired."

"You will be tomorrow," Kume warned sagely. Getting to her feet, she lidded the jelly and put it away. "Come on. Upstairs and to bed with you."

Natua chuckled. "You sound just like you used to when I was in grammar school and didn't want to go to bed on a school night."

"Ah, but you were a stubborn child." Kume put one hand over her heart for dramatic effect.

Giggling, Natua wrapped an arm around her mother's shoulders and pulled her along to the stairs. "You used to say I got that from Papa." She stopped walking when Kume's smile faltered. "You miss him, too, don't you."

"Every day." Kume lifted a trembling hand to wipe away an errant tear. "We married late, you know. His career. My pride." She shrugged. "He would have retired next year. If he'd lived."

Natua hugged Kume's shoulders and rested her cheek against her mother's. "I've always wondered something, Mama. But I've never known how to ask you."

"Oh? What's that?" Kume squeezed Natua's arm encouragingly.

"You gave away his things, Mama. All of them." Natua's voice cracked and she paused to regain control of it. "You never asked me if there was something I wanted to keep to remember him by."

"Your papa was a military man, Natua. We owned precious little beyond the clothes on our backs." Kume tried blinking back the tears, but it wasn't enough. Several spilled down her cheeks, leaving her to try to mop them up with the kerchief she took from her pocket. "I knew a man about his size who could use his old uniforms. And there was a young officer at Fort Baim that he'd taken a shine to, so I sent his sword and some other equipment to him. Surely you didn't want any of those things?"

Natua dabbed at her eyes with her cuff, then took her mother by the hand. "There's something I need to show you." Leading the way up the stairs, she entered her bedroom and seated her mother at the vanity. "I remember that young officer you mentioned. I thought he was so dashing." Her laughter was choked with tears as she knelt by her bed and reached for the case. "He looked particularly handsome when he brought this to our home one day after the funeral."

Kume crumpled her kerchief as her hands moved to cover her mouth. She hadn't seen her husband's sword case for nine years, yet she recognized it instantly.

"He kept the dress sword and a few other odds and ends. But he told me he thought it should stay in our family." Natua opened it, showing her mother the medals and other things.

"You've had this all this time?" A flood of memories washed over Kume as she stroked a battered, standard-issue sewing kit. How often had she teased her husband about his lack of sewing skills? Whenever he came home from field exercises, she inevitably had to unpick his efforts so that she could mend things properly. "And you never told me?"

"I was afraid, Mama. You gave it away once before.

I thought..." Natua shook her head and lapsed into silence.

"You thought—" Kume's shoulders slumped as the realization hit her "—that I would just find another way to get rid of them? Oh, you poor child." Setting the case aside, she gathered Natua close. "Darling, I was never trying to erase Papa. It just didn't occur to me that you would want these old things. After all, my dear, what use do we have for that sword?"

"It was Papa's." Natua choked on the mixed emotions welling up inside her. Most importantly, her treasures weren't a secret anymore. "We can share these things now, Mama. We'll both have something to remember him by."

Kume half-laughed, half-sobbed. "I didn't give all of his things away." She gave Natua a lop-sided smile as she drew back. "I still have his shaving kit. A few pictures. Our wedding cups."

"You do?" Natua sniffled and wiped her face. "May I see them?"

"Of course, darling. I should've shown them to you long ago." And so they stayed up a little longer, their bond deepening still further as they reminisced in the moonlight streaming through the window of Kume's room.

"Ah, now." Kume patted her daughter's hand the fourth time Natua yawned. "It's past time you were asleep." Closing the small album of tinsheet pictures, she helped Natua to her feet and began unwinding the gerri that she wore.

"Mmm, high time we both got some rest," Natua countered drowsily. Slipping her arms around her mother, she whispered, "Thank you for tonight, Mama."

"Thank you, Natua." Kume kissed her daughter's cheek and gently guided her over to her bed. "Now lie down. We'll talk more tomorrow."

Natua was surprised the next morning to find herself still in yesterday's clothes, but laughed it off when she thought of the marvelous conversation she'd had with her mother. When she'd cleaned up and dressed for the day, she hurried downstairs.

"There you are." Kume finished peeling a small, prickly fruit and handed it to her on a plate. "I had some of this at the Motruns the other day. It's quite good with the buttered bread."

"Mm, yes, I have it and it's delicious." Natua handed the plate back with a wink. "You eat this one. I'll peel one for myself. It's a new day, remember?"

"Well, I..." Kume stuttered a little in her surprise. "It's one thing to have someone come in and help with the chores. Surely I can still make your breakfast."

"I hope you will sometimes." Natua agreed readily as she sat opposite of her mother. "If I'm running late or you just feel like you want to, that's grand. But on a hot day, which is all there ever is in Marroi, a light breakfast like this will carry me through to lunch just fine."

"Gracious, I never thought." Kume shook her head and reached for the butter knife. "Oh, dear."

"What's wrong?" Natua saw only the bread and the butter when she looked over.

"We seem always to be nearly out of bread." Kume placed a buttered slice of bread on Natua's plate, then prepared one for herself.

"We do, don't we?" Natua relaxed, glad it was something so simple. Or was it? "It's easy to get bread from the marketplace. In fact, we would do well to get as much of our food from the marketplace as possible."

"Oh?" Kume frowned and set clasped hands on the table, waiting for Natua so they could eat together. "Are you sure that's wise? I recall several people warning me after we first moved here, about both the prices and the quality of food we would get from the local market."

"It pays to be careful," Natua agreed. "Some places are particularly bad about trying to take advantage of foreigners." She smiled when Kume tsked softly. "I should probably check with some of my friends at work. They can recommend the best places to shop. Maybe they'll also know where we can find a reliable person to help around the house."

Kume shifted a little uncomfortably in her chair. "That really isn't necessary. I don't mind doing housework. It's just this infernal heat."

"Mother." Natua put her hand lightly on her mother's. As she looked at her mother, truly looked at her for the first time in a long time, she saw a sprinkling of gray hairs in "You've done so much for me. All of my life you've been there for me. Let me do this little thing for you."

Kume relented, her eyes suspiciously moist as she murmured, "If you're going to put it that way."

"I am." Natua squeezed her mother's hand, then patted it.

"In that case, I could ask around here, too. I know at least a few of the families in the quarter have housekeepers." Kume chewed in silence, her eyes thoughtfully narrowed. "I do hope the local market is less expensive than our previous arrangements." Her eyes twinkled as she continued, "With the way we're going to be throwing money around, we'll need to economize somewhere. Otherwise we'll never be able to afford all of those parties."

"Ah, yes, the parties." Natua finished her food and wiped her fingers on a napkin. "I expect you to have a tentative date for the first one by the time I get home tonight. That way we can start inviting people." Stacking her mother's dishes with her own, Natua carried them to the sink. "I'd better get going."

She paused to kiss her mother's cheek, then hurried out the door.

Chapter 11

The second time Natua caught Kaloe staring at her, she put her quill down and motioned for him to join her at her desk. "Is something wrong?"

"I don't think so." He peered into her face. "Judging by the light in your eyes and the fact that you can't stop smiling, I would say something was very right."

Putting one finger on his chest, she pressed gently until he straightened away from her. "Have I ever told you about Lurrak?"

"Your homeland?" His happy mood plummeted like a rider fallen from their dragon's saddle. "Is that why you're so happy? You're going home?" The words were bitter in his mouth.

"What?" She wrinkled her nose in confusion. "I have *no* idea what made you think that." Her mind replayed part of last night's conversation and she sat back a bit in her chair. "Although. You *are* the second person in less than a day to suggest that."

"Suggest?" Kaloe gripped her free hand. "I'm not suggesting anything of the kind. You must stay." He stopped when he heard his own vehemence. Saw how her eyes were widening. Gentling his hold on her hand, he tried to smooth over his gaffe. "You must stay. Here, at the copy center. Helping us."

Natua struggled to breathe, for rather than maintaining his distance, he'd come even closer. Her back pressed against her chair, she had nowhere to retreat. And no matter what he said next, there'd been nothing particularly professional about the heat flickering in his gaze mere moments ago.

"Kaloe, please." She freed her hand and once again pushed him back to what passed for a 'respectable' distance in Lurrak. "I'm not going anywhere, alright? I want to stay in Marroi. I only meant to tell you that, where I come from, people don't stand so close to each other. It makes me a little uncomfortable."

"Oh." Embarrassed, he withdrew even further. "How's this?"

"Better, thank you." Picking up her quill, she made a shooing motion. "Get back to work."

He turned to go, then turned back. "Do people in Lurrak ever stand close to each other?" He hoped so.

"Well. Yes, sometimes." Natua did her best not to blush. "If they're good friends or, um, on special occasions."

His brow puckered. "I sort of thought we were friends."

"We? You and I?" Nonplussed, Natua shifted in her chair and brought her forearms to rest on the desk. She'd be lying if she said she didn't think of him as more than a confrere. However, they weren't the kind of 'friends' who stood as close as he had just now. "We," she pointed her quill at him, then herself, "should be working."

Kaloe still hesitated a moment, studying her as he tried to decipher her message. One of the benefits of being raised by a single mother was that women rarely confused him. Natua managed to, occasionally, but he blamed that on his growing feelings for her. He had to be careful not to interpret what she said and did the way he wanted them, but rather how she meant them. Take now for example. She hadn't said they weren't friends. Actually, she'd leaned forward before she'd spoken, closing the distance between them marginally. Satisfied, he smiled.

"Yes, of course." He was here to work, not flirt. That was better saved for later, when he didn't have to worry quite so much about a potential audience. "Let me take those." He picked up the files she'd stacked to one side as she finished translating them.

As he walked away, Natua took a deep breath. Frowned. Did she feel…sad? No, not sad. What then?

Exasperated with herself, she dipped her quill to

resume her translation. Pyr had cleverly brought her favorite dictionary along with the files, the one with multiple languages in it, and now she stared unseeingly at it.

Lonely. That was it. Sitting there, in a room with over twenty people in it, she felt lonely. It didn't make sense. She'd felt fine, even a little crowded, until... Natua lifted her eyes, looking through her lashes to where Kaloe stood sorting the new translations into the assignment box.

Wait. What was he doing? Her jaw dropped as she watched him working with the files. At that distance she couldn't actually tell what he was doing, but judging by the flashes of color she saw, she thought she knew. The very first time she'd investigated the assignment box, she'd had to consult the assignment sheet in the back of each jacket to verify the copy due dates. To save herself time going forward, she'd rearranged things so that the nearest deadlines were in the same color jacket, then the next due, and so on. She'd been too busy to give it much thought, but now it occurred to her that since then the files had stayed in that order.

Because of Kaloe. Without being told or asking for praise, he'd simply stepped in and followed her lead, saving her time and effort. Extraordinary.

Ridiculous. She gave herself a little shake and turned her attention back to the translation. Not only was she no longer a child to go dreaming over a fellow, she was this fellow's boss. Indirectly, anyway.

Her quill froze, poised over a half-written word. *She* might be too old for that, but—what about Kaloe? He was only... Well, she didn't know how old he was, just that he was several years younger than herself. Oh, dear. Did that mean he was young enough to confuse one feeling for another?

"Head Translator." Pyr waited politely for a response. "Head Translator?" He repeated himself with a smidge more volume. "Manager Mirko would like to see you."

"What? Oh." She put her quill down. Picked it back up and finished the word. What was the matter with her? At her age, she should certainly be rational enough to differentiate between a growing friendship and a budding romance. "Sorry." Wiping the quill clean, she set it in the box with the others. "Let's go."

Only the faint swish of her slippers on the floor accompanied her past the door to the main building, for Pyr had other tasks to accomplish, but Natua didn't mind. Her term at the copy center was half over. It was high time she met with Mirko again.

Korrez didn't bother looking up from his work as she approached the office. "He's expecting you."

She privately acknowledged her own annoyance with his disrespectful attitude and walked past without saying a word. As usual, Mirko was seated behind his monstrosity of a desk when she entered the office.

"Prezio." He gestured at a chair. "So nice of you to take time out of your busy schedule to meet with me."

The rebuke in his tone drew her up short. "I've been busy working on the translations you sent. However, I came as soon as you sent word."

"Oh, come now." Selecting a shaping rod from his top drawer, Mirko draped one leg over the other and began filing at a rough spot on one of his nails. "Supervisor Gusari has made a number of appointments with me over the last few weeks. I'd venture to say I've seen more of him since you transferred to the copy center than I have in the past year."

Natua gritted her teeth. It didn't take much imagination to picture Gusari sitting in the same chair she now occupied, whining about the changes she'd made. Now that she knew Mirko was a party to, or at the very least, aware of, Gusari's embezzlement and the horrid way he treated his staff, she was hard-pressed not to tell him exactly what she thought of them both.

"Then you already know things have changed for the better at the copy center." Despite the intensity of her feelings, she somehow managed to speak softly.

"Changed, yes." Mirko intentionally devoted the next few seconds to perfecting the angle on the nail he'd finally smoothed out. He'd sensed a change in Gusari during their last meeting, as if the idiot might do something drastic to get rid of Prezio. Naturally, Mirko warned him to be circumspect in his actions, but for the first time in all his years doing business with the man, he didn't believe Gusari would do what he'd been told.

Natua, fractionally older yet vastly wiser now than on the occasion of her last visit to this office, found his actions oddly amusing. Two dozen scribes depended on the copy center for work and what did Mirko care about? His vanity. Her already-low opinion of the man dropped drastically.

At last satisfied with the results of his grooming efforts, Mirko set the rod down and turned back to Prezio. He didn't care for what he saw. She was so still, too still, too perfectly in control for someone who'd just been humiliated by waiting while he'd tended to his manicuring.

"You say things are better at the copy center. I will admit, the efficiency is improving. On paper." He skipped straight to the crux of his plan, the whole reason he'd called her in. "The irony of it all is that we have just received notice that our paper supplier is overbooked. We're going to have to turn down over a dozen lucrative translations related to the royal wedding because of it." He shook his head and endeavored to assume a grave countenance. "If we aren't able to source enough of the right kind of paper quickly, we may not even be able to serve our regular customers."

"I don't understand." Natua cut in sharply. She knew, without knowing how she knew, that Mirko was circling around to threaten someone's termination. "We have a contract with them that they are legally obligated to fill."

"We do?" Mirko's eyebrows shot up. Inwardly he triumphed even as he seethed with resentment for her. This was more like the Prezio he knew and hoped to manipulate. "A contract? I wonder why I didn't think of that. Ah, wait. I did." Reversing course, his eyebrows drew sharply down, until he bore an odd resemblance to the narrow-faced 'smoker' dragon, so-nicknamed because it expelled smoke with each exhalation, even from between its teeth at times. "I also had the foresight to file a supplementary contract with them as soon as I gathered enough evidence to believe we would get the royal translations." Yanking open a drawer, he pulled out his copy of the supplementary contract and threw it down on his desk.

"But then how…" She started to express her confusion, only to stop when he flung up a hand.

"Allow me to anticipate your next question." Steepling his hands, he glared at her. "While Itzuli Communications may be the best translation and copy house in Koroa, we are not the only one. Our supplier signed many such contracts and, if you read ours carefully, you will find that they made provision for exactly this circumstance. They will fulfill the delivery of their contracts in the order that they were signed, no exceptions."

Natua couldn't help it. She picked up the document and began flipping through it.

"Page twelve." Mirko supplied wearily. "Subparagraph 2A. Can you truly believe I did not read it for myself?"

She didn't dignify the question with a response. Locating the spot, she marked it with her finger. "May I take this with me?"

"I suppose. It's only a duplicate." Mirko chuckled dryly. "I should warn you, though, that you're wasting your time. Our lawyers went over it with me this morning."

Natua bit back the question of why they hadn't reviewed it *before* he signed it. This was not the time for pointing fingers. No, she had to keep her focus on not losing business—or co-workers—and fanning Mirko's flames could burn that house down around her ears.

"I'll read it after work tonight. Perhaps I'll find a mistranslation somewhere." She smiled sweetly. "Was that all?"

He huffed, annoyed that she was taking the news so well. "Wasn't that enough?"

"It's a huge obstacle to overcome." She agreed demurely as she rose, still intent on protecting the others. "We will at least accept the translation portion of the translations, I hope?"

"Another excellent idea, Prezio, where do you come up with them all?" Mirko scowled. "There are no half portions here. Either we do the whole job, or we get nothing."

"Then take the whole job," she countered. "If we take the jobs, then the other companies can't. They will scramble to cancel their paper orders and our supplier will have to fill ours." Her blood chilled when his scowl shifted to a smug smile.

"It could work. Yes. Very well. I will notify the palace that we will accept *all* of their business." Mirko smoothed his hair, enormously pleased with himself. They could never handle so much work in such a short time. He would enjoy watching her drive herself to exhaustion. As she approached failure, he would naturally fire her and take over the project himself. The timing couldn't be more perfect, for he'd just begun attempting to persuade Director Rysl to sell Itzuli to him. He couldn't offer much for a business about to lose its reputation, now could he?

Natua gripped the back of the chair for support. How many translations did his heavily stressed 'all' include? How many copies? "Excellent. The translators and scribes alike will be glad for the overtime." It was the best strategy she could come up with on such short notice.

His smile dimmed. "Yes. I suppose it will come to

that."

"If there's nothing else?" Relieved that he'd essentially agreed, Natua tentatively released the chair. Flexed aching fingers as soon as they were safely hidden by the chair back.

"No, that's more than enough. As usual." Mirko pulled the chord behind his desk, signaling for Korrez. He'd already dictated a letter declining the royal translations and wanted to call it back.

Natua gave Mirko a tiny bow while she waited for Korrez to bustle through the door. Naturally she heard Mirko demand the letter.

"What do you mean you already mailed it?" Mirko's bellow echoed through the stone halls. "Well, don't just stand here. Go and GET IT!"

Stifling a laugh, she hurried back to the copy center. She couldn't guess how things were going to turn out, yet she had a good feeling about it. Surely Mirko and Gusari would have to pull their own weight to get this handled properly. Who knew? They might even get a taste for making an honest living.

"Tetsu. Bariux. My desk, please." Trading her finger for a scrap of paper to mark her place, Natua set the contract aside and focused on the men approaching her desk. She barely spared a glance at Gusari's desk, which was empty, as usual. "Gentlemen. I've just learned that we're going to get a lot more work. Tetsu." She addressed Kaloe even as she picked up her quill and a blank page. "I want you to go through the assignment box. Evaluate it based on due date, number of copies required, languages, and so forth. Bring me an estimate on how quickly we could clear it out with the resources on hand. Don't include the trainees in your calculations." Seeing Bariux stiffen from the corner of her eye, she looked at him directly. "Underestimating our capacity may be the only thing that saves us in the long run."

"Understood." Kaloe nodded to Bariux, who looked slightly mollified, and went to work.

"Bariux. I need you to gather information. Or record it, if you already have it." Natua rotated the page so he could see the columns she'd made across the paper's long edge. "These are the more difficult languages that we most often copy. I want to be able to use this to see at a glance who is proficient in these languages. After you've finished," she handed it to him, "I'd like to discuss putting you in charge of the training group for the languages you are proficient in. If you're willing."

"Yes, Translator." Bariux, now apparently quite rejuvenated, set to his task with alacrity.

Meanwhile, Natua took a seat at the training table. She reviewed their work daily, but things were about to change, and quickly.

"Are we ever going to get back to real work?" asked the youngest scribe as he handed over his practice page.

"Sooner than you think. Sooner than I would've liked, actually." Natua nodded with approval at his copy. "You've all improved. Your handwriting is better. Your skill with these new languages has grown. And, soon we won't be able to afford the luxury of four scribes in training status." She gave them a moment to digest that, then cleared her throat to regain their attention. "I'll check your work going forward, just like everyone else's. Alright?"

Satisfied with their eager nods, Natua got to her feet. Gusari was still off doing something somewhere else, so she moved to stand in front of his desk, which was where the scribes were accustomed to looking for updates.

"May I have your attention, please." She waited semi-patiently for them to all finish their thoughts and look up. Only when she had everyone's attention did she proceed. "I wanted to inform you of another change to the way things are done in the copy center. I hope to resume training groups after the royal wedding, but soon we will all have as much and probably more work than we can handle." That created a bit of a stir, which she did her best to ignore. "We are no longer going to have the entire staff working on a project until it is completed. Going forward, projects will be assigned based first on your accuracy and second on your language proficiency. The third consideration will, of course, be the assignment itself; its due date and size. Working together and to the best of our abilities, I believe we will be equal to the task ahead. Thank you."

Ending with a smile and nod, Natua retook her seat, where she resumed the translation she'd interrupted to meet with Mirko. She hadn't gotten much further with it when Kaloe approached.

"Nice speech." Kaloe winked and handed her his written assessment.

"Wait." Natua skimmed the sheet, nodding to herself. He'd done a good job, organizing the assignments by due date first, then number of copies and how many of which languages. She blew out a breath. "This won't be easy."

"Futile comes to mind." Kaloe lowered his voice, but kept back a bit. "Even as we speak, the translators are preparing more files for the assignment box. We'll never see the end of it."

"I should hope not," she agreed, holding the sheet out to him. "The point isn't to work ourselves out of our jobs, Kaloe. It's to clear as much of this as we reasonably can now, before we are drowning in projects for the wedding."

He pursed his lips, but narrowly refrained from whistling in surprise. "We'll be doing work for the royal wedding? What an honor!"

"I'm glad you feel that way." She rattled the sheet she was still holding until he took it. "I'll get these translations done as quickly as I safely can, but I expect more are coming. Which means that, for the time being, you are in charge of keeping the assignment box in order. I also want your recommendation as to what projects to work next. We'll talk a bit more once Bariux brings me his sheet. Right now, if you'd finish your current copy, please?"

She smiled at him when he mock saluted before leaving. It was only as she bent over her translation again that she remembered with a gasp— "The parties! When am I going to find time to plan, organize, and co-host parties?"

Chapter 12

"Kaloe, you don't have to walk me home!" Natua protested, but he didn't seem to be listening. "It's the third time this week."

"So?" He unceremoniously took her lunch pail from her as they walked out into the courtyard. "What you should be worried about, what I know I am worried about, is what would I tell my mother when she asks if you got safely home?"

"Well, I guess I can't argue with that." Maybe she could've, if she hadn't been so tired. "Does she really ask you that?"

"Of course." He linked his arm through hers to steady her as she stumbled. If he hadn't seen her eating lunch every day, he would wonder, for she was now definitely thinner than when they'd first met. "She also asks if Tilla is doing a good job."

"Tilla?" Natua dragged her mind away from the translation she was working on. "Oh, our new housekeeper! The wonderful woman who not only cleans *and* cooks, but is also teaching my mother some new recipes!"

"You are satisfied with her, then?" He couldn't help grinning at her, pleased to hear his mother's friend was appreciated.

"We couldn't be happier. Well, except for one thing." Natua tried to keep a straight face but couldn't. "I'm going to have to speak to her about her cooking. It is much, much too delicious. If I eat much more of it, I'm going to have to buy a whole new wardrobe!"

Kaloe hooted with laughter at that, completely unperturbed by the friendly glare on her face. She was in no actual danger of exceeding the comfortable limits of anything he'd ever seen her wear.

"I see what's going on. Yes, it's all becoming clear to me now." She wagged a finger at him. "You deliberately recommended her, trying to drum up business for your mother's shop!"

"Drum up?" He enjoyed her teasing but didn't understand it. "Why would a tailor shop need a drum?"

"What? No, it. Um." She took a deep breath while she arranged her scattered thoughts. "It's a Lurrakian expression. We have traders there, too, that travel from town to town. When they arrive in a new town, they put on a little show. You know, to make a little noise. Let folks know they're there and open for business."

"Ah, I begin to understand. You think Tilla and I shill for my mother's shop." He quirked an eyebrow at her. Some shops, even some stalls, used the tactic of sending a wandering spokesman throughout the marketplace or city in the hope that they could direct business to them.

"Yes. Exactly." Natua snapped her fingers as the market came into view. "Speaking of Tilla. I have to pick up some things. Um. Dried…dried." She pulled out the list and squinted at it. Fortunately for Tilla, she didn't work at the copy center or Natua would've had her at the training table until her handwriting improved.

Kaloe brought them to a halt at the edge of the food stalls. "Is it an herb? Or a spice?"

"I think it's some kind of a pepper. What do you see?" She turned slightly so they could both read, mmm, *try* to read it.

"Let me look." His eyebrows shot up in surprise. "She must've been in a hurry when she wrote this."

"Can you read it?" She asked doubtfully.

"I can. The first item is a pippera."

"Aha! That stall over there has an entire wall of those!" She pointed.

Wait, wait." He held her in place. "I know where we can get a better quality pippera and for a better price. Come."

He kept helping her interpret Tilla's scribble, but

he let her do the haggling once they arrived. She spoke Marroi well enough and he trusted her to give a fair price, which gave him a chance to browse between stops. It would soon be his mother's birthday and he hadn't settled on a gift for her. She'd never worn jewelry during his childhood, but in the last few years she'd relented, starting with when her boss scolded her for not dressing the part.

Women come here to buy pretty things. What do they think when they see how plainly you dress? Hmm?

Just as he was about to go check on Natua, a necklace caught his eye. Tiny iridescent bitxi stones were spaced evenly along a cord made of the darkest ergmo ore and burnished until it fairly glowed in the sunlight. It was one of those rare ornaments that would go with any outfit, yet tasteful enough to suit any occasion at which jewelry should be worn.

"A lovely piece, yes?" The trader addressed him in clumsy Marroi. "I give fair price." He beamed as he quoted a figure.

"Lovely necklace, yes." Kaloe carefully replaced the item on the display. There was no point in haggling over such a sum. It would take months of extra work at the copy center for him to save up even half of it. "I'm sure you will sell it easily." Inclining his head politely, he turned to walk away and bumped into someone.

"Oh! Oh, excuse me, please." A short woman with gray streaks in her blond hair apologized in Lurrakian as she backed away from the tall stranger. "I'm terribly sorry."

"It is forgotten." Kaloe responded graciously, offering her a slight bow.

"You speak Lurrakian?" She stopped retreating. "Could…could you help me, please? I came to buy something and, um." She looked very small as she eyed the chaos that was the market. "I'm rather lost, you see." As if she heard how desperate she sounded, she drew herself up. "I will pay you for your services as a guide, naturally."

His pride smarted a little at her presumptuous statement, but he took a deep breath. Tourists often made such mistakes.

"Seeing you safely along will be payment enough." Kaloe bowed gallantly.

"Mother?" Natua stopped walking to look back and forth between her mother and Kaloe. "Do you two know each other?"

"Natua, my dear." Kume closed the gap between them and gripped her daughter's arm as if afraid of being forcibly separated from her. "No, I cannot say that I've had the pleasure of learning this young man's name, but he is most kind." Turning to Kaloe, she repeated, "Sir, you are most kind. However, I find that I will not be needing your services after all."

"'Mother." Natua interrupted before her mother tried to walk away with her.

"Hmm?" Kume, still relieved to be in familiar company, smiled brightly at her daughter.

"Mother, I'd like you to meet my confrere and friend, Kaloe Tetsu. His mother recommended Tilla to me." Natua gestured to him, then back to her mother as she continued, "Kaloe, please permit me to introduce my dear mother, Kume Prezio."

Recovering from his shock, Kaloe bowed as grandly as he had to Doctor Oneko. "Dragon's whiskers, how stupid I am. I hope you will forgive me for not recognizing you at once."

"Recognize me?" Kume frowned. "Have we met before?"

"This is the first time I have seen your enchanting face." Kaloe straightened. "But have I not spent every day for the last five weeks with your daughter, whose beauty so closely resembles your own?"

Kume's eyebrows rose exponentially. "Indeed. Have you?"

"Yes, Mother. I did mention he was my confrere." Natua fought bravely against blushing, and lost. Trying to salvage the situation, she improvised, "Don't mind his talk. Flattering the boss is something of a tradition here."

"Natua!" Doctor Leuna Oneko, who'd witnessed most of the conversation from one aisle over, hailed them as she approached, her annoyed guards hot on her heels. "Kaloe. It's so good to see you both again."

"Doctor." Kaloe greeted her.

"Leuna. What a pleasant surprise." Natua repressed a grimace when her slightly overwhelmed mother tightened her hold. Flexing her fingers to make sure blood was still reaching them, she asked, "May I present my mother, Kume Prezio?"

Acting quickly, Leuna gave Kume a slight bow in deference to the other woman's seniority. "Always a pleasure to meet new friends."

"The pleasure is mine, naturally." Kume demurred, returning the bow. "What brings you to the market?"

"Gift hunting." Leuna lifted one shoulder, trying to downplay her discouragement. She had it on good authority that King Txoko's gift for her, whatever it was, was already being handmade. "I keep hoping to find something that will inspire me with the perfect wedding gift, but so far nothing seems quite right."

"I wonder." Natua hesitated, reluctant to advise a bride on such an important matter. "We, that is, my mother and I, were talking recently about when she got married."

"Oh, that's nothing to bother her with." Kume broke in hastily, startled to hear Natua bring it up to such an important person. "It was a long time ago and really, a very small ceremony. Nothing fancy."

Leuna smiled and gently countered Kume. "Go ahead, Natua. What were you going to say?"

Natua took a deep breath. "She's right, it wasn't fancy. All my father could afford was the license and a set of plain wooden wedding cups."

"Wedding cups?" Leuna frowned thoughtfully.

"Yes. Though they were quite ordinary when he

bought them, he spent hours carving them before the ceremony." Natua waited anxiously for Leuna's response.

"What a wonderful story. It reminds me." Leuna's eyes narrowed slightly as she looked back on a memory. "It reminds me of my parents. They were fresh out of college when they married; had more prospects than money." Returning to the present, she ventured an opinion. "I don't suppose anything is ever truly ordinary that plays a part in bringing about such happiness."

"No, you're right." Kume's voice had a hint of tears in it. "You are absolutely right, Your Highness."

Leuna blinked, then laughed softly. "I suppose I should get used to that title."

"You'll barely have time for that before you become Your Majesty," observed Fiantza cheekily.

"Fair point." Leuna laughed a trifle nervously, then relaxed as the others joined in. "It's been nearly a year since Txoko proposed, yet I can hardly grasp everything that's coming." The wedding itself was still two months away, and a good thing, too. It was far too late to ask her grandparents to fetch anything from her hometown of Herrixka when they returned to Marroi. She'd have to send a special dragon messenger. Hmm, the sooner the better. "It's been delightful seeing you again. And meeting you." She nodded politely to Kume.

"You as well." Kaloe, sensing that she needed to leave, was quick to bow.

"Have a good evening, Doctor." Natua followed suit, thrilled to think that her suggestion might be the reason behind the faint smile on Leuna's face.

"We hope to see you again sometime." Kume blurted the cliché without thinking.

Leuna stopped. So did her guards, who'd been preparing to follow her. Lately, she thought she knew what a pebble dropped into a pond felt like. Ever since she'd agreed to marry Txoko, she hadn't been able to do more than breathe normally without creating ripples.

"I'd like that. I'll send invitations 'round. You must join us for supper at the palace."

Kaloe opened and shut his mouth twice without managing to squeak a word out. "Me? At the palace?"

"You do eat, I trust." Leuna smiled at her own joke. In her experience, it was always the tall, slender fellows that ate the most. She'd have to give the staff advance notice.

"Oh, yes." Natua nodded vehemently. "I've seen it with my own eyes and it's quite a marvel. In fact, just the other day his mother was telling me that if sand was edible, he'd lay the desert bare."

"She did not." Kaloe tried to sound gruff, but it was hard when he wanted to laugh. "She was talking about her friend, Tilla, and saying that she was such a good cook, she could even make sand taste good."

Leuna flicked a glance between them, trying to pinpoint what it was that made the simple banter sound like so much more. It ended as quickly as it had begun, leaving her intrigued.

"You're too kind to suggest it." Kume bobbed an awkward curtsy. "We couldn't impose. Especially not with everything you already have to do."

"Now that's no reason not to come." Leuna ducked her head sheepishly. "It's no strain upon *me* to have a few extra guests. I get in terrible trouble if I even try to turn a hand. And it would be so nice to have you. Please come."

Natua bravely lifted her chin. "We'll look forward to it. Thank you."

"Stupendous. Is this week too soon?" Leuna fingered the whistle she wore on a loop about her wrist. She wouldn't dream of trying to order the half-wild distira dragon about, but they had reached something of an understanding on certain matters.

"That would be fine." Kume, accepting her fate as a guest at the palace, of all places, accepted as graciously as she could.

Kaloe...hesitated.

"Kaloe Tetsu, isn't it?" Leuna promised, "I'll be sure to send invitations for your parents as well. I can't wait to meet them."

"Thank you." Kaloe appreciated her quick grasp of the reason behind his reluctance. "I know my mother will be glad to come."

"Well, I'll see you all then." Leuna bowed and left.

"Goodness me." Kume half-covered her mouth with one hand. "I know we said we'd tour the palace, Natua, but this… This is more than I'd bargained for! Whatever shall we wear?"

"You don't have to worry about that. Please, allow me." Kaloe helped himself to Natua's packages, wishing he'd thought of it sooner rather than just letting her stand there and hold them. "My mother has many customers who have eaten at the palace. She can help us decide what to wear."

"What a good idea." Natua agreed before her mother could object. Taking advantage of the fact that her mother still had a firm grip on her arm, she started walking toward home. "And if we don't have anything suitable, she manages a tailor shop. It's perfect."

"Yes." Kume needed a minute to warm up to the thought of having a complete stranger advise her on her wardrobe. Granted, it would be worth a little awkwardness to not spend an entire evening at the palace wishing she'd worn something else. "Does the shop make Lurrakian-style clothing?"

Natua turned to Kaloe, who shrugged.

"For such a special occasion, of course. Though you might be more comfortable wearing a palantzia." Kaloe was genuinely curious why anyone would choose to wear the heavy, stiff style of clothing she seemed to prefer. On the other hand, it helped explain why Natua sometimes chose it instead of the lighter, looser Marroi clothes she wore so beautifully.

"We are Lurrakian." Kume reminded him proudly. "We will go as Lurrakians."

"That's true, Mama, we are. But I don't think it was

Leuna's intention to have us come as political ambassadors." Natua steered her mother to one side so the cart that had been following them could rattle past. "Didn't you get the feeling that she just wanted a relaxing evening? Good food, some pleasant conversation. That sort of thing?"

"I…I see what you mean." Kume yielded the point reluctantly. Mindful of Kaloe's presence—and impressed that he was going out of his way just to carry packages for his boss—Kume said no more. It would be embarrassing enough to admit to Natua that ignorance of how to wear the clothes was intimidating her. Spotting their gate, she announced, "Here we are. Oh! Oh, my."

"What is it, Mama?" Natua gestured to Kaloe that he could put the packages down by the door, but he shook his head. *Stubborn.* "Is something wrong?"

"It's Tilla. I mean." Kume hastily corrected herself. "There's nothing wrong with Tilla. It's just that I volunteered to pick up some things at the market for her. She made a list last night, which somehow went missing this morning and, well." She threw up her hands, disgusted with herself. "I was going to try to buy as many of the things as I could remember, but I got lost. Then we met the queen." Actually, that last was a pretty decent reason to forget about a mere shopping list. At the end of the story, however, one fact remained. "I'm afraid I've muffed it all up."

"Mama." Natua slowly pulled a piece of paper out of her pocket and showed it to her. "Is this the list you couldn't find?"

"It is!" Kume stared from the list to Natua and back again. "You mean, *you*…"

"I'm sorry, Mama, I should've told you. I saw it on the hallway table as I was leaving this morning and thought you'd forgotten to ask me to pick things up on the way home from work."

Kaloe held up the packages he was still holding. "We got the whole list."

"You did?" Kume's lips twitched. Then her shoulders started to shake. The laughter bubbled up, up inside her until it spilled out. "I'm sorry. I can't seem to help myself. I spent all day wracking my brain to try to remember everything Tilla asked me for. And now you ha-have it and it's taken care of!"

Natua put an arm around her mother's shoulders and squeezed. The cares of the day seemed to roll off her shoulders as she started giggling, too.

"I'll take these inside," offered Kaloe, grinning. He winked at Natua as he passed, then came to a full stop inside the house.

"What is it, Kaloe?" Natua paused beside him, releasing her mother to go on ahead. "Is something wrong?"

"Wrong?" He turned toward her, but his eyes continued scanning the strange room on his left. "No. I just." Shrugging, he admitted, "I've never been in a house like this."

"Is it so very different from your home?" Natua took advantage of his distraction to try to retrieve the packages.

"Not so fast." He gave her his full attention as he moved his hands to one side, away from her. "I'll carry them."

"Thank you for bringing them from the market, but it's a really short walk to the kitchen from here." She pointed at the hallway. Seeing his eyebrows rise slightly as he followed the direction of her finger, she gave in. "Alright. Come on, and I'll give you the short tour."

"Wait." Shifting the packages all to one arm, he caught her sleeve.

"Now what?" She wasn't sure if she was impatient or amused or both. Tired, mostly.

"Start the tour here." He waved at the room that had first captured his attention.

"That? It's the sitting room."

"You…have a room just for sitting?" Kaloe stared

at the room with renewed wonder. He'd noticed the chairs, of course, but still.

"No, it's, um." Natua laughed and rubbed her forehead. "It's not for us to sit in. It's for guests. I mean." Taking a deep breath, she tried a third time. "Anyone can sit in here. But we invite guests to sit in here with us so we can talk and…and things. It's the largest room in the house."

"Ah." He nodded, beginning to understand. "Where do you sit when you do not have guests?"

Chapter 13

"Do you think we should invite the Motruns to the first party? We could make it a birthday celebration for you!" Kume mused aloud as she made a final adjustment to her hair. They were only going to the tailor shop, but she wasn't missing a chance to practice when they had so little time to prepare for a night at the palace. Only three days to sort out what to wear!

"A birthday party? I'm too old for those." Natua laughed and shook her head. "But, we should absolutely invite the Motruns. I know I suggested having them over weeks ago." Natua peeked into the mirror over her mother's shoulder, trying to reassure herself she'd done a good job with her mother's hair. She hadn't tried a hairstyle this fancy since her roommate's 'terribly important date' back at university. Good thing she had a few days to practice it. "I'm sorry I've been so busy."

"Your new position is very demanding." Kume smiled at her daughter's reflection and got to her feet. "I look forward to your return to regular translating."

"Yes, I…I suppose so." Natua deftly secured her pale blue gerri as they descended the stairs. Catching the surprised expression on her mother's face, she explained, "I won't feel easy leaving the copy center in Gusari's tender care."

"But your two months are nearly completed." Kume frowned and followed her into the courtyard. "You don't have much time to effect a change."

"That's true." Natua hesitated. She hadn't told anyone she was considering taking the matter straight to Director Rysl. Given any other choice, she would rather not disturb his partial retirement. And if she did approach him, what would she say? One bottle of diluted ink and the testimony of a few scribes might persuade him to discipline Gusari, but it wasn't exactly compelling evidence for termination.

"Don't worry, my dear." Kume patted her hand. "I know you'll figure it out."

"Thank you, Mama." Natua linked her arm with her mother's. "Enough about work. Let's go pick out some new clothes!"

Kume faltered where the road changed from weathered stone slabs to cobblestones. "You're sure you know where we're going?"

"I'm positive." Natua squeezed her hand. "Here, see? Kaloe drew us a map." She handed it to her mother. It would've been a slightly shorter walk to cut through the marketplace, but she was hoping to catch a cycle carriage. Not only was Patare Tetsu squeezing them in on short notice, she was staying late at the shop so Natua could come after work. It wouldn't do to keep her waiting.

"Ah." Kume sighed in relief. "He's actually quite a nice young man, your confrere." A few steps later, she suggested, "I wonder if he and his mother would enjoy coming over for supper."

"They might." Natua smiled, remembering the way Kaloe pestered her with questions about all things Lurrakian during the short tour she'd given him of their home the night before. She'd countered with questions about Marroi until her mother announced she was going to bed and they'd both realized how late it was.

"That's a nice smile." Kume cocked an eyebrow at her. "Have you thought of someone else you'd like to invite? Someone you want me to meet?"

Taken completely off-guard, Natua tried to laugh it off. The noise came out so strained that she stopped as abruptly as she'd started.

"Oh, look. A carriage!" Putting two fingers to her lips, Natua whistled for the carriage, which promptly stopped, turned around, and came back for them. She helped her mother in, then gave directions in Marroi to the driver.

Once they were settled and on their way, Kume

touched her daughter's arm lightly. "Darling, I'm sorry if I seem pushy at times. It's just that…as much alike as we are, we're still so different." Kume sighed. "I told my mother about every crush and every beau. Of course, when I was your age, I was not providing food and shelter for anyone. The only job I've ever held was housekeeper for you and your father. I never knew the level of exhaustion I see you dealing with until after you were born. I…I loved you both so much." Kume swallowed hard. "What I'm trying to say, and I think I'm failing miserably, is that when I talk about you, your future and marriage, it's only because I want you to have someone just as wonderful to share your life with. Alright?"

"It's nice to hear you say that, Mama. And it isn't that I don't want what you had. I just don't seem to have the time or energy after work to pursue such a future." Natua blinked back the tears that threatened. "I'm afraid I'm something of a lost cause. Unless there's someone hiding, waiting to pop out at me, I honestly don't see how that could change."

"Hello! There you are!" Kaloe bounded out of the shop toward them, the broad smile on his face easily visible even in the fading light as he opened the carriage door. "I was afraid I'd miss you."

"Miss us?" Kume gently tugged at Natua's arm, for she sat motionless. "Wasn't it you who arranged the time and place for us to meet with your mother?"

"True enough." He chuckled, but kept an eye on Natua, whose eyes had gone as large as dinner plates. "I'm sorry if I startled you."

"No. I… Not exactly." Natua gave herself a shake and pasted a smile on her face. She'd only been joking before. And Kaloe was just, well. His usual, exuberant self. The timing was decidedly odd, there was no arguing that.

"We'd best be getting inside," Kume suggested, her own eyes taking in a great deal, "or we'll have your mother out here looking for us as well." With a little effort, she got them shepherded safely into to the shop where his mother was indeed waiting for them.

Once she'd been introduced to Kume, Patare beckoned for her to follow. "We shall start at the beginning, please."

"Meaning me?" Kume clarified with an uncertain laugh. "I'm not sure I qualify as the 'beginning,' but I suppose we do have to start somewhere."

Natua nodded encouragingly to her mother as they stepped around a screen to take some measurements. Finding that she was more or less alone with Kaloe in a room lit only by moonlight and lanterns, Natua developed a sudden fascination with the drawings on the table.

Kaloe, unable to stand idle, once again set himself to sharpening the pins and needles. As often as he'd done it, he should've been able to do it with his eyes closed. Tonight, however, his eyes were neither trained on his work nor closed.

Natua, sensing his gaze, turned her back on him. Distractedly, she ran her fingers through a tray full of beads and buttons, watching them glitter even in the weak light. By rights, she should've faced him and struck up a conversation. A little laughter would've eased the inexplicable tension in her shoulders, and...

"Ouch!" Natua jerked her hand away and stared at the needle protruding from her fingertip.

"What is it?" Kaloe came to his feet as if the chair had bucked him off. "Are you hurt?" Seeing in an instant what had happened, he caught her by the wrist.

"It's nothing, just a loose needle." Natua tried to step away, but all at once his arm was about her waist and she was being held firmly in place. He spoke and his breath stirred a curl at her neck.

"Keep still. Don't go swinging it about. I'll have it out in a moment, alright?" He promised, mistaking her sudden shiver for pain or fear. Tenderly, he eased the needle free, then pushed it safely into a cushion, where it should've been in the first place. Blast a careless needleworker! "It's not bad. It's not too bad." Kaloe recklessly threw things around, searching for a strip of cloth left over from a cutting, anything he could wrap around her wounded digit.

"Is that an aid kit over there?" Fairly hemmed in, she nodded toward it even as she pressed her fingers together to staunch the slowly seeping blood. "Let me get it."

"No, no you mustn't move." His arm tightened about her waist. "I had a handful of pins and needles in my lap when I stood up. They're scattered all over the floor by now."

"Then hadn't I better be the one to go?" She tapped the toe of her boot on the floor, the sound frightfully loud. "You're wearing slippers. And so are both of our mothers."

Kaloe shot an uneasy glance at the changing screen. A fine impression her mother would have of him if she came out unexpectedly to see her daughter in his arms, and bleeding in the bargain.

His arms dropped at last and Natua drew her first real breath since… Was it really only moments since she'd been quietly minding her business? Her heart was racing like a runaway supply cart on the hill south of the market.

Stepping away from him, she retrieved the kit and set it on the nearest table to open it.

"Do you need any help?" Kaloe watched anxiously—helplessly—from where he stood, trapped by his thin-soled slippers. He was on the verge of risking impalement to join her when she sighed in frustration.

No matter how hard she tried, Natua simply couldn't hold the pad in place and tie the ends all with one hand. Of course, she might use her nose as another finger, but that did seem a trifle silly with help standing so nearby. Reluctantly, Natua brought the bandage and a lantern over to him. "Would you mind?"

Their eyes met over their joined hands as he worked, and the instant he finished Natua hastily moved away. "Here, take this." She pushed the lantern at him.

"What are you doing?" Kaloe held the lantern high so he could see her better.

"Kaloe, you're blinding me." She lifted a hand to shield her eyes until he lowered the lantern. "Good. Now hold it closer to the ground." He complied despite wearing a comically confused expression. Stooping, she began to examine the floor. "How many pins and needles am I looking for?"

"A handful," he answered, a tad blankly.

"So more than three and less than twenty?" She pushed her hair back out of her face as she bent to study the floor. "Aha! Here's one!"

"Twenty? No, just five. How many fingers do you think I have?" He demonstrated his point by extending one finger at a time until his right hand was spread out.

"Hmm." Spotting two silver lines on the floor, Natua picked them up carefully. From that angle it was easy to see the last two. "And these make five." Straightening, she poked each of them into the nearest cushion. "There. You may walk safely now, good sir."

Whatever he might've said—or done—was abruptly preempted by the sound of their mother's raised voices.

"Stop saying that, it doesn't make any sense!" Kume sounded exasperated.

Patare responded in Marroi, not unkindly, but apparently at her wits' end.

"Excuse me." Natua brushed past Kaloe to go stand by the changing screen. "Mother? Patare? Can I help?" They both answered at the same time, and in their native languages, giving Natua a headache as she tried to keep up with them both. Tentatively, she peeked around the screen.

"I think it's time we left." Kume had both arms wrapped tightly around herself and refused to look at

Patare.

"I don't understand what's wrong." Patare's exclamation was heartfelt. "I merely suggested she wear a palantzia to the dinner."

"Wait. Please." Natua rubbed her forehead. "Mother, what happened? Why are you so upset?"

"It's nothing. I just want to go home."

"We'll go home as soon as you've explained." Natua moved closer and lowered her voice. "You're going to tell me anyway."

Kume fidgeted with the sleeve of her shirt a moment, then relented. "I suppose I'm overreacting a bit, but. I didn't come all the way over here to be told that I'm" —she glared at Patare over Natua's shoulder and lowered her voice— "that I'm overweight."

"Overw…" Stunned, Natua gave her mother a quick once over even though she already knew it wasn't true. They might eventually gain a few pounds with the way Tilla was feeding them, but it hadn't happened yet! "Patare." Turning back to Kaloe's mother, she asked in Marroi, "Do you remember exactly what you said about wearing a palantzia? Word for word?"

"Word for word?" Patare tapped two fingers on her chin as she thought. Switching to Lurrakian to be precise, she repeated, "You will enjoy wearing the palantzia because it fits so much more loose."

"There, you see?" Kume sniffed.

"Oh, Mother." Natua hugged her spontaneously. Whispered in her ear, "That was a statement on fashion, not on weight. Think about it. It can't be good business to go around telling your customers, um, what they don't want to hear."

"What?" Kume's jaw nearly dropped. "Fashion?"

"Yes, that's all she meant. Here, look at what she's wearing." Natua was relieved when Patare held her arms out to her sides, demonstrating her willingness to model and displaying exactly what Natua was trying explain. "Marroi clothing is designed to fit differently than Lurrakian clothing does. On everyone."

"Well, I." Kume blinked uncertainly, her cheeks pinking. "How embarrassing."

"Please, no." Patare lowered her arms to take Kume's hands in her own. "If you are embarrassed, then I have to be embarrassed, too. It was I who spoke, yes?"

"She has a point, Mama." Natua tried to nudge things in the right direction. "Let's just write it off as a mutual mistranslation, hmm?"

Kume nodded once, then again. "Thank you. I'd like that."

"Good." Patare relaxed, satisfied that things were sorted out with her most important new customer. She trusted Kaloe to make what he could of his relationship with the boss-woman, but knew it would be easier for everyone if she could make friends with Natua's mother. "Now, young lady, you come at good time. It is your turn." She brandished her measuring tape.

Natua laughed and good-naturedly mimicked Patare's stance of a moment before, arms out to her sides, shoulders back and chin level. "Can you really have new clothes ready for us in only three days? I wouldn't want to take you away from your regular customers."

"You are kind to worry, but," Patare completed her measurements and jotted them down, "it is no trouble. It is good for business, in fact." Choosing her words carefully, she continued in Lurrakian. "I have customers who order cloth for fancy clothes. An accident by the carrier ruins half the shipment, so I must send for more. Now all the cloth is here and my customers have gone." Tossing the measuring tape over her shoulder, she opened a cupboard to show them. "It will take no time to make two palantzias for you."

Kume gasped, delighted with the vibrant colors she saw.

"For you I suggest the blue of the sea and the

green of the idetea plant." Patare lifted down two bolts of filmy cloth and nodded at Kume. "For Natua, the blue of the sky and the red of the ripe fruit." An artist in her own way, Patare could hardly wait to see her clients in their new outfits.

Kaloe, meanwhile, had resumed carefully sharpening pins and needles—one at a time. He was naturally curious about the colors, but knew better than to peek around the screen. For now he would have to be satisfied with the knowledge that Natua and her mother were happy with the selections.

"Good. You come here before the dinner." Patare folded the screen back out of the way. "We will try on the clothes, then go."

"Are you sure?" Kume paused, more annoyed with her inability to speak Marroi than usual. "I beg your pardon. I only wonder if we shouldn't come by a day earlier, for fittings?"

Natua did her best to interpret, though 'fittings' wasn't a word she'd ever needed to know in Marroi previously. Patare reassured her that wouldn't be necessary, which she relayed to her mother.

"Let me walk you home," suggested Kaloe, getting to his feet.

"That's alright." Natua rubbed her injured finger without realizing it. "You should go home and rest. Both of you." Her smile included Patare as well. "Busy day tomorrow."

"At least let me find a carriage for you." Kaloe frowned out at the empty street. Street lamps and moonlight kept it from being totally dark, but he still didn't like it.

"Thank you, young man." Kume hadn't been looking forward to the long walk, lights or no.

"I'll be as quick as I can." He bowed and hurried out the door.

Natua watched him out of sight, then realized that both other women were looking at her. "I'll be glad to go home and sleep." She said the first thing that came to mind. "We've had so much work at the copy center lately that I get more tired just thinking about it."

"Kaloe tells me you are now running the center?" Patare half-stated, half-asked.

"Oh, no. Not exactly. Supervisor Gusari," she noted the frown that appeared on Patare's face at the mention of his name, "is still in charge. I'm just trying to help."

"Yes." Patare's expression softened and she nodded. "Kaloe has told me of your help. Since you came, there has been no docking of pay. No extra hours worked for free. He says the work goes much more smooth now."

Natua felt her cheeks pinking at the implied praise.

"Natua? You did all that and haven't told me?" Kume slipped her arm through her daughter's and squeezed gently. "Why, I'm terribly proud of you."

"I haven't done anything alone. Kaloe's help has been invaluable. He learns quickly and more than once has made the difference between success and failure on a project. But this." Natua's voice shook with frustration. "It isn't permanent. In two more weeks, I'll return to translating full-time. And Gusari will undoubtedly return to his old ways. In fact, things may very well be worse." He'd been so obliging the last few days, almost to the point of being cooperative, that she couldn't shake the feeling he was plotting something particularly nasty.

Patare's smile faded. "Kaloe has also told me this. He says maybe you will find the path?"

"A way to make things better? Make them truly better?" Natua didn't intend to scoff, but there it was. "I think about it every day. It's more than Gusari, though. It's." She reigned herself in before she could accuse Mirko.

"There, there, my dear." Kume patted her hand soothingly. "If it can be done, you'll sort it out."

"Thank you." Natua forced a smile and once more asked herself what she would need to have in order to convince Director Rysl to intervene. "I do hope you're right, but I'm afraid we're running out of time."

Chapter 14

"Are you ready?" Kaloe stood by Natua's desk, both of their lunch pails already in his hand. His forehead creased with concern as he considered her pale face and heavy eyes. If not for their supper appointment at the palace, he would've taken her straight home to rest. Perhaps this was Gusari's latest plan. Do nothing and watch them run themselves ragged trying to defend against what he *might* do. He certainly wasn't helping. The wedding copies continued to pile higher and higher.

"In a minute." Natua set aside the file she'd just triple-checked. "We'll have to watch the assignment box more closely. Gusari seems to have caught on to the colored jackets."

"Here." Kaloe put the pails down, took her carefully by the wrists and led her over to sit on the nearest bench. Everyone else had already gone and the sandglass was still. "I'll do that in the morning. Come, let's wipe your fingers."

"But…" She twisted toward her desk, thinking of all the things she still needed to do.

"Don't argue." He seated himself close enough that their knees brushed. Twisting open the bottle of ink remover, he wet a bit of rag. "Give me your hand."

She should've been upset with his audacity in giving her orders, but somehow she wasn't. Still. "I'll do it."

"It's faster this way." Kaloe didn't ask again, just captured one of her hands and began cleaning it. "You work too hard."

"Me? *I* work too hard?" Natua arched an eyebrow. "Who has been here every morning when I arrived? Who has stayed late every day for the past week and a half, plus walked me home after?" Her heart stuttered when he looked up at her.

"Who creates work for herself?" He countered

gently. Finished with one hand, he picked up the other. And just held it, his thumb lightly stroking its back. "You knew I would check the assignment box in the morning. It's the best time, for anything can happen after we leave for the day."

"Yes." She dropped her gaze. "I know. I just thought I saw Gusari over here earlier and…"

"Gusari is letting us chase shadows." Noticing a slight flinch as he wiped her hand, Kaloe held onto it after he'd finished removing the ink. Kneaded her muscles to loosen them. "Is that better?" Would she never learn to stretch her hands? If he was being honest, a tiny part of him hoped not.

"We should go." She'd never expected to get into the habit of holding hands with him, even for so innocuous a reason as his pain-relieving hand massages.

"You have to take better care of yourself." He released her hand and got to his feet. "Now that Mirko has agreed to let you stay until after the wedding projects are completed, we need you more than ever." That guaranteed her another month at the copy center, maybe a little more—and yet not nearly enough. *I need you.*

"I'm fine." The room tilted a little as she rose. "Really."

"Fine? You're fine?" Kaloe barked the words as he wrapped an arm around her to keep her upright. Literally carried her over to their lunch pails, where he knocked the lid off of hers and stared inside in dismay. "Have you eaten anything today?" Selecting a small fruit, he brought it to her lips. "Take a bite."

She obeyed, then rested her head against his shoulder while she chewed. The sweet juice trickled down her throat, reviving her.

"Have another bite." When she'd complied, he closed his eyes and pressed his cheek to her hair. "Are all Lurrakian women as stubborn as you are?"

Rousing enough to realize exactly where she was,

Natua carefully extricated herself. "Thank you for your help, Kaloe. I guess I did forget to eat lunch." Needing to change the subject, or at least jar him loose from the way he was looking at her, she forced a laugh. "It's a good thing we're going to a dinner, isn't it? I can eat all I like and…"

"You have to eat more than once a day!" Kaloe threw up his hands, finally losing his temper. "You have to sleep more than a few hours a night!" He exhaled raggedly. "Buying the success of the copy center at the expense of your health is far too high a price. Do you not see that?"

"Kaloe, I." She stared at him for a moment, trying not to know what burned in his eyes. "It's nice of you to worry about me, but must you also shout? I'm fine now." Turning away, she put a few strides of space between them. Found him blocking the path to the door when she would've started toward it.

"I shouldn't have shouted. I'm sorry." Kaloe's lips twisted in a wry smile. "How do Lurrakian men act when they're in love?"

Natua's knees gave way and she sank down onto a bench. *He said it. Right out loud, he just…said the words.*

"I don't know what else to call it." He lifted a leg over the bench, straddling it so he could face her. A strange peace settled over him as he accepted that this was his moment of truth. "You make the day brighter just by walking in the door. If you ask me to do something, anything at all, knowing you will smile at me when I finish makes me work a little harder. A little better."

"I'm very flattered, but as you said, you work for me." Natua finally lifted her eyes to his. "What you're feeling isn't love, Kaloe. It's gratitude. Things have changed a lot since I came and it's only natural that you…"

"It's more than that. So *much* more." He spoke quickly, afraid she was going to get up and walk away again. Afraid he'd never get another chance to speak if he failed to convince her now. "I miss you when we're apart, so much that I make excuses to walk you home, just so I can spend a little more time with you. I notice details, like how you hate to eat roast lizard and that your favorite color is yellow. You look beautiful in it, too." He felt a surge of hope when he saw the faint blush rising in her cheeks. "I want a great deal more than merely to work with you, Natua Prezio. Won't you give us that chance?" Her answer smashed his hope like a glass ball.

"I'm so sorry." Natua drove the words through stiff lips. "I see that you truly believe you are in love with me." Folding her hands in her lap, she pushed her own feelings down. Whatever he thought he knew now, time would change all that as he watched her grow old before he did. It would be less painful—for them both—to end things before they got started. "You're so young, Kaloe. Life must seem very straightforward. People fall in love, get married, and live happily. At my age, I see things differently."

"That's not how I see things, either." He rubbed his hands on his pant legs, suddenly sad. "Maybe I did, when I was a child. Before my father died in a wrangling accident."

Her stomach twisted in painful empathy. Losing a parent had changed everything for her, too.

"He wasn't well that day. I think it was his stomach, but he made excuses." Kaloe tried to swallow the tears crowding his throat. "I can still hear him telling my mother he was too excited and that was why he couldn't eat. That he would have a big meal after he'd worked the last dragon for the buru. We were all certain this was the big day. The buru would be so pleased with my father that he would offer a permanent position in his stables." A tear slipped past Kaloe's defenses, but he didn't seem to notice. "They had plans for our new, permanent home. I had plans to make friends with every child in the city."

Natua didn't think, she just reached out and slipped

her hand into his, gripping it firmly. "I didn't know." *One more thing we have in common. We've both experienced loss.*

"And now that you do?" Unshed tears stung his eyes as he searched her face. "Natua, I can't offer you the heart of a careless boy because I don't have one. And if you tell me I am alone in my feelings, I will never speak of them again. So far you've said I work for you. That I'm grateful, or maybe just young and foolish." He rubbed his thumb lightly over the hand she'd placed his. It might've been an expression of her pity, though he hated to think so. "But you'll have to tell me, in your own words, why *you* think we are a bad match." He let go of her hand and straightened his shoulders. "That you feel nothing for me."

With the best of intentions, Natua opened her mouth. Tried to shape the words that formed the key that would release him from his infatuation with her—but they wouldn't come. Why not? He wouldn't listen to reason, so now she had to tell him she didn't… That they couldn't, because… Her mind refused to complete the thoughts, leaving her tongue-tied.

Kaloe waited as long as he could bear, then prodded. "What's the matter? Can't you do it?" Getting to his feet, he took both of her hands in his and pulled her up to stand beside him. "If you truly cannot tell me no, then I must ask again. Will you not dare with me?"

"I—" Natua bit her lip. What was she doing? "I can try."

He inhaled sharply. Was he hearing things? "Did you just say yes?" His only answer was a tiny, lopsided smile on her face. Giddy with joy, he pulled her close.

"Kaloe!" She couldn't draw a breath. Struggled ineffectually to free herself before he cracked her ribs in his heartfelt enthusiasm. "Kaloe. Please." The words came out as pained gasps.

He released her promptly. "I'm sorry." Raked his fingers through his hair and struggled to curb the desire to whoop with joy. "I forgot."

"No. Fine." She put a hand on her waist as she sucked in lungfuls of air to replace what he'd squeezed out of her. "It's fine." Bruised. Her ribs were just bruised, not cracked. What a relief! Not until after he'd turned to collect their things when it occurred to her to ask, "What did you forget?"

"That it is not the custom to be so close together in Lurrak." Claiming one of her hands, he lifted it to his lips. "Come. We are late."

Before she could collect the thoughts he'd scattered, let alone begin to explain that this was one of the exceptions to that unwritten rule, they were already outside.

Spotting an empty carriage as they turned onto a main street, Kaloe flagged it down and swung Natua inside. Giving directions to his mother's shop, he dropped onto the seat beside her and burst out laughing.

"What are you laughing about?" Confused, Natua tried to tug her hand free. Had it all been a joke?

"Ah!" He stopped laughing and leaned close. "Don't people hold hands in Lurrak, either?"

"Yes, of course they do." She gave up and sat back with a huff. "But they don't laugh like that right after making such a serious decision."

"They don't?" He tsked as if to say he was sorry for them. "Then maybe they don't feel as overjoyed as I do. Maybe they don't deserve to, because it was too easy for them." Noting the faint creases between her brows, he asked softly, "And what about you? How do you feel?"

She was saved from having to answer by their arrival at the shop. It was easy for her to tell that Kaloe was disappointed when she climbed down and hurried inside, but if he'd insisted on the truth right then, he might've heard entirely too much of it. Her emotions were still whirling and bubbling, far too chaotic to be understood properly, let alone solidified into a short answer.

"There you are!" Already dressed and ready to go, Kume pointed at the changing screen. "Quickly. There's barely time to make alterations!"

Natua paused an instant to ooh and aah at her mother's gorgeous new outfit, a dark blue base color with emerald green accents, then allowed herself to be herded over to the screen and helped to change.

"I asked the carriage to wait." Kaloe burst into the shop, looking for Natua. Then, realizing where she must already be, he jerked his attention instead to the galtzak that waited for him. Thankfully, the shop was big enough to have a second changing screen, which his mother was already shooing him behind.

"Just drape your work clothes over the top," Patare ordered her son. "I'll hand you your new outfit."

Slipping out of his tunic, he quickly rinsed with the scented water that waited for him. A finely woven tan shirt appeared at the edge of the changing screen and he donned it. Next came a dark brown bata with embroidered cuffs, a pair of trousers the exact same shade, and a brilliant blue gerri.

Wrapping and tucking at lightning speed, he stepped out at the same time as Natua.

"Oh, my." Natua wasn't sure whether to be pleased or dismayed at what she saw. Her own outfit fit like she'd come in for half a dozen fittings, but Kaloe. He looked as if he'd been dipped in chocolate, then sprinkled with star dust. She almost couldn't blame the shopgirl for goggling at him. Almost.

Natua gave herself a little shake and looked away, pretending to check her reflection in a nearby mirror. That was when it hit her. His gerri! It was the exact same shade of blue as the base color of her palantzia. Anyone who saw them would think it was done deliberately, to pair them as a couple! Which…well. They *were*. Recently. Very, very recently!

Wasn't she even going to have time to get used to the idea before everyone else figured it out?

"Don't stare, Kaloe." Patare adjusted her own gerri

and patted her hair. "Are we all ready? Very good." Nodding at the needleworker who'd volunteered to help—no doubt in the hopes of making eyes at Kaloe, poor thing—Patare instructed her to take care in locking up, then swept the others out the door. "Carriages are a fine thing and I'm grateful for them," she reminded them all pragmatically, "but it is not cheap to keep them waiting."

Kume laughed with her, appreciating the point, then spent most of the ride complimenting the outfits. "And you were able to get them done without a single fitting. I'm so amazed. I will have to tell all my friends where to find your shop."

Natua let the words drift over her, wishing with every revolution of the carriage wheels that she were somewhere quiet so she could think. She was dating Kaloe. Officially. As of less than an hour ago. Her lips curved up in a rebellious smile that baffled her.

Dating didn't have to be all surprises and mystery. At the very least, she should've seen it coming. Should've been waiting for it, wondering when he would finally ask. Instead, it had somehow snuck up on her and taken her wholly unawares.

Her heart leapt into her throat when Kaloe's hand touched hers.

"You look lovely," he murmured in Marroi.

Oh, she didn't stand a chance tonight. If he didn't give them away, her burning cheeks would.

Yet, entirely without her head's permission, her heart and lips whispered back, "And you are very handsome."

"Here we are." Patare announced as the carriage drew to a halt, mostly to distract Kume. While it didn't take a mother's intuition to sense that something had changed between her son and his boss, the one thing Patare was absolutely sure of was that she should keep her speculations to herself.

"Where is here?" Kume looked around, puzzled. "I don't see any entrance."

Kaloe stepped down first so he could help the others. "The entrance is high above us, Madam. Do you see the lights?" He pointed.

"But that's halfway up the mountain!" Kume wriggled her toes in her thin slippers and tested her left knee, which bothered her some days. "Are we expected to walk that far?"

Hearing the plaintive note in her mother's voice, Natua came to her side to soothe her. "I'm sure that isn't it, Mother."

"We will fly, of course." Patare turned from paying the cyclist to indicate a small cluster of liveried servants. "The dragons are coming."

Natua took an involuntary step backward. "M-must we fly?"

Kaloe caught her eye. "The only alternative is to go back around the mountain to the entrance the public tours use. From there, the walk to the level where the royal family entertains would take an hour, easily."

"I would estimate closer to two hours." A servant, the same who had personally delivered their invitations, bowed in greeting. He indulged in a little light humor to ease the palpable tension. "I'm afraid the food would be quite cold by then."

Kume managed a laugh and Natua smiled.

"I suppose we fly, then." Natua admitted defeat.

"An excellent choice." Pleased that things had been worked out so simply, the servant motioned at nearby benches. "Please make yourselves comfortable. We will leave as soon as the other guests have arrived."

"Sir?" Kaloe hurried after him. "Can the young lady ride with me?"

"I'm sorry, but these dragons only carry two passengers." Curious, he looked past Kaloe to the woman in question. "I assure you, our riders are the best in the country. She will be quite safe with them."

"Of course." Kaloe offered a humble bow. "I would never suggest otherwise. It's just." He broke off, unwilling to share their secret with a stranger before either of their parents.

The man chuckled softly. "No need to explain, my boy. I've seen young love before."

"Then, perhaps. Perhaps I could guide a dragon, and she could ride with me? That would be only two passengers, and…" Kaloe stopped when he saw the servant begin to shake his head.

"Special approval is required to fly so near the palace." He was about to go help one of the other guests when Kaloe stopped him.

"There *must* be a way. What about when guests fly in from far away?" Kaloe brightened. "Are they not met by palace guards and guided in?"

"Well, yes. That is true, but…"

"Look around us! We are surrounded by palace guards." At the last moment, Kaloe decided against pointing at them. Soldiers had been known to take exception to such things. "Is it not the same for them to guide me in from here as it would be if I'd flown in from far away?"

Impressed with the boy's persistence, the servant seriously considered the idea. "Ask the head guard," he directed at last. "If it's alright with her, I will raise no objections."

Chapter 15

Natua watched, confused, as Kaloe motioned for her to stay put, then fairly sprinted over to talk to the group of soldiers. He bowed so hard, so fast that she worried he would knock his head against his knees. One of the soldiers suddenly pulled away from the group and went over to inspect a dragon. She couldn't clearly hear what he called back to the others, but the dragon was led away and another brought in to replace it.

Kaloe was grinning as he returned to Natua's side.

"What was that all about?" she asked when he reached her.

"You don't have to worry about the flight," he promised. "You will be perfectly safe. Each of the riders tonight is exceptionally skilled."

"Including the one whose dragon was just taken away?" She couldn't help sounding a little skeptical.

"Ah, yes. Well. The dragon is ready to lay and should avoid flying for a few days." The quizzical tilt to Natua's head prompted him to expound. "She was taken to a nesting area, where she can lay her eggs safely."

"Oh. Oh, I see." Natua paused. "But if she's ready to lay, why was she out here, prepared to carry guests?"

"Her rider didn't notice the signs." Kaloe shook his head in mild disbelief. The head guard had obviously known, for she'd had another dragon waiting and ready. It was a very good night *not* to be the rider who'd made the mistake. "I imagine he will be kept tending the nesting areas for some time, to make sure this never happens again."

"Good." Natua studied the remaining guards. "But who will ride the new dragon?"

"I will." Kaloe stood calmly while she stared up at him.

"You? *You* will?" Her heart stuttered at the thought. "By yourself?"

He took her hand in his and held it firmly. "Do you recall that my father was a dragon wrangler? He taught me everything I would ever need to know to fly such a well-trained dragon such a short distance." Her eyes darted from one dragon to another until he stepped in front of her. "I arranged it so I could ask you to ride with me, but only if *you* want to."

"Then…it would be alright if I rode with one of the guards?" She felt churlish just voicing the question, yet she appreciated the steady way he held her gaze when she asked. "Even though we're dating now?"

"Yes, of course. Whatever you choose, you will be safe. And that is the most important thing." Bowing, he added apologetically, "If you will excuse me? I must see to my dragon."

Natua watched him go. Observed the ease with which they interacted. In a matter of moments, they seemed perfectly comfortable with each other.

"I can't sit another moment," Kume announced as she joined them, Patare in tow. "Those benches are plain metal, not an ounce of covering on them to soften the experience."

"A covering would not survive long here." Patare cast an interested glance toward Kaloe.

They all looked around as another cycle carriage rattled up and dropped off two more guests.

"Hegalak gora!" The head guard shouted the order as she strode toward Kaloe. "You have a good eye for an expectant mother. How are you at keeping your seat?"

"It depends." Kaloe forced himself to keep a straight face despite the excitement swirling in his blood. Had his father lived, he might have joined the Dragon Guard. "I wouldn't even try to mount a wild dragon."

"Really." The ghost of a smile appeared on the head guard's face. Or was it just a playful shadow?

"No point. They'd have me off in half a heartbeat." He patted his dragon's neck and she nuzzled him back. "This one, though. I think we'll get along fine."

"You've got some sense, I'll give you that." She poked a stiff finger into his chest just the same. "One false move out of you and you'll spend the night in jail. Royal guest or not."

"You don't have to worry about that." Natua countered, stepping up beside him. "I'll be riding with him."

"Are you guaranteeing that you can keep him out of trouble?" The guard wasn't impressed.

"Actually, I'm trusting him to keep us both out of trouble." Natua answered serenely and slipped her hand into Kaloe's.

"You've been warned." The guard stalked away rather than let her astonishment show.

"So." Natua's grip on his hand tightened as she eyed the dragon they were going to ride. "What do we do now?"

"It's time to go, so we must get on. I'll mount first, then help you up behind me. Alright?" He waited only for her nod before gathering the reins and swinging aboard. "Now, it's your turn."

Natua felt horribly clumsy as she tried to mimic his graceful movements, and settled in behind him greatly relieved not to have kicked the poor dragon. Speaking rationally, she doubted that the guards would select an ill-tempered dragon for guest transport. Emotionally, however, the simple fact that the dragon *would* destroy them all on a whim gave her no comfort whatsoever.

"Don't squeeze. Just let your legs relax, alright?" Kaloe patted Natua's knee. "If you're nervous, hold onto me, as tightly as you wish. But know that most dragons don't appreciate even slippered heels in their ribs."

"Oh." Natua was working on it when the first dragon of their flight lifted off. Their dragon began spreading its wings in anticipation. Her stomach did the opposite, clenching itself into a ball. "Oh, dear."

Kaloe felt her face against the back of his shoulder and took a moment to squeeze her hand before speaking softly to the dragon. Natua's arms were an iron band about his midsection as they rose into the air and he was only able to take shallow breaths. Was there no way to ease her distress?

"It's alright." He kept both hands on the reins now, in case the dragon decided to test its new rider. "We're all up and we'll land soon. This is probably the shortest flight you'll ever take." If she responded, it was too muffled for him to hear, so he directed his attention to a smooth touchdown on the narrow shelf. "Good girl."

Sensing the cessation of motion, Natua straightened, embarrassed to have spent the entire time hiding. It couldn't have been all that unusual, however, for nobody seemed to care in the least.

"When you're ready, I'll hop down. Then I'll help you dismount. Alright?" Kaloe surrendered the reins to the servant who'd appeared, but was in no hurry. Letting Natua make decisions about dragon riding, even tiny ones, would help in the long run.

"Alright." She withdrew her arms. Watched in amazement as he threw his leg over the dragon's neck, and slid lightly down. "You make that look so easy."

"It isn't." He laughed and placed both of his hands on her waist. "It can take a fair bit of practice to become comfortable with all that dragon riding entails."

Startled, and perhaps still a bit numb from the shock, she didn't resist when he lifted her down.

"Well, that was unexpected." Kume touched her hair, convinced that it was a windblown mess.

"You look fine, Mama." Natua stepped back from Kaloe and moved to reassure her mother. "We were only airborne for a few moments."

"Yes, and you with a scribe at the reins." Kume

sighed dramatically. "My dear girl, what were you thinking?"

Anything Natua might've said in Kaloe's defense was preempted by a senior servant, who clapped his hands to get everyone's attention.

"Welcome to the palace." The man bowed in general greeting to the group. "Please, come this way."

Natua wisely let the matter drop for the time being and allowed herself to become part of the group as it swept along a long marble hallway. Well, one side was marble. The other side dropped off precipitously, giving them all a jaw-dropping view of an enormous cavern, filled with sculptures and statues and banners.

One of the other guests saved them the trouble of asking about the display and they all learned it was representative of the reign of Txoko's father, King Egiaz.

"Will we be able to see it more," Kume retreated from the edge, where she'd been drawn by sheer curiosity, "um, closely after dinner?"

"That will depend upon King Txoko." The servant was polite, though not optimistic. "I will ask."

Kume nodded her understanding and the group resumed wending its way to a reception area.

Natua found Kaloe at her side again as they entered the spacious room. "Are we going to be expected to meet the king?" she whispered, wondering that she hadn't thought to ask before.

"It is possible." Kaloe considered the room and its fine appointments. "I think tonight is meant to be more of a casual affair."

"Casual?" Natua echoed in disbelief. "Do kings *have* casual gatherings?"

"Sometimes." Kaloe gestured around the room as he explained how he knew. "Look at the small flags over there. The Marroi flag is up, but not the king's. And then the servants' gerris. They're wearing palace tan, not the royal purple."

"That's it? That's how you know this is an informal

get-together with royalty?" Amused and impressed at the same time, Natua laughed and looked around to check on her mother. It was a relief to see her talking with Patare.

"Well. That and I sort of doubt we'd be invited if it was strictly formal." Kaloe glanced at his toes, then back up at her to watch her reaction.

Natua did a double-take at his slowly growing grin. "You're teasing me." As awful as it was to realize that she'd been taken in, it sort of took the edge off her anxiety, too. If Kaloe was comfortable enough to kid her, she could relax as well.

The doors, which had closed behind them without anyone taking much notice, were suddenly thrown wide. A tiny gasp escaped Natua as she turned to face them. Two servants entered first, and she was confused by their relatively rough attire. Instead of palace colors, they wore desert browns and grays, with what looked like real swords at their sides. Guards, perhaps? Certainly they weren't guests. Her father, she knew, wore only a short sword—which he'd laughingly called a 'letter opener'—when attending formal functions.

"Please, no." A man to her left murmured in Alna and shifted position so that he stood a little between the woman at his side and the newcomers.

As if on cue, all conversation ceased as a muscular older man stalked through the doors. The woman accompanying him had such a haughty glare on her face that the temperature in the room seemed to drop ten degrees. Together they stood in the middle of the room, glowering at everyone. The space around them gradually grew larger as folks edged away from them.

"Who is it?" An elegant older woman asked the man beside her.

There was a moment's hesitation before he quietly responded, "Buru Tipo Baden and his wife."

"Ah." The woman nodded knowingly. "The parents of the king's first wife. Do they still blame him for her death, do you think?" They moved off, murmuring quietly to each other.

When it was her turn to be scrutinized, Natua's Lurrakian pride asserted itself and she met the buru's hostile gaze without flinching. They were not dragons, after all. She didn't know them herself, but was learning a lot from the whispering going on in various languages around her. It was quite different from reading the written words, but she caught enough to realize that everyone who actually knew what was going on was stiff with disapproval at 'the audacity' of their bringing armed guards into the palace.

"The king and future queen of Marroi!" Announced a voice from somewhere.

Natua relaxed fractionally when she saw Leuna walking in on the arm of a dashing man about her age. The man could only be King Txoko, who would surely sort things out.

"Please." King Txoko held up his hands when the bowing began. "We can either stand on formalities or sit down to supper." A round of laughter, encouraged by his friendly smile, swept the room. "I, for one, am in favor of the latter."

Natua watched with interest as two palace servants opened a second set of doors, much taller than the first, revealing another room. She could see part of a knee-height table, complete with plush cushions on the floor by each place setting.

"In a minute we'll all be invited to walk past the royal couple to get to our seats. A smile, a handshake, and perhaps a word or two. Won't take long." Kaloe was about to offer her his arm when he saw the arrogant buru and his wife sweep across the room and take up a stance beside the king, effectively joining the receiving line.

"What's going on?" Natua asked uneasily. While she didn't hold with judging people based on gossip, something about them created the same anxious feeling in her as seeing a precariously balanced bucket of paint.

"I'm not sure what they're up to." Kaloe didn't much care for the airs they were giving themselves. And, judging by the way the tension had gone up in the room, he wasn't the only one. "I'd say they were here for the wedding, but it's still some weeks away."

All the guests tried not to eavesdrop as King Txoko leaned over to speak to his father-by-law. Unfortunately, no one could miss the heated nature of the conversation; on the buru's part, at least.

"They'll not make things easy for the doctor," Kaloe muttered as a palace guard advanced on the buru's guards.

Natua watched the silent power struggle between the armed guards with equal parts interest and unease. "Where are the other palace guards?"

"Don't worry." Kaloe was confident. "There are more about if need be. The point here is that one palace guard can rout two of the buru's guards." As softly as he'd spoken, some of the nearer guests began nodding their agreement.

"I see." She didn't like it, but she definitely understood it. A buru could not be allowed to successfully challenge the king.

King Txoko returned to Leuna's side and, smiling as though nothing was amiss, moved to greet the nearest guest.

Natua wondered if she could be so bold while dealing with Gusari and Mirko as to turn her back on them. It was educational to watch the buru deflate slightly when things began moving around him as if he wasn't there. Granted, he and his wife still looked angry even as they allowed a servant to direct them to their seats. Yet it all put Natua in mind of a spoiled child who threw a tantrum to get their way or just to gain attention, then meekly did as they were told when met with gentle but firm resolve.

Even the buru's guards lost some of their fierceness as the guests resumed chatting normally. A pleasant-faced servant approached and spoke to the palace guard, who relayed the message to her erstwhile opponents with the barest hint of a bow.

"He's done it." Kaloe's whisper was filled with both awe and triumph.

"Who's done what?" Natua had obviously missed something, for she had no clue why all three guards left together.

"King Txoko." Kaloe took her hand and began guiding her over to where their mothers stood in the loose line edging its way toward the royal couple. "The buru's party has joined everyone for supper, and the guards are going now to have their own meal."

"You mean," she dropped her voice to where even she could barely hear it, "he saw them trying to force their way in and invited them in instead?"

"Yes, exactly. Robbed them of their excuse for a squabble, for the moment at least." Kaloe was positively delighted. "Clever fellow."

"Ah, there you two are." Kume claimed Natua's near arm, but not before noticing that Kaloe was acting more like a beau than a confrere. "I hope they don't split us up. They used to do that at the large military functions I attended with your father. I think the hope was that we would all become instant friends." Her disbelieving tone stated quite clearly that this tactic had never worked out well for her.

"With such a long table, I'm sure they can find us two seats together," she reassured her mother. She relinquished Kaloe's hand reluctantly. It would've been nice to have spent the evening at his side, particularly given their new understanding; yet it would be too unfair to abandon her mother in a room full of people from all over Jatorri, who might or might not speak a word of Lurrakian.

"Darling," Leuna's voice intruded on Natua's hectic thoughts, "these are the friends I was telling you about."

Txoko bowed and greeted them all warmly,

thanking them for coming as if they were his old friends, instead of his betrothed's new acquaintances.

Leuna turned as they edged out of the way of the next group, but only long enough to nod at a senior server.

"This way, please." The man guided them to one end of the long table, placing Natua and her mother on one side and Kaloe opposite, beside Patare. Like everyone else, they remained standing, waiting for their host and hostess to finish greeting their guests and join them.

"Oh, how marvelous." Kume sighed in relief when she saw her soon-to-be seat. Most of the cushions at the table were plain cushions, but a few here and there had a sort of attachment that included a legless base and a chair back of sorts. "I'm not sure my back would have held out with nothing to lean against."

Natua smothered a giggle, then straightened as the king led Leuna over. Surrendering her to the same senior servant who'd shown them to their chairs, Txoko kissed Leuna's hand, then retreated to his own place. Natua's heart twisted a little when she saw the calm resolve in Leuna's stance, and she wondered if they ever got to eat together when they could be simply themselves, two people deeply in love. For they were—she'd seen it in their eyes.

Gracious, did that mean she gave herself away whenever she looked at Kaloe? But no, she supposed not. As yet they had merely agreed to walk together along the path that might lead to love. Txoko and Leuna had reached the edge of the cliff, joined hands, and jumped off together.

Kaloe thought he saw a flicker of panic on Natua's face, which disturbed him. Short of walking around the table and trying to talk to her while everyone else was busy following the royal example and seating themselves, there was nothing he could do about it right then, which disturbed him even more.

Patare allowed her son to steady her as she lowered herself onto her cushion, then bumped his knee lightly when he seemed disposed to linger in a standing position. They'd all waited long enough to eat, and he could stare at his ladylove just as easily sitting as standing.

Chapter 16

Natua admired the calm way Leuna navigated the dinner topics; accepting compliments; returning them; and yes, discreetly changing the subject where needed. She was so engrossed in listening that she didn't think twice about jumping in when a foreign dignitary stumbled over a word.

"I quite agree, Baksil Isim." Natua lifted a bite-sized wrap, stuffed with seasoned meat and cheese then fried to golden perfection. "The flavor is superb."

"Ah. Yes." Baksil Isim nodded in relief at the rescue, then lifted a wrap from his own plate. "The flavor is so much."

Leuna politely promised to pass their approval on to the kitchen staff, but sent Natua a grateful smile when Baksil Isim was distracted by something his wife said. "Remind me where it is that you work, Natua? In communications?"

"Itzuli Communications." Natua supplied the missing detail, mindful of the rare opportunity to make the name of the company known to so many who might have translation work for them.

"Do you manage?" Baksil Isim returned to the conversation.

"Manage?" Natua wasn't quite sure how to answer that. *Yes, I manage, but it would be easier if I wasn't sandwiched between a crook and a backstabbing bully.*

"Kude tahm." Baksil Isim lowered his next bite back to his plate and his brows knit thoughtfully.

"Manager? Am I a manager?" Thinking back to the answer she'd toyed with giving, Natua chuckled softly. "No, just a translator."

"A head translator." Kaloe made the correction mildly. "Who currently oversees…" He paused to wipe his mouth and choose less difficult words. "She also helps us work better at the copy center."

"A woman of skill." Baksil Isim pronounced,

approval evident in his tone.

Natua accepted the praise with a smile and slight nod.

"Of course, I remember now." Leuna's eyebrows rose marginally as if something about the memory startled her. "We've sent rather a lot of projects your way. Would it be boorish of me to ask how things are going?" Speaking to the other guests in hearing, she explained, "We just signed with Itzuli Communications to prepare all of our wedding documents and paperwork."

Several of the guests nodded or even lifted their glasses in Natua's direction, confirming the effect of royal approval on their opinions.

"Not boorish at all." Natua leaned to one side so a servant could remove one dish and replace it with the next. Thank goodness she had Pyr to keep her informed! "The translations and copies alike proceed apace."

Leuna clapped her hands softly, then blushed. "I hope you will all forgive my enthusiasm."

Baksil Isim and his wife exchanged a look of loving understanding and everyone else smiled and spoke sympathetically.

"Itzuli." A gentleman a few chairs down took a sip of his drink. "Is Mirko still managing that?"

Natua didn't understand his slightly acerbic tone, but responded, "Yes, he is."

"I am surprised." He continued speaking while he sawed at his meat. "The last time I spoke with him, he gave me to understand he'd soon own Itzuli."

Natua was so startled that she nearly dropped her napkin. She shot Kaloe a look and shook her head firmly to silence the angry protest raging in his eyes. When she was quite sure she could control her own tone, she asked, "And when was this?"

"A few months ago, I can't remember exactly. I believe he said he was planning to buy out the owner." The fellow gave Natua and Kaloe a slightly pitying look, then turned to answer the woman to his left and the subject dropped.

Natua tried to do the rest of the meal justice, but all the taste had gone out of it for her. This course was warm. The next cold. Even the pudding made no more impression on her than that it was soft and easy to swallow.

Kaloe likewise ate in a trance. Twice he lifted his fork to his mouth only to notice—barely—that it was empty.

As the meal wore on, and the shock wore off, they roused themselves enough to resume exchanging pleasantries and small talk with those around them.

Leuna, apart from being grateful that the buru and his wife were behaving civilly, was curious about the odd effect a casual remark had on the younger two of her special guests. Natua looked more determined than downcast, but neither of them seemed to be enjoying themselves any longer. She would've let it go until their next encounter at the marketplace were it not for two things: firstly, she'd selected her wedding gift for Txoko and wouldn't be visiting the marketplace nearly as often; and secondly, something about the arrangements they'd made with Itzuli bothered her.

When supper was taken away and they all returned to the conversation room where they'd begun, Natua and Kaloe moved off to one side a bit while their mothers discussed the marble columns that lined one wall, each of which had been shaped into a statue.

"Did you know about Mirko's plans?" Kaloe wanted to know.

"I had no idea. I don't even want to believe it." Still reeling from the revelation, Natua shook her head. "But I've made up my mind. I have to go see Director Rysl as soon as possible. Leaving Mirko in charge when he retired was awful enough. Selling the company to him would spell disaster for any number of the employees."

Indeed, Gusari's present tyranny would seem like a

gentle pat on the head compared to Mirko's unregulated squeezing of resources to his own profit.

"I will go with you." Kaloe declared firmly. "Together we will convince him that…"

"No, you mustn't." Natua interrupted unapologetically. "He'll be reluctant enough to let a head translator barge in on him unannounced. Anyway." She softened a bit then, remembering how things had changed between them. "I need you to stay at the copy center while I'm gone. Keep things running smoothly. Just remember, Bariux is still a bit miffed about being 'taken to class,' as I heard him call it. Oh, and whatever you do, don't let Tryun…"

"You don't have to worry. Not about any of it, but especially not about Tryun." Kaloe touched her arm, partly to reassure her and partly to reassure himself. Dating a boss was going to take a lot of getting used to. "I won't take my eyes off him, not for a minute."

"Then you will stay and look after things for me?" Natua was anxious enough about convincing Director Rysl without having the added pressure of worrying what state she'd find things in when she returned to work.

"Of course I will." He gave up and took her hand in his. He'd been wanting to ever since they left the supper table. "Only please don't make it sound like you're leaving for good. If Gusari can take seven hour lunches, you can be a little late tomorrow morning. And I want to hear exactly what happens when you get back."

"Back?" Leuna inserted herself into the conversation, cheerfully slipping her arm through Natua's. "Are you taking a trip?"

"Um." Natua shifted her weight from one foot to the other uneasily. "No, not exactly. It was just something for work."

"Work?" Leuna pretended to pout. "Truly, I am a failure as a hostess." From the corner of her eye, she saw the buru's wife smirk as if she'd overheard, and

Leuna's heart sank. Would she never learn to keep her guard up when they were about? She stiffened at the sight of the woman shifting toward them, as if to join them!

Kaloe, observing the same thing, objected promptly to Leuna's assertion. "On the contrary. This evening has been delightful." He caught Natua's gaze and held it as he spoke, willing her to agree with him.

Natua, embarrassed enough at having disappointed her hostess, wasn't entirely certain how to interpret the intense look in Kaloe's eyes. It wasn't romantic, which was…a good thing, under the circumstances?

Leaving that to be sorted out later, she returned her attention to Leuna. "You mustn't blame yourself, Leuna. I can't seem to help it. Ask anyone. Ask my mother." Natua gestured vaguely in her mother's direction. "I have a positive talent for bringing work home—and to parties—with me."

Leuna released a relieved breath when her adversary abruptly changed course and walked away, nose in the air. "Thank you."

"You are most welcome." Kaloe bowed politely. Detecting confusion on Natua's face, he mouthed, 'buru' while Leuna was still distracted.

"Now that it's just us, I have a question for you. And I'm sorry to say it's about…." Leuna jumped a foot as an arm slipped around her waist. "Txoko! You startled me!"

"Oh? Should I have sent a note to warn you I was coming?" Txoko smiled fondly at his future wife. To distract himself from the ever-present desire to kiss Leuna, he directed his attention to their guests instead. "Are you enjoying yourselves?"

"Yes, of course." Kaloe answered first.

"We are. Thank you for asking, Your Majesty." Natua was acutely conscious of the fact she was still holding Kaloe's hand.

"Your Majesty? Such formality." Txoko winked at

Leuna, whose cheeks pinked, but only slightly. She'd grown tan during their time together over the last ten months, and was slowly becoming more accustomed to the small familiarities he sometimes displayed in public. "Please, call me Txoko. All of Leuna's friends do."

"I'm not, um, sure." Natua looked from Leuna to Txoko and back again. From the corner of her eye she saw a slight frown on Kaloe's face and thought she understood it. They could hardly presume upon a friendship that consisted of a few random encounters in the market. Except, Txoko had every right to decide for himself. "Are *you* sure?"

"Yes, of course." Leuna's smile came easily. "Though—back to my question."

"Your Majesty?" A voice called from a nearby group. "Might we have a word?"

Txoko nodded to the voice, bowed his apologies to Leuna and their group, then went to join the others.

"Does that happen a lot?" Natua asked, feeling sorry for Leuna, who looked incomplete without Txoko beside her.

"Often enough." Leuna managed a soft laugh. "He's always being asked to give an opinion on things he doesn't know much about. One of the 'perks' of being king, he says." Glancing around the room, Leuna excused herself. "I should probably go mingle with our other guests."

"Of course." Natua and Kaloe answered at the same time, making Leuna smile.

Before she left, though, she whispered something to Natua, who nodded her understanding.

"What did Leuna want?" Kaloe leaned in to ask as Kume moved off to study something else, Patare at her side.

"To talk with us." Natua looked from one wall to the next, but in vain. "Aren't there any sandglasses in the palace?"

"Dozens." Kaloe shrugged. "However, they are specifically banished from conversation rooms such as this."

"What? Why?" Natua glanced at the windows and nearly groaned. "Never mind. It's later than I thought." The second moon was up, she could tell by the mixed colors of the moonlight.

"Don't worry." Kaloe soothed. "We'll stay long enough to speak with her, then go home and rest."

"Yes. Of course." Natua accepted his reassurance wearily. "I only hope we can get a carriage home."

"I'm sure we'll manage." Kaloe exchanged a smile with his mother, who was now near enough to overhear their conversation. While he wasn't exactly surprised that Natua didn't know they'd be flying home, he did look forward to her surprise when she found out. "Now. Come over here and have a look at this mural."

"Mural?" Kume, who had been coming to speak with them, seized on the idea. She'd completely missed the royal couple, but nevertheless was thoroughly enjoying herself. "Where? What's it about?" She clasped her hands in near child-like delight. "Oh, isn't everything delightful? I really must write to my cousin and tell her all about tonight! Every detail!"

"What a lovely thought. I'm sure she'll appreciate hearing from you." Natua hastily smothered a smile, knowing full well that her mother would in fact write something approaching a tome on the subject of the party. A little polite revenge for all the times Cousin Hani had done the same thing to Kume.

Natua paid less attention to the mural than she did to Kaloe as he explained it to her mother in great detail, marveling at his patience with the never-ending questions. Belatedly, she remembered she was holding hands with him. At approximately the same instant, she realized Patare was watching them.

"Oh!" Natua rocked to one side when someone jostled her. She accepted the apology in the language it was given, earning a look of pleased surprise. Somehow she was drawn into a conversation by the fellow, an older gentleman whose keen plum-colored eyes belied his snow-white hair and age-lined face. The others were still engrossed in the mural when she checked on them, so Natua indulged her elder, though she stumbled a bit over her words.

"I'm terribly sorry." Natua laughed after mispronouncing one word rather badly. "I've never spoken these words before, only read them."

"You read Remen, also?" He clasped his hands behind his back and appraised her very seriously. "In that case, perhaps you would do me the honor of visiting my home. Borrowing some of my books?"

"You are far too generous!" Natua couldn't believe her ears. "Oh, but I'd be afraid of damaging them. I know how difficult it is to find books in Remen here. They're so heavy, and costly to transport. And I…"

He waved one hand lazily, dispersing her objections like a wisp of smoke from an extinguished candle. "I am in the business of transport, and have been for the past thirty years." His eyes twinkled as he leaned a trifle closer to add, "Multiply that by two or three dozen shipments per year and you will begin to grasp the size of my library."

"But that's." She passed a hand over her eyes. "So. Many. Books!"

"And they are not all in Remen. No, I read a bit in other languages, too. I vowed long ago to never stop learning." He bowed slightly and pressed a card into her free hand. "Ah, but I have kept you too long. Thank you for your time."

Natua's shock was compounded by Leuna's sudden appearance at her side.

"I have to know," Leuna whispered in Lurrakian. "What did you say to make Master Ganten smile?"

"Say?" Natua shook her head, bewildered. "Nothing. We just talked a little."

"Well, you must've done something special." Leuna allowed herself a tiny sigh. "I've spoken to him on several occasions. He's unfailingly polite, but in a distant, detached manner. When he *does* smile, it's the socially obligatory sort. You know, like this."

Natua winced at Leuna's demonstration. "Oh, that's awful." She groaned, exasperated with herself. "I mean, it's…"

"Awful to have that to look forward to every time I speak with him?" Leuna didn't take offense at the verbal misstep. "I agree. Especially when he comes to so many royal functions."

"How do you mean?" Natua hadn't thought the day could hold any more surprises for her—after Kaloe's confession and the alarming news that Mirko might soon own Itzuli, everything else should've seemed more or less uninteresting. Except here she stood, intrigued by the story of a complete stranger.

"Well, you see." Leuna caught herself. "I'm sorry, I can't explain it properly right now. Could you stay for a while? Once everyone else leaves, we can talk as much as we like."

"I'm tempted, I really am." Natua's thoughts strayed for an instant to the subject of sleep and she struggled to suppress a yawn. She hadn't expected Leuna to ask them to stay after. Whatever it was, it could surely wait, at least a little longer. "Unfortunately, I have work tomorrow. I'd love to discuss it another time?"

"Yes, of course." Leuna's brow furrowed. "Your work. That's actually what I wanted to speak with you about."

"Oh, dear." Natua made a stab at humor. "I've been a bad influence on you!"

Leuna clapped a hand over her mouth to keep from laughing out loud. Pulling Natua away from the others, she found a semi-separate spot in the slowly emptying room.

"No, honestly. I wanted to hear details about how things are going." Leuna tried to rest her hand on her aid kit, but Fiantza hadn't allowed her to bring it tonight, so instead she let her arm fall to her side. "We've got a few million wedding details to take care of and right now everything is somewhere between theory, contracted, and, 'Don't worry, it'll be done in time.'" She sighed and patted Natua's arm. "I guess that's what I actually wanted to talk to you about. Just. Things."

Natua's heart constricted. "I'd be happy to stay and talk." A little girl-talk would actually be quite welcome.

"No." Leuna shook her head. "No, you're right. It's ridiculously late for someone who has to do such an important job in the morning." She winked, deciding to end the evening on a cheerful note. Making Natua feel sorry for her had never been Leuna's goal. "We are so happy that Itzuli accepted the contract. When I heard that we were considering other companies, I was concerned. After all, yours is the best translation company in all of Koroa. It was such a relief when we received the counteroffer."

"Counteroffer?" Natua wrinkled her nose. "What do you mean?"

"Why, Manager Mirko's counteroffer. I'm told he only accepted the contract once we agreed to the extra fees." Leuna clarified.

"He added fees after submitting the original quote?" Natua leaned back against the wall they were 'hiding' by and folded her arms across her chest. What was Mirko up to?

"You mean you didn't know?" Leuna was genuinely puzzled. "I mean, yes, that's right. He said they would cover the supplemental manpower and supplies necessary to complete such a large contract in a timely fashion."

"I'm sure he did." Natua took a deep breath. How much could she—*should* she—share? And yet, in a roundabout way, Leuna was her employer. "I knew we'd decided to take the job, it was I who pushed for it. But something is wrong about these extra fees. Itzuli Communications charges a reasonable price for our work, but it's all carefully calculated before we ever submit a quote. Every translator, every scribe, every scrap of paper and drop of ink is taken into account." At least, that was how her friend in accounting always made it sound.

"Ah, I see. How disappointing." Sadness tugged at the corners of Leuna's lips, turning them down. "I suppose someday I'll get used to it, but after almost a year in the palace I am still astonished each time a company tries to take advantage of the palace's supposedly bottomless coffers."

Chapter 17

"I'm going to visit Director Rysl in the morning." Natua announced her decision abruptly, without meaning to. Not only did she have a concrete complaint against Mirko now, she had the added impetus of needing to dissuade Rysl from selling to him. "He will have something to say about this, I am sure."

Leuna eased herself into a leaning position beside her. "Who is Director Rysl?"

"At present, he is the retired but legal owner of Itzuli Communications." Natua glanced around the room, looking for Kaloe and their mothers.

"And what do you hope to accomplish?" Leuna asked, openly curious. "The contract is already signed. The funds have been transferred."

"Hmm?" Natua exhaled as the other woman's words sank in. "Yes. Yes, that's true." How much did she dare say? Certainly not more than she could prove, which was—nothing. Nothing that would interest anyone but herself and those directly concerned with Itzuli.

"Natua?" Leuna watched emotions flicker across her friend's face with growing concern. While she hadn't gotten used to people asking her for favors, either, she had a sneaking suspicion that was about to happen. There were certain downsides to becoming royalty, like never being sure why people were nice to you. "What's wrong?"

"Wrong?" Natua pasted a smile on her face, having made up her mind not to bother Leuna with it all. "I was just thinking. About your question."

"And?" Leuna really, *really* hoped she was wrong about what Natua would say next.

"I am going because I need to know if Director Rysl approved these fees." Natua blew out a breath. "I'm sure that sounds strange to you, because as you say, the deal has been finalized. Nevertheless. I think it speaks to a pattern of goings-on that he is unaware of."

"I see." Leuna waited a beat, in case Natua was building up to asking for a favor. When no such request was forthcoming, she gently asked, "What if he does know?"

Natua grimaced and straightened away from the wall. "He doesn't. He can't."

"Why are you so sure?" Leuna copied Natua's move and faced her. "What aren't you telling me? This is about more than the fees. 'A pattern of goings-on,' you said."

"It doesn't matter." Natua shook her head. "There's nothing more I can say until after I speak with Director Rysl." Ah, but wait. She couldn't just walk in and tell the director what she'd heard at a dinner party. Which couldn't happen until after she got copies of the original quote and the current contract from her friend in accounting. A friend she'd been neglecting of late, unfortunately.

From the corner of her eye, Natua saw a party of five waiting with hopeful expressions on their faces. "Please forgive me. I've taken up too much of your time."

Leuna caught her arm as she was about to walk away. Searched her eyes. "Thank you for coming tonight."

Natua bowed, feeling a need for formality after all she had—and hadn't—told Leuna. She offered Kaloe a tight smile as he moved to rejoin her.

"I feel like I missed something important." Kaloe looked from Natua's stern expression to where Leuna was bidding her guests a good night. He didn't dare take Natua's hand as he inquired, "Is everything alright?"

"Not exactly, no." A glance at her mother confirmed that Kume and Patare were chatting happily with another woman, so Natua decided to tell Kaloe what had happened. Of course, she had to explain why the fees were so important, and ended with, "I don't know what, if anything, Director Rysl will choose to do once I've told him. I just know I have to try to stop him from selling Itzuli to Mirko."

"That must be prevented at all costs." Kaloe agreed fervently. "This creating of fees is something I could see Gusari doing. Like servant, like master perhaps?"

"Perhaps." Natua shook her head, still uneasy.

"What is it? You look worried." Kaloe bumped her elbow with his. "Once he sees the proof, how can Director Rysl fail to admit that Mirko has acted badly?"

"As you say, Mirko has a lot in common with Gusari and will surely at least try to wriggle out of it. He stands and walks like a man, but deep down he has a wide streak of gutter rat." Natua scrunched her eyes closed. "I can't believe I said that."

"What is a gutter rat?" Though Kaloe didn't recognize all the words, he knew the tone all too well.

"Never mind." She opened her eyes. "I'll have to be at Itzuli early tomorrow to beg copies of the quote and contract from my friend. Otherwise, I'll end up at Director Rysl's with only words to convince him."

A slow smile spread across Kaloe's face. "We do need more than words, don't we?"

"Forget it." Natua shifted to face him. She could just imagine him trying to find a way to sneak into the large, stone building after hours. And failing, one way or another. "I mean it."

"It would be simple!" he protested. "There are so many windows and vents. All I would have to do is…"

"No." Natua was acutely aware of the fact that their mothers were approaching, thankfully deep in conversation with each other. She didn't know about Kaloe, but she hadn't told her mother about their 'adventure' with the ink bottles and didn't plan to if she could help it!

"It would be even simpler with your help." He arched his eyebrows, thinking back to the last time they'd had this conversation. "You could loan me your key."

"I don't have a key." She reached up to smooth her hair and smile at their mothers, who were almost there. "And we're sticking with my idea of borrowing copies from Accounting."

"Natua. *Honestly.*" Kume groaned as she linked arms with her daughter. "I leave you alone for five minutes and you're talking about business?"

"I'm afraid it was my fault." Leuna smiled as she reappeared near the group. "I asked her how the wedding contract was progressing."

"Oh, I see. Well, that's not quite the same as talking about work, is it?" Kume withdrew her objection gracefully. Her nod took in Kaloe as well as Natua. "I'm sure they will do everything in their power to get things done in good time."

"Of course." Kaloe bowed slightly. "It is our honor to be even a small part of helping prepare for the royal wedding."

Txoko joined them just then and slipped an arm around Leuna's waist as he grinned at Kaloe. "Do you work at Itzuli Communications as well?"

"I do." Kaloe confirmed.

"Do you like your work?" Txoko couldn't imagine spending a full day at a desk, let alone liking it.

"It's..." Kaloe shot Natua a look. Should he be painfully honest and speak of Gusari? No, better not. Diplomatically, he responded with a smile, "I do now."

Txoko followed the line of Kaloe's gaze to the lightly blushing woman at his side—who just happened to be wearing colors that complimented Kaloe's galtzak. A small smile played around his lips as he drew his own conclusions.

"Come." Leuna intervened before the fellows could resume talking about business. "We'll walk with you."

They exchanged pleasantries as they went, laughing and chuckling and making a concerted effort not to discuss work—or yawn.

"Good night." Natua accepted a hug from Leuna, who went on to hug the other women in the tiny group.

"Rest well. And," Leuna spoke for Natua's ears only, "good luck with Director Rysl tomorrow."

"Thank you." Natua watched the royal couple leave, arms around each other's waists and Leuna's head resting on Txoko's shoulder.

"They look happy, don't they?" Kaloe ventured to take Natua's hand again.

"Better than that." Natua looked up at him. "They look content to be together."

"Content is better than happy?" He heard the scraping of dragon claws and tails on marble and knew it was nearly time to leave.

"Mm." Natua rubbed her tired eyes. "I think so. I couldn't be happy if I'm not content, could I?"

"I suppose not." Looking over her shoulder, he nodded at the waiting guard. "Let's get you home." Placing his hands on Natua's waist, he lifted her up, into the saddle. "It's alright," he promised when he felt her tense. "It's my turn next."

Natua relaxed and stayed where he'd put her while Kaloe stepped into the stirrup and climbed aboard, bringing his leg up over the dragon's neck. With a little help from him, she repositioned herself so that she was riding astride, and released a sigh as she rested her head on the back of his shoulder.

On the other side of the ledge, Kume was dismayed to see Natua once more calmly sitting behind Kaloe. The boy seemed nice enough, it wasn't that. Kume stopped breathing when the dragon she was to ride turned to look at her. Was she going to be eaten?

"Steady." The rider patted the dragon's neck and smiled reassuringly at the wax-white guest. "She's just eager to be off."

"I should've waited," Natua whispered to herself. "Should've made sure my mother was safely settled before getting aboard." From her perch behind Kaloe,

Natua watched Patare coaxing Kume to mount.

"That might've helped her." Kaloe patted her hand, where it already rested on his waist. "Yet surely it does her good to see that you are not afraid." Kume was situated now, which left only his mother and the head guard.

"Not afraid?" Natua eased closer to him as all the dragons began to spread their wings. "You must be joking."

Kaloe chuckled and they were off, diving off the ledge with the others. He thought he heard a muffled scream and suddenly her arms were like iron bands around his waist. Of all the idiotic… How could he not have thought to prepare her for the sudden downward plunge?

"It's alright." He called to her over his shoulder as they leveled out. "We'll soon be there." Snatching quick glances are the other riders he saw that Kume was pressed so tightly against her rider that, if he hadn't known it was a person, he might've assumed the rider was a hunchback. It was sad, really. They were both missing a marvelous view—Koroa lit only by moonlight, the sloped metal roofs glittering as they flew over them.

Natua clung to him and forced herself to breathe. Kaloe was obviously not afraid. And, even before today's confession of love, she'd trusted him to keep her safe. The wind plucked at her sleeves and trousers as they flew, teasing her for hiding her face from it. That, and curiosity at how long the flight was taking, prompted her to peek around Kaloe's shoulder.

"It's…so beautiful." Natua watched, entranced, as an enchanted city slipped past beneath them. Here and there dragonglass skylights caught a moonbeam and joyously reflected the color back at the stars.

"It is, isn't it?" Kaloe took his first deep breath since they embarked and threaded the fingers of one hand through hers. He couldn't have asked for a more picturesque ending to their day.

"But where are we?" Natua blinked as she realized the palace lay well behind them. "And where are we going?"

"It's too late to find a carriage, so we're going straight home." The flight began to split up now as guards escorted the other guests to their homes. Even he and Natua would've ordinarily parted by now, half of their group going to his home and half to Natua's, except that they represented two households on one dragon. Not too surprisingly, the head guard stayed with them, keeping an eye on him. "We'll stop at your home first."

"Oh." The empty marketplace swept by, shutters and curtains stirring in the wake of powerful dragon wings. She snuggled in closer, but this time because she wanted to. "I think our secret is probably out. And it wasn't even a secret for very long."

"Do you mind?" Kaloe didn't have to ask which secret. They were less than a minute from her house and he waited anxiously for her answer.

"Yes and no." Natua sighed. She would've preferred a little more time to get used to the idea herself before being called upon to confirm—and possibly even justify—a romantic relationship with a much younger man who also happened to be under her authority at work. "You'll have to tell me what your mother says."

"I will." He eased back on the reins, bringing the dragon to a soft landing in front of Natua's house.

"Aren't you getting down?" she asked when he didn't do so right away.

"No, the others are waiting to escort my mother and me home. Here, take my arm." He helped her down, but kept her near the dragon a moment when her feet had touched the ground. "Good night, my darling."

The endearment prompted her to look up at him and she nearly gasped when his lips brushed hers.

"Let's go!" called the head guard, softly so as not to disturb those sleeping in the houses surrounding them.

Kaloe used his knees to move the dragon away from an apparently stunned Natua, then they leapt into the air and were away.

Natua would've watched them out of sight except that her mother took her hand and gently towed her inside.

"Well, that was quite an evening." Kume closed the door behind them. She was fairly bristling with questions about Kaloe, including when they were planning to tell her they were dating—and maybe how old he was—but she kept them to herself as she ushered Natua upstairs and into bed. "Sleep quickly, my dear. Dawn delays its arrival for nothing and no one."

"Goodnight, Mama." Natua rolled onto one side, convinced she would be unable to sleep now that Kaloe was swirling through her blood. What had he been thinking, stealing a kiss like that? And then vanishing into the night sky! Scoundrel.

What if she'd wanted to kiss him back?

Cheeks flaming in the dark, she flung an arm up over her eyes. She *did* want to kiss him back.

Perhaps not with both of their mothers for an audience, though.

She tossed and turned the night through, sleeping only in scattered snatches. When she woke up from a dream where a gezi wearing Mirko's face chasing her through the streets of Koroa, screaming, 'You tattle-tale! You nasty little tattle-tale!' she wasn't sure whether to laugh or cry.

Either way, she doubted she'd get any more 'sleep' before the gray horizon turned into a blazing gold. Sitting up with a groan, Natua allowed herself a moment of self-pity before rolling out and starting her day. While washing her face and doing her hair, she mentally selected her outfit—a smoke gray tunic over a butter yellow shirt and matching trousers. For added confidence, she wound the sky blue gerri from her brand new palantzia around her waist, draped one end over her right shoulder, then tied it so it couldn't fall forward and trip her.

"And where," a yawn stopped Kume mid-sentence, "are you going so early?"

Natua grimaced apologetically. "I'm sorry I woke you, Mama." She gave her mother a quick peck on the cheek and started down the stairs. "I have an important meeting this morning and need to stop by work first."

"A meeting? Are you sure you're up to that after staying out so late last night? Darling, you should've told me! We could've gotten home sooner." Kume frowned as Natua continued toward the front door. "Wait! What about your breakfast?"

"I have an entire clowder of gezi dragons performing aerial acrobatics in my stomach right now." Natua laughed and shook her head, blowing another kiss as she walked out the door. "No room for food!"

"Natua!" Kume folded her arms across her chest and raised one eyebrow. "Will your confrere be at this meeting?"

Taken off guard, Natua blushed fiercely. "No, he'll be at the copy center. The meeting is…somewhere else." She didn't have time to explain where or why she was going, let alone that *she* was the one calling the meeting.

"I see. Well, let's have a long talk when you get home, alright?" Kume didn't feel the need to specify a topic.

"Of course." The gezis in Natua's stomach doubled in size as she tried to predict how that 'talk' would go. Exactly what she needed today, one more thing to worry about.

Naturally, now that Kaloe was on her mind, she had to stop by to see him.

'What are you doing here? Did something go wrong with your friend in Accounting?" Kaloe hurried over from the assignment stack and met her at her desk. They were the first to arrive, so he spoke freely. "Did you sleep at all?" He touched the back of his hand to her forehead. "I think you're feverish." Some boyfriend he was. He could've made their excuses to King Txoko much earlier, could've taken Natua home to let her rest. But no, he'd been so eager to impress her mother that he hadn't taken care of her.

"Good morning to you, too." Natua pushed his hand aside and barely resisted stealing a kiss of her own. Moving past him to her desk, she positioned herself so that it was between them. "I just wanted to make an appearance here this morning. Gusari will know something is afoot when I'm not here later." She spoke quickly, trying to take her mind off the way her heart was somersaulting through her chest. The gezis in her stomach, however, were curiously still.

"Assuming he decides to grace us with his presence." Kaloe watched her rearrange her stacks and had a sneaking suspicion she was just pretending to be busy to keep him at bay. It was for the best, given the open doors, but oh, how badly he wanted to talk with her!

"Good point. You'll be in charge while I'm gone." She flicked a glance at him and almost laughed when she saw the startled expression on his face. "Don't do anything drastic, just keep the assignments moving in order and tell everyone I'll be back as soon as I can. Oh, and don't let Tryun out of your sight. I don't know what Gusari and he are up to, but it can't be good."

"Don't worry." Kaloe began edging around the desk. "We're almost done with this project. It should ship out today and make room for the…" His progress toward Natua halted when he heard someone whistling just outside the courtyard door.

"Hey, hey, early risers!" The woman who usually sat across from Kaloe greeted them cheerfully. "Are you here for overtime, too?"

"Could anything else drag us here before the usual starting time?" Kaloe retorted with a half-laugh, half-snort.

"Good morning." Natua nodded to her, then directed her attention back to the files she was pushing aimlessly around her desk. She'd noticed Kaloe trying to get closer to her and was glad he hadn't succeeded. Especially since she was still so uncertain about her decision to date him.

Take their present states, for example. It was so terribly unfair. They were both up most of the night. They both had a lot on their minds. And she apparently looked 'feverish'—while he looked ready to go play pilota. It did nothing to reassure her of the wisdom of dating a younger man.

"I better get going. My friend should be in his office by now."

"Wait." Kaloe moved quickly to intercept her. "I wanted to tell you that my mother and I talked when we got home."

"Oh? Oh." Natua peered anxiously into his eyes. How could they look so clear with everything they had going on? "What did she say?" The gezis were back in her stomach, moving faster than ever.

"That she likes you. A lot." One side of his mouth quirked up in amusement at their cryptic conversation. He was frustrated, too, though. He wanted so much more than a whispered conversation. He wanted to hear her laugh, see her smile. "Is it my turn to buy lunch today?"

"I don't remember." She looked past him at the trio of scribes that had just arrived and suddenly felt very shy. "Either way, I'd like to have lunch with you. If the meeting doesn't last too long."

"Don't worry. I'll wait for you at the usual food cart as long as I can. If the meeting does go over long," he shrugged, "we can have supper together instead."

"Not exactly." She wrinkled her nose apologetically. "You see, I was too tired to talk with *my* mother last night. As I was leaving this morning, she made it clear that tonight would be different."

"Ah. Yes." Kaloe nodded his understanding. "Alright. Would you like me to go with you? To be there while you talk?" He could at least do that much. Answer any questions Kume might have for him.

"I..." Natua shook her head slowly. "I can't predict how the conversation will go, so. I think it would be best for us to speak privately first." There was still so much her mother didn't know, let alone like, about Marroi. Whether she meant what she might or might not say, words had a way of sticking in a heart like barbs.

Kaloe started to say something, then remembered their audience and took a deep breath instead. "Natua. If she says no, what will you do?"

She closed her eyes and looked away. "Try again, I suppose."

His heart sank. 'I suppose' wasn't terribly encouraging.

"I'll see you later." Natua took a step back. Her heart felt like an over-worked weathervane this morning, pointing one way and then the other as far as 'they' were concerned. She was glad he hadn't asked what she would do if she happened to agree with one of her mother's arguments, because he wouldn't have liked the answer. Tonight's conversation might be the perfect excuse to do what she probably should've done in the first place—tell him to find someone his own age, someone he wouldn't have to worry about looking sick after a late night.

To the others, who were already hard at work on the copies, she announced in passing, "I have a meeting this morning. I'll be back as soon as I can." Which might be sooner than she expected, if Director Rysl wasn't home or if he refused to see her. Cheerful thought.

"Ah, that explains it." One of the younger scribes who had filtered in while they were talking gave her a quick once-over. "I thought you were awfully dressed up for just another day with us."

A few of the women chimed in with pleasant comments and Natua thanked them all with a smile. Now, why couldn't *Kaloe* have said something like that?

Chapter 18

Natua chewed her lip as she stared at Director Rysl's house. The weight of the copies in her lap seemed to be anchoring her to the carriage seat. Her friend in Accounting was appalled when she told him of Mirko's plan to buy the company, and eager to help however he could.

"Getting out?" The cyclist asked impatiently after waiting several seconds longer than usual.

"Yes. Yes, I am." Natua paid the cyclist, including a reasonable tip, and climbed down.

He vanished in a faint whir of gears, leaving her standing alone on an empty street of lovely jaio homes. Made strictly of local materials, a mixture of sand and limestone, then heat-treated with dragonfire, the walls all bore unique striations of colors and texture. One home might have a streak of burning purple, while another shone green when the sunlight hit it just right. The brown courtyard walls, built to the height of the average man in an attempt to protect the carefully cultivated plants from the sandstorms that passed through, were boring in comparison.

The difference between the bare street and the courtyard as she entered was enough to make her stop and catch her breath. Teryn trees did their best to cast shadows with their sparse branches, and fruit bushes gave the air a delightful tang. The irrigation system made dripping sounds as deliberately fashioned pools of water slowly overflowed into the next pool of water, all sheltered within metal pipes to protect the precious liquid from evaporating before reaching its destination.

"Good morning." The voice came from behind a bush off to Natua's right. A man she hadn't noticed knelt there beside a mesh basket half filled with ripe truip fruit, his head covered by a floppy hat. "May I help you?"

"Oh, no. Thank you, but no, I wouldn't want to

bother you." She hesitated. "Is Director Rysl home this morning?" His harrumph sounded somehow familiar and she took a step toward him.

"I haven't heard that name in a while." Gloved hands pushed the thorny branches aside and plucked another of square pome to be added to the basket.

The gezi dragons tucked their wings and hit the bottom of her stomach en masse as Natua turned to look at the house. "Do you mean that he's moved?" It was so rare for a Marroi to relocate once they had selected a permanent home!

"Is that what I said?" The man braced his hands against his knees and grunted as he clambered to his feet. "Really, Head Translator. I am disappointed." His head slowly lifted and Director Rysl's familiar face grinned at her from under his wide-brimmed hat. There were a few more wrinkles around his eyes than when she'd seen him last, and the smudges of dirt were definitely new, but overall he looked absolutely wonderful.

"Director Rysl!" She was so glad to see him that Natua spontaneously closed the distance between them and gave him a hug.

"Well!" He chuckled and patted her back. "Yet another perk of retirement."

They laughed together even as they parted.

"Forgive me, sir. I just. I'm so glad to see you!" She looked down when her foot struck something. Gasped. The files! She must've dropped them in her surprise. "Oh no!"

"What's all this?" he asked, removing his gloves as she stooped to pick up the scattered papers. "You finally come to visit me and you bring paperwork?"

Red-faced, and not just with exertion, she straightened to face him. "Forgive me. I know it's terribly bad manners." It was getting to be ridiculous, too. She was going to have to make a concerted effort to just have fun at the party she and her mother were hosting in a few days.

"It's worse than that." Picking up his basket, he gestured toward the house. "I haven't had my breakfast yet. And you know I hate to talk business on an empty stomach."

"How could I forget?" She found herself smiling despite the delay she could hear coming. "I used to bring you hot truip rolls on the mornings when you had client meetings."

"Ah, I am drooling just remembering." Chuckling, he offered her his arm. "Now, if you'll come inside, we can eat, and then we can talk." He paused. "Unless, you have eaten already?"

"Um, well, no. I was too nervous." The second thought slipped out and she held her breath, awaiting his response.

"Then you *must* join me." He inclined his head toward her as they walked. "My wife is away, visiting her sister, and my son is in the Dragon Soldiers, posted halfway across Marroi. I'm glad you are here." He smiled as he opened the kitchen door and stepped back to let her pass. "I was dreading eating alone again."

Natua found herself put to work washing the fresh fruit and squeezing juice from it while he cooked ground meat with tubers and mild peppers in a light oil.

"I don't understand," she admitted as they sat down to what he had prepared plus bread, jams, and three different kinds of cheese. "Do you often cook for yourself?"

"Sometimes." He shrugged as he slathered butter and jam on a slice of bread. "I enjoy it when I have the time. And it means the cook can have the morning off. So long as neither of us tells my wife, everyone is happy."

Natua hid a smile behind her napkin. Oh, how she'd missed this warm, kindly man. He had always made time for her, guided her as she navigated her new job. She considered him a friend, of sorts. Her nerves were a thing of the past now that she was here, so close to telling him about Mirko.

Rysl directed the flow of conversation as they ate the delicious meal, keeping to light, friendly topics, then drained the last of the juice with a satisfied sigh.

"Alright. I believe I am now ready to discuss the bad news you have brought." He produced a pair of glasses from a drawer and slipped them on. They made his eyes seem bigger than usual in his dark face.

"Bad news?" Natua eyed the dishes on the table with some trepidation. It was one thing to borrow official copies and quite another to return them with grease spots and jam on them.

"I assume it must be." He tilted his head to one side curiously. "Am I wrong?"

"No, not exactly." She tapped her fingers on the table, found a sticky spot, and wiped them on her napkin. "In fact, you're absolutely right."

"Ah." He stacked some of the dishes and carried them over to the sink. "If it's as bad as all that, perhaps we should adjourn to my office. Come."

Rising from her cushion, she followed him gratefully to the far corner of the house. Unlike his old office at Itzuli, this room had a mound of plush cushions, a comfortable-looking lounge, and a desk with just enough room to lean two elbows on.

"Have a seat, my dear. And tell me what is worrying you so." Sitting on one corner of the lounge, Rysl rested his shoulders against the wall, prepared to listen.

"Sir, is it true that you're planning to sell Itzuli?"

He frowned and tugged at one earlobe. "Yes, but how did you hear of this? I haven't told anyone because I didn't want to unsettle the employees." Lifting his hands, he continued, "Always before a sale, everyone worries. They worry about their job, about what a new boss will expect. It makes such a mess."

"I understand, but." She lowered herself onto the other corner of the lounge, body turned toward him as much as the arrangement would allow. "Must you sell to Mirko?"

Rysl's eyebrows went up. "Don't you want me to?"

Natua hesitated. Laughed a little and shook her head. "For what it's worth, no."

"And why is that?" Rysl, surprised at her negative response, probed for more information. He'd always been able to trust her to tell him the truth, at least, as she saw it.

"Where to begin?" She shuffled the papers she'd brought, trying to smooth bent corners. "I honestly believe that the company will fail under his hand. More importantly, he uses people badly, sir."

Rysl didn't answer immediately. "I will not ask if you know what you are saying. Aware as I am of your skills, I am confident you could say exactly what you meant in over a dozen languages."

"Thank you, sir." She lifted one shoulder. "I would probably mispronounce the words, though."

"That may be." He chuckled. Indicated the papers she kept fiddling with. "Now, tell me what those have to do with our discussion."

"Ah." Natua flipped through them once more to make sure she'd put them back in the right order. "You know, of course, that Itzuli recently accepted a contract from the palace."

"Yes, a proud day for us all." Rysl fairly swelled with pride at the honor to his company.

"Very proud," she agreed. "But I am not proud of the way Mirko handled things."

"How so?" Rysl sat forward, concerned.

"After submitting the original quote," she handed over the applicable document, "*and* telling the palace we could not do the job, he then submitted a second offer." Natua held up the other document. "With added, and as I understand it, exorbitant, fees."

Rysl scowled. "Fees? What sort of fees?" He scanned through the original quote and noted the price.

"See for yourself." Natua watched anxiously as he adjusted his glasses and began reading the actual contract. And kept reading—well, skimming, actually, judging by how quickly he was moving through it. Her heart stuttered to a halt when he closed the file, took off his glasses, and began studying her instead.

"Have you read this?" He tapped the contract with his glasses.

"No, sir." Dread pooled in her stomach, drowning the remaining gezis. Something was wrong. Had her friend given her the wrong contract? But no, she'd checked that before she left Itzuli and both documents were what she'd asked for.

"Then you didn't know that this contract," he held it up, "is for the exact same price as the original quote?" Rysl lifted the other file so that they were side by side.

"What?" Flabbergasted, Natua reached for the contract. "But that can't be." Turning pages rapidly, she stopped at the section that stated the price. Accepted the other document from him and opened it for comparison. "I don't understand. This can't be right!"

"Natua." He spoke her name gently. "Is it possible that you misunderstood?" Resting his hands on his knees, he opened them both questioningly. "Where did you hear of these extra fees? Can you trust your source?"

"I do trust her." Natua sank back against the wall, her mind whirling. "She has no reason to lie."

"Then." Rysl glanced at the paperwork in her lap, still trying to find an explanation for the situation. He had already determined to investigate Natua's declaration that Mirko wasn't treating the employees well, but felt the need to resolve this matter now, while she was here. "Are you certain she understood? That," he shrugged, "she had the right information?"

"She must have." Natua stopped herself before she revealed her source. She was embarrassed enough for two people already, there was no need to drag Leuna into it. Besides, Rysl had a good point. Whomever it was that told Leuna about the extra fees could've been talking about some other contract. An honest miscommunication, the sort of thing that happened a hundred times a day.

Rysl looked up as a bell rang. "Well. Looks like this is my morning for visitors." He patted her knee in a fatherly way. "Wait here, my dear, while I go to see who it is."

"Wait." Natua put her hand on his arm and sat up as he began to struggle into a standing position. "Let me go, sir."

He sighed and nodded. "Thank you, my dear."

Smiling, she set the papers on his desk and hurried back down the hallway to the front door. Opening it, she found none other than—

"Natua!" Leuna grinned at her. "I'm so glad you're still here."

"What are you doing here?" Natua quickly stepped outside, pulling the door mostly closed behind her.

"After last night, I was worried about how things would turn out. I, um, couldn't wait, so I came over." Leuna pointed at the door, confused. "Aren't you going to invite me in?"

"I was going to, but there's been a terrible mistake." She pressed a finger to her lips when Leuna started to respond. "I brought copies from Itzuli to show Director Rysl, the quote and the contract both so he could see for himself."

"Good! What did he say?" Leuna kept her voice down even as she interrupted.

"What could he say?" Natua rubbed her forehead in distress. "The prices are the same. Exactly the same!"

Leuna's chin dipped while one eyebrow rose. "That's impossible." She brought one hand up to her chest, showing Natua the files she held. "They're completely different in my copies."

Natua let go of the door, oblivious to its motion as it swung slowly open again. Reached out for the copies, which Leuna relinquished. Ignoring the quote, she opened the contract.

The rustle of the papers sounded loudly in her ears as she paged through it, looking for the price. Her heartbeat slowed as she found the right section. The writing got larger and larger as she followed her finger down the page and read the price listed there.

"Natua?" Director Rysl poked his head out his front door and looked askance at the odd little scene. "Is everything alright?"

"I think she needs to sit down," suggested Leuna, taking Natua by the arm.

"I'm fine." Natua cleared her throat of the squeak and tried again as she handed the file. "I'm fine. Really." Pointing at Leuna, she asked, "May we come inside?"

Rysl turned one hand palm up, surrendering to the strange events of the morning. "Why not?"

Natua ushered Leuna inside and closed the door behind them. "Sir, may I introduce Doctor Leuna Oneko, the betrothed of King Txoko?"

Leuna, feeling a little out of place in her casual sunset orange palantzia and simple braid, squared her shoulders. "Forgive me for intruding upon you this morning, sir."

"Intruding? Not at all!" Rysl, who had heard only good things about his future queen, bowed gallantly. "My humble home is honored by your presence! Please, come in! Come in and make yourself comfortable."

"I think," Natua intervened before he got them seated in the main room, "that she would be most comfortable in your office."

"My office?" Rysl didn't try to conceal his surprise. "She knows about…"

"I'm afraid I was the one who told Natua about the added fees." Leuna supplied the answer to the question he hadn't finished.

Rysl silently motioned for them to precede him. Once they were all resettled, Leuna on one of the cushions and Natua beside Rysl on the lounge, Natua took a deep breath.

"I believe the files on your desk are the official copies from Itzuli's own Accounting department. Is that correct?" Natua waited until he nodded.

"Yes." Rysl nodded again. "I saw our marks on the pages."

Leuna, sensing her cue, bowed slightly. "I also have a copy of the contract. I brought it with me from the palace."

Rysl's smile trembled as he accepted the file from her. The room seemed eerily quiet as he once more flipped to the correct page to check the price. The blood drained from his face as he read.

"I—I see it. But I cannot believe it." His fists clenched, crumpling the pages he held. "Here the price is half again as much as the quote."

Natua silently took the office copy and handed it to Leuna.

"This isn't right. The price listed here is identical to the original quote." Leuna reported, bewildered.

"Exactly." Natua touched Director Rysl's arm, troubled by how pale he was. "Sir, it appears that Mirko has falsified the records. Accepted money from the palace as part of the contract, and failed to report it."

"Yes, yes. That is how it appears." Rysl hated to think ill of his employees—especially the one he had hand-picked for a position of power. Brightening, he suggested, "Perhaps there is another document in Itzuli's files. An amendment to the contract, listing the fees."

"It would be a simple thing to check, sir," Natua pointed out gently.

"And so I shall. At once!" He allowed her to help him to his feet, then paused, looking down at his clothes. There was dirt on the knees of his trousers and oil spots from the kitchen on his tunic. "I, um. I'll change and meet you there."

"Yes, sir, and thank you." Natua picked up the

copies she'd brought. "That will give me time to get these back into the files and check on things at the copy center."

"Good thinking." Rysl reached out and helped Leuna up from the cushions. "I'm sorry to have to ask you this, Your Highness, but could you possibly let me borrow your copy of the contract?"

"I'll do better than that." Leuna smiled graciously. "I'll bring it myself, along with the agent from the palace who finalized it with Manager Mirko."

"Marvelous." Rysl rubbed his hands together. "We'll get to the bottom of this today!"

Natua assured him that they could see themselves out, so he took himself off to get cleaned up. It wasn't until she reached the street with Leuna that she gave a thought to how they might be traveling.

"Dragons." She sighed the word, more in resignation than fear this time.

"Wait right here. Stand still when I bring her over to meet you." Leuna patted her arm. "She's quite sweet." She chuckled at Natua's muttered response.

Natua did as she was told, holding her ground while the large, alabaster dragon sniffed her, then shook its magnificent, multi-colored ruffles. "Can you drop me at the copy center first, please? I mean—*take* me to the copy center?"

"Yes, of course." Leuna mounted first, then helped Natua clamber up behind her. "Well done." Leuna used a small stone that hung from her saddle to scratch the distira's scales under her ruffle. It was one of her favorite spots. "Here we go."

It was just a short hop over to the copy center, but they were both frowning by the time they landed. Someone was shouting, their words unintelligible after being bounced off the building's metal walls.

"Should I come in with you?" Leuna eyed the door, and winced at the next roar that emanated from it.

"Thanks, but no. I can handle Gusari. We'll need

your help with Mirko." Natua swung down with surprising ease.

"I'm off to the palace then. See you soon." Leuna clucked to the distira, who spread her wings and shot up off the ground in a burst of power. "Showoff!!!"

Natua stared after them in concern, but her attention was jerked back to the copy center by the sound of Gusari shouting again. Sprinting toward the courtyard door, she burst in.

Chapter 19

"What's going on here?" Natua demanded. Her heart dropped to her toes when she saw Kaloe and Gusari standing beside his desk—where Mirko was sitting!

"Aha! Look who has finally decided to join us!" Gusari planted his fists on pudgy hips. "I trust you slept well."

"You're one to talk. Where were you when I stopped by earlier?" All eyes were on her as Natua strode across the room. She pointed at the stacks of crates near the double doors. "What are those still doing here? They should've been picked up over an hour ago!"

"That is precisely what we are discussing." Mirko smoothed one hand over his perfectly flat hair. "What have you to say for yourself?"

"Me?" Natua

"Yes, you." Lazily, Mirko took a page from Gusari's desk and held it out to her. "It was you who failed to renew the transport contract, was it not?"

Suddenly remembering the files tucked under her arm, Natua hesitated to accept the paper. She couldn't let him see them.

"Here, hold these." Feigning impatience, she fairly slapped the quote and wedding translations contract against Kaloe's chest. Took the page from Mirko and glanced at it. "This is our agreement with the delivery company. It expired last week! But I've never seen this before," she protested, looking up.

"I tried to tell them that," Kaloe inserted bravely.

"And yet, it was found on your desk." Mirko picked up a second page and rattled it. "As was this, the renewal." He cocked his head at her, looking for all the world like a hungry gezi. "I send you to the copy center to improve things and you let this slip past? Tell me, Head Translator. What good is efficiency in the center when the work stops here?" A meticulously manicured finger pointed accusingly at the crates of work.

Natua took a deep breath and let it out, expelling her disbelief and anger with it. Mirko and Gusari weren't stupid. They both knew that Gusari was in charge of procuring supplies and arranging delivery of their work. It followed, too, that they—or at least, Gusari—had some plan for rescuing the situation. But not before they'd achieved their mutual goal of getting rid of her.

"What did I ever do to you?" she asked calmly. "I know I changed things at the copy center, that I have prevented Gusari from continuing to bilk the company for money. But you, Mirko. What makes you so hostile toward me?"

Shaken by the way she'd torn aside his subterfuge and cut straight to the heart of the matter, Mirko didn't know what to say. At first. "I don't know what you're talking about." Standing, he tugged automatically at the front of his tunic. "I see clearly that there is no point in continuing this discussion. You think you can distract me from your dereliction of duty by maligning Gusari and myself, but you couldn't be more wrong." He waited for her to protest. Then, "Consider yourself terminated."

"No, you can't!" The words burst out of Kaloe, who had been silent long enough. "You think we don't know…"

"Kaloe." Natua cut him off sharply, only to be drowned out by the others.

"If you fire her, I quit!" One of the scribes jumped to her feet.

"Me, too!"

"I won't go back to working under Gusari!" shouted a third.

The protests rose in pitch and fervor until Natua turned to face them. The serenity radiating from her soothed the group so that their cries grew softer and less and eventually petered out.

"Please, trust me a little longer." She gestured to the partially completed copes on their tables. "This project is so terribly important. Won't you finish while I make arrangements to have these crates delivered?"

"Then, you aren't leaving?" Kaloe moved to her side, his expression a comical mishmash of disbelief and relief.

"Not just yet." She squeezed his arm reassuringly as she took the files from him, tucking them securely under her arm again. "Back to work, everyone. I'll take care of things, I promise."

The scribes looked at each other uncertainly. She'd never broken a promise before, but.

"How?" Bariux stepped forward and bowed. "We know you mean well, it's just. You don't work here anymore."

"Exactly." Mirko snapped. He was about to order her off the premises when he realized she was ignoring him. How dare she!

A terrific screeching sound rent the silence and a gasping Pyr dashed into the room. "Manager Mirko! Manager!" Skidding to a halt, he braced his hands on his knees and tried to catch his breath while delivering his message. "You. Your office. Now."

"Are you presuming to give me orders?" Mirko raised his hand, prepared to cuff the boy for his insolence.

"Mirko!" A booming voice spat the name so that it bounced off the walls far beyond the room's natural capacity to create echoes.

"Director Rysl!" Mirko let his hand fall to his side, but he knew it was too late. The man standing in the doorway left open by Pyr had seen him for what he really was. "What a, um. A surprise! A pleasant one, of course." Lifting his hands to his chest, he clasped them together and bowed obsequiously. "Please, come with me to the comfort of my, um. Of *your* office."

"I don't think so." Rysl stalked into the room, brushing past Mirko and claiming Gusari's chair for himself. "Your secretary was kind enough to inform me where you were and what you were doing. You obviously wanted witnesses. Alright, we'll have witnesses." It was not in his nature to be vindictive, but his outrage at Mirko's actions was such that he determined to let the man have a taste of his own medicine. "Head Translator Prezio."

"Yes, sir." Natua moved to stand before the desk. Perhaps it was just as well that she hadn't had the opportunity to return the files to Accounting.

Predictably, Mirko tried to wriggle off the hook, but the return of Leuna brought that to a spectacular end. The large, muscular guards that followed her into the room might have had something to do with his abrupt change of tone.

"Mirko, do you honestly expect me to believe that you had no idea there was a discrepancy between the copies in our files and the copies in the palace files?" Rysl tapped the contracts, which were each open to the appropriate page. "And the fact that there is no amended contract nor any legal addendum in our files is just," he spread his hands, palms up, "an oversight?"

"I don't know why you're so angry with me." Mirko fairly whimpered. "Anybody could make a mistake."

"Was it a mistake that sent the entire sum of the extra fees to your accounts?" The palace agent produced a paper and set it on the desk before Rysl.

"How…?" Mirko started to blurt out a question, then lapsed as abruptly into a sullen silence.

"I happened to be in the file room this morning when Doctor Oneko came looking for a copy of our contract with Itzuli." The agent folded his arms across his chest, file jacket and all. "As soon as I understood that there was some question regarding your business practices, I began making inquiries. The bank was most cooperative."

"So." Rysl glowered at Mirko. "As soon as I agreed to sell you Itzuli, you were planning to use money that was rightfully mine to fund the purchase."

"Such an underhanded scheme." Gusari tsked and looked at Mirko with such disapproval that Natua nearly laughed out loud. "I hope you don't think I had anything to do with this."

"Don't be ridiculous." Mirko snorted disdainfully. "You dare to suggest that your petty thievery is in any way comparable with my plans for gaining control of this company?" Several jaws swung loose in shock at his admission of guilt. "This isn't over. While Gusari sweats off his debt to Itzuli, I shall hire the best lawyer in Koroa. In Marroi! I'll own this company yet, just wait!"

"I think you'll find there are no better lawyers than those currently employed by the palace." Leuna gestured to the guards she'd brought back with her. "Take them to the lawyers." She returned the agent's bow, knowing that he would need to give his official statement as well.

Mirko went silently, unlike the trembling Gusari.

"But what have I done?" whined Gusari, edging away from the stern-faced guards. "I know nothing about his crimes!"

"No, I'm sure you are quite innocent in this." Natua responded quietly. Now that the time for his punishment had arrived, she almost felt sorry for the man. "However, you may recall that former-Manager Mirko has made allegations of thievery against you. I, myself, intend to bring formal charges of embezzlement and willful destruction of company property. And while it will be up to a judge to decide your fate once the evidence has been examined, I feel confident that the bank will be equally cooperative when called upon to provide your financial records."

"This is a mistake." Gusari plead with the guards as they led him away. "I haven't done... I'm... Let go of me!"

"What a dreadful affair." Rysl wearily sat back in the chair. He gasped as it reclined further than expected, nearly dropping him on the floor. Bolting to his feet, he smoothed his clothes as casually as he could. "Let's…let's adjourn to my office, shall we?"

Natua looked over her shoulder and winked at Kaloe, who promptly winked back.

"Show's over, folks. Time to get back to work." Kaloe clapped his hands.

A cheer started somewhere in the scribe pool and followed Director Rysl, Natua, and Leuna as they walked out the double doors.

"I think they rather like you, my dear." Rysl chuckled.

"It's mutual, sir. I admire them for their grit in surviving as long as they have here." Natua paused to turn her face to the sun. She'd found no delight in deposing Mirko or Gusari, only a grim satisfaction that they would no longer hold sway over the translators and scribes for whom she cared so much.

"You must tell me how bad things were. Spare no detail." Rysl emphatically slashed his hand down from left to right. "Recompense must be made for the wrongs done."

"I'm glad you feel that way, sir." Natua playfully quirked an eyebrow at him. "May I ask, does this mean that I still work for Itzuli?"

"What a question." Rysl chuckled. "From what I saw in there, I doubt I could run the place without you!"

"In that case, sir, our conversation will have to wait." Natua pointed over her shoulder at the copy center. "We have a completed project waiting to go out. I don't know how Mirko or Gusari were planning to get it done, given that our contract with our usual transport company was allowed to lapse, but I have an idea that might even work."

"Oh? I rather thought I would send someone over to them and ask them to make today's pickup in good faith, then sign a new contract with them as soon as possible." Rysl looked to Natua as if to encourage her to explain her position, so she did.

"They would probably be here before we could blink, but…I worry about signing with the same company that has worked with Gusari for so long," she admitted. "You may eventually decide to do just that—but for today's situation, at least, I'd like to try something different. We might find that a different company is a better fit going forward."

"Yes, I see your point. Very well." Rysl made shooing motions. "Get along with you, then. The copy center will never pay for itself if we leave completed projects lying around!"

Leuna cleared her throat as a grinning Natua turned to leave. "Need a ride?"

Natua blew out a breath. "I'd appreciate it. If you have the time."

"It's my pleasure." Leuna winked. "Especially if you're planning to see Master Ganten?"

"He's the only person I know in the transport business." Natua wondered vaguely if she could truly say she *knew* someone she'd only met the night before. As she gingerly climbed up behind Leuna, she asked, "Are you sure you want to come along? He might not be happy that I'm only visiting him to ask for a favor."

"Then don't make it a favor." Leuna urged the distira into the air and turned her toward Master Ganten's home on the edge of Koroa. "What can you offer him?" Even though it was just the two of them now, Leuna's guards being more interested in providing protection than conversation, they continued speaking in Marroi almost as a matter of course.

Natua spent the rest of the short hop examining that question from every direction she could think of. When they landed, she slid down almost easily.

"You're getting better at this," teased Leuna as she joined her on the ground.

"I've been practicing." Natua struggled to keep a straight face for a few seconds, then they laughed together.

"Would you like me to wait here?" Leuna volunteered graciously.

"I'd prefer you came along, actually." Natua linked arms with her friend and started toward the courtyard gate. "You've known him longer and can help if I get myself in a tangle."

"That's not very likely." Leuna opened the latch and pushed the gate open. "Mm, isn't it beautiful?"

Nearly twice the size of Director Rysl's courtyard, Mater Ganten's boasted five varieties of fruit trees, cunningly shaped bushes, and a white stone path to the front door that featured a handful of narrow offshoots for those seeking solitude.

"Listen." Soft tones shimmered through the air, the sweet sound tempting visitors to leave the path in search of their source. But Natua hesitated, reluctant to step on the carpet of tough-looking scrub grass that separated her from them. "I think I see the bells. Is there no walkway to them?"

"None." The women whirled to face the deep voice and found Mater Ganten watching them from a little further up the path.

"Oh." Feeling a little foolish for forgetting her mission, Natua squared her shoulders. "Your windcatchers make such pretty music. I wanted a closer look."

"There are no obstacles." He graciously spoke in Marroi for Leuna's sake as he nodded across the distance.

"Yes, but." Natua shook her head. "I know how hard it is to cultivate grass here. I don't want to walk on it just to satisfy my curiosity."

A slow smile played across his lips and he bowed to her. "You are most welcome in my home, Natua Prezio. Doctor Oneko. Please." He stepped aside, bowing again for them to precede him up to the house.

"You're most kind, sir."

In typical Remen fashion, Master Ganten refused to discuss business until after he'd given a short tour of his large home. A young servant bowed as they entered a final room and, as soon as the guests were seated, served them food and drink.

Natua chose a roll of meat and cheese inside a dark green leaf instead of the triangles of bread slathered with an unusual-smelling brown spread.

Satisfied that his guests were attended to, Master Ganten dismissed the lad with a nod and helped himself to a crumbly, lightly sweetened roll. "So. Now that the pleasantries have been observed, shall we discuss the urgent matter that has brought you here?"

Leuna managed to keep a straight face, but Natua choked on her bite of…of incredibly salty something.

"However did you know?" Natua coughed and pressed one hand to her chest.

Ganten finished chewing the bite he'd taken, swallowed, and then answered. "'Tis midday. You mentioned that you work for Itzuli Communications and, as everyone in Koroa knows, your company is up to its metaphorical eyebrows," he wriggled his own, slightly bushy ones, "in work. So for you to be here, now, something must be amiss."

Set at ease a bit by his playful wording and action, Natua ventured to explain. "We've had a rather eventful morning, it is true." From the corner of her eye she saw Leuna hastily hide a smile behind her cup. "I suppose you've already deduced that our problem is one of transport." At his nod, she continued, "The project is crated and ready to be picked up. Unfortunately, it should have left hours ago for the five main border cities."

"I know them." Ganten's eyebrows rose slowly. "They are quite a distance from Koroa. You were transporting via dragons?"

"Dragons are fast and reliable, but also the most expensive method of transport. For this sort of thing we generally use a kleir pack train." Natua tried to drown her anxiety—and the blasted bite of food— with a healthy swallow of sweetened, flavored water, but it only sort of worked.

"Mm, yes. I know kleirs well. Sturdy beasts, well-suited to long, overland treks." Ganten nodded his approval, then stroked his chin. "Ordinarily, I would not be able to help on such short notice. Happily, the situation presents an intriguing opportunity for me."

"An opportunity?" Leuna smiled and leaned forward in a display of polite curiosity.

"The details don't matter." He waved the subject away with his free hand. "Tell me when the items must be delivered by and let us settle on a price."

"Of course." Natua wiped her hands on the cloth napkin. It was easy to relay the facts of the shipment, all of which he assured her were no problem, and after a little haggling, he graciously agreed to welcome her back the next day with a firm price.

Leuna sat by as an interested spectator through most of it, though at the end she commented, "I must say, your estimates are more than fair, given the circumstances." She meant it as a compliment, especially after Mirko's duplicity.

"I agree, I am being most generous." Ganten's purple eyes twinkled. "This is because I have a small favor of my own to ask. Natua Prezio." He smiled broadly. "I want you to consider coming to work for me."

Natua's cup started to slide from numb fingers and she caught it just in time to keep it from wobbling—empty, thankfully—across the floor. "I'm sorry." She scrunched her eyes closed for an instant as she shook her head. "Did you just ask me to work for…"

"Me." He finished solemnly. "A person with your skills would be very valuable to my organization."

"I'm just a translator." The words slipped out without her meaning for them to. "I mean. What could I do that your current staff or a company such as Itzuli can't do much better?"

"Ah, yes, just a translator—who easily carries on a conversation in a tongue she has only read." He set his cup and saucer aside, then rose to collect theirs, signaling that their interview was at an end. "I think, over time, you could become an excellent interpreter. It wouldn't be easy. As for the job itself, there would be some travel involved. And, as in most places, travel in Marroi includes a degree of danger."

"Are you trying to persuade me or dissuade me?" Natua asked as she and Leuna rose.

"I wish simply to be honest." He moved over to a door made of perfectly clear, uncolored dragonglass and pointed at something. "If you go through here, the path will take you by the windcatchers. Then follow it around to your right and you will reach a side door in the wall."

"Thank you." Natua didn't move. "I would need to know a good deal more about the job you are offering before I could possibly make a decision. And," she hurried on when he seemed about to speak, "I cannot abandon Itzuli when she has so much work to do. Could you wait for my answer until after the royal wedding?"

"Now it is you who is being honest." The corners of his lips twitched as he bowed. "I can wait."

Natua returned the bow, then followed Leuna outside. They didn't speak as they walked, not even when they stopped to admire the windcatchers—tubes with flared, rounded bottoms and made of some metal she didn't recognize.

Chapter 20

Only after the door in the wall was closed firmly behind them did Leuna risk whispering, "Did you just agree to consider leaving Itzuli?"

Natua struggled to breathe around the weight on her chest. "I think I did."

"Do you want to leave?" Leuna was surprised.

"Not really." Natua looked around, still a little dazed, and turned to her left to follow the wall back to the street where they'd landed. "I didn't say I *would* leave. Just that I was willing to discuss it."

"True." Leuna linked arms with her and they walked in silence until they reached the corner. "It might be kind of nice. Having a job that pays you to travel around Marroi."

"It might." Natua had her doubts. The dust and heat were difficult enough to tolerate in familiar surroundings, where she'd already found the cool spot in the room.

"He was right about you, by the way." Leuna walked ahead to greet the distira, who could still be a bit touchy about people she didn't know well. "I watched you at the party last night. Your language skills go beyond translation."

They went back and forth on the subject for most of the return trip. As they soared over the marketplace, Natua scanned the crowds near the food carts. She wasn't hungry, not after eating at Ganten's, but it was close enough to the midday meal that she was surprised not to see Kaloe.

At her request, they took a short detour around Kaloe's second favorite food cart, which was parked in the business section of town. It was quite convenient to Itzuli, especially on days when they were rushed, yet there was still no sign of Kaloe.

"Could you drop me off here, please?" Natua groaned and rephrased. "I mean, could you set me down here?"

"Don't worry." Leuna laughed as she coaxed the distira to land in a nearby alleyway. Dust was the one constant ingredient in Marroi food, but landing near a food cart during business hours could only be described as stupid. "I haven't lost a passenger yet." She'd come a long way since meeting her first dragon, a scrawny little orphan gailen, in the woods near her home in Herrixka.

"Thank you for going out of your way for me." Natua eased herself off of the dragon, sighing with relief when her feet touched solid ground again. "For coming to Director Rysl's. And everything." It had been quite a morning.

"Of course. And for the record—if you can't come to terms with Ganten, I'll gladly make an offer. I send a fair bit of private correspondence and could use a good confidential secretary." Leuna grimaced. "Sorry to give you one more thing to worry about. There's no rush, though; I'll wait as long as you need to make up your mind."

"I… Thanks." Natua's mind was whirling again, but she was growing accustomed to the feeling. "Thank you for everything."

Leuna nodded, then left, her ever-present guards close behind her.

Natua hurried over to the food cart, where she asked about Kaloe.

"The tall boy? The one you come with?" The owner deftly rolled up an order for a customer and served it out. "Him I don't see today."

"Oh." Well. She still wasn't hungry, but Kaloe probably was, so she ordered his favorite dish and took it with her back to Itzuli.

The scribes welcomed her with clapping and huge smiles, which left her blushing in the doorway until Kaloe rescued her.

"You just missed the authorities," he told her as he ushered her over to her desk. "They took every scrap of paper from Gusari's desk."

"They tried to take Tryun, too!" Yelled one of the scribes.

Tryun hung his head, but made no reply.

Kaloe waved them back to work. "It's almost time for lunch, you chattering kraebirds. Finish your pages quickly so I can hang them up to dry."

"Speaking of lunch." Natua spoke quietly as she set the box of food on her desk. "I thought it was later than it is and didn't know if you'd been able to get away. So. I brought you that."

"Thank you." His back to the others, Kaloe covered her hand with his and squeezed. "That was very kind of you."

"You're welcome." She turned her hand so that it was palm up and loosely wrapped her fingers around his hand as well. Their eyes met and he smiled. In the middle of the weird chaos that was her life, peace stole over her.

It stayed with her throughout the rest of the work day. She met with Director Rysl long enough to iron out a firm offer to Master Ganten's services. Returning to the copy center, she spot-checked copies as usual. Soothed fears about who would replace Gusari. It wasn't easy, but she even completed one of her smaller translations.

And every time she looked around, there was Kaloe. He seemed to be everywhere at once: at his seat, diligently making copies; bringing fresh supplies; hanging pages to dry; or simply answering questions.

It was only as the final bell rang and she rose to pop her back that she remembered—her mother was waiting to talk with her when she got home.

"Ready?" Kaloe asked as he joined her at her desk.

"I doubt it." She laughed and shook her head when he raised his eyebrows. "Because you're going to tell me everything that I missed while I was gone this morning while we walk."

"Or," he countered with a smile, "you could tell me everything that you did while you were away." He offered her his arm.

"Goodness, that would be a long conversation." Natua took a deep breath and let it out slowly. "Are you walking me home or once around Koroa?"

Taken completely by surprise, he laughed out loud. "We can go wherever you wish. But, if it's to be once around Koroa, you must allow me to hire a cycle carriage."

Relaxing, she tentatively set her hand in the crook of his elbow. She could do this. She could give their relationship a chance.

"Shall we go?" Gently, he took her hand and tucked it more comfortably in place.

They didn't talk about much of anything at first, for both were too busy with the new experience of being together. It was their usual route, and to Natua it felt as though everyone stared when they walked past.

Kaloe, meanwhile, was having trouble keeping his feet on the ground. With Natua at his side, even the stars seemed close enough to touch.

"Isn't it wonderful?" Natua sighed. "We don't have to double-check everything in the morning to see if Gusari has been interfering."

Disappointed that her mind was still preoccupied with work, Kaloe didn't answer immediately. Summoning a smile, he returned, "Or Tryun, either."

"Oh, about that. What did they mean when they said the authorities tried to take Tryun, too?" Natua frowned. "I've been puzzling over that all day."

"Poor Tryun." Kaloe shook his head. "I guess, to hear Gusari tell it, everything was Tryun's doing."

"What!" Natua stared at him so hard she tripped on an uneven spot in the street.

"Careful." He steadied her. They stood there for a moment, alone in the crowd of people moving around them as if nothing had happened.

"Thank you." Natua stayed close to him as they resumed their walk, allowing herself to enjoy the experience. It *was* nice to have someone looking out for her.

"Of course." Kaloe took hope from her continued proximity, but was still worried. He had only a few more minutes to convince her to do more than *Try again, I suppose,* if her mother opposed their relationship.

"Kaloe." How should she tell him about Master Ganten's offer? "Do you ever think of leaving Itzuli?"

Amazed, he stopped walking to look down at her. "Leave? Now? When things have finally taken a turn for the better?" Kaloe edged them out of the way of an oncoming cart. "I've been hanging on at Itzuli for so long, hoping things would improve. With a decent supervisor in charge, I'm sure that I can make Chief Scribe, and the wages from that would be more than enough to support a family."

She blushed and looked away. This was an unexpected turn of conversation!

"Hey." Taking her chin in his hand, Kaloe turned her face toward him again. "I used to love to watch my father work with his maps, checking our course or updating landmarks to share with other travelers. We could travel for thousands of miles without getting lost. I thought he was the most amazing man in the whole world." Since she hadn't pulled away, he brought both hands to rest lightly on her waist. "Then we visited a city, the first one I can remember. I wandered off and got lost, just for a little while. When they found me, I was in tears, telling a nice old woman that I was hopeless. I'd never be as smart as he was."

"But you were just a child." Natua moved closer without realizing it, a part of her wanting to comfort the lost child from all those years ago.

"Yes. A child who didn't know where he was, let alone how to get to where he wanted to be." He tapped her lightly on the nose. "You and I, we are like I was then. Everything is new. We face so many decisions, so many right or wrong turns." Kaloe paused, conscious that he needed to tread lightly here. "What

I said a minute ago, about supporting a family. I could tell it worried you, but it shouldn't. That's a crossroads so far away, I can't even see it from here. Alright?"

Natua could feel herself blushing again, but didn't retreat from the topic. "I don't want to disappoint you. Won't it be worse to get there and find out that…" Her cheeks were on fire now. "Kaloe, I'm so much older than you are."

"Wait, wait." He interrupted kindly. He hadn't planned to discuss such an intimate subject on the side of the road, any more than he had planned to shout at her moments before telling her he loved her. Yet now, as then, he sensed that this was a moment to be seized. "If you insist upon worrying, let's worry together. What if I wait a few years and marry a woman half my age, hmm? What if she doesn't want children? Or, what if we both want children, but are never blessed with them?" He paused and raised his eyebrows, hoping to impress her with his sincerity. "'What if' is a road that no traveler has ever found the end of."

She looked up at him curiously, her embarrassment easing like someone had loosened the lid on a boiling pot, letting the built-up pressure out. "How can someone as young as you are still be so wise?"

"I don't know." Now he winked, wanting to lighten the mood. "I must get it from my mother." Pleased by her answering smile, he took a step back, wary of carts and foot traffic. "Come. We mustn't keep *your* mother waiting."

They traveled the rest of the way in a companionable silence, happy just to be together.

Kaloe hesitated at the courtyard gate. "You're sure you don't want me to stay?"

"Thank you for offering but…" Natua smiled and nodded. "I'm sure." She reached for the latch when he lingered. "I'll see you in the morning."

"It will be a long night for me." He made no move to follow her. "Wondering how things went."

She hesitated. "Will this help?" Slipping her arms

around his waist, she rested her head against his chest. His contented sigh as he returned the hug told her more than words could ever have expressed.

If she was being honest, she'd needed the hug as much as he had. She wore it like an invisible protective shield as she walked through the door—where she found her mother waiting for her in the sitting room. Noises from the kitchen announced that Tilla was hard at work in there, so Natua took a seat near her mother.

"Welcome home, dear." Kume sprinkled a little cooling powder in the glasses of juice she had waiting and slid one over to Natua. "How was your day?"

"Busy." Natua frowned as she stirred her juice. How could she condense everything that had happened into a few short sentences? They needed to be as short as possible, because she was anxious to get past the small talk. "My meeting went very well. Gusari and Mirko won't be a problem anymore."

"That's wonderful! However did you manage that?" Kume sipped her drink and leaned back, a little concerned that work was more important to Natua than her new boyfriend. Finding the liquid too warm, she added two pinches of cooling powder and stirred them in while she waited.

"Well." Natua took a deep, calming breath, then related the events in an outline format. When she got to the part about arranging transport with Master Ganten, she accidentally let slip about his job offer.

"Oh, my. Would that be wise?" Kume inquired. "After all your time at Itzuli, especially after you've worked so hard to improve things at the copy center, are you really considering taking a different job?"

"I don't know." A small laugh escaped. "So much has happened so quickly, Mama, that I haven't even had time to decide if I want to start wondering about that."

"I see." Kume patted her hand lightly. "You'd better go upstairs and get changed, dear. I'll bring up a tray in a minute and you can go to bed early."

"What?" Natua set her glass down harder than she

meant to. "Are you serious?"

"Goodness!" Kume pressed a hand to her heart. "You startled me!"

"I'm sorry." She felt about two inches tall as she released the glass and folded her hands in her lap. "I just thought. I mean, this morning you seemed to want to talk about…something specific." Her mother *did* know she was in a relationship with Kaloe, didn't she? More than a 'working relationship.'

"That's right, I did." Kume studied her daughter's face and decided they were both confused. "But you haven't brought him up once, so I thought," she lifted hands and shoulders, "that perhaps I misunderstood."

"*I* haven't." Natua sputtered. "Why would I bring him up? You're the one who wanted to talk about it."

Kume's brows drew together and she gave a little headshake. "Does that mean you do *not* want to?" In her youth, she'd shared everything with her mother. At least, everything of note. Surely having someone to hold hands with counted?

"I…" Natua sagged into her chair. She was tired. Too tired for word games. "How much can I tell you about something that's just begun?"

Kume didn't answer, preferring to let Natua continue at her own pace now that she'd begun.

"He surprised me, Mama. I didn't know he felt. This way." Natua's gaze dropped to her hands. "Shouldn't I have?"

"Not necessarily, my dear." Kume lifted her heels, then settled them back on the floor, rocking her body slightly. "It's actually quite easy to mistake growing fondness for mere friendship. I did that myself, once."

"I didn't know." Natua bit her lip. "Was it Papa?"

"Sakes, no. I never had to wonder whether your papa was just being polite." Kume's cheeks went a lovely shade of pink. Then her eyes saddened. "There was a man, though. He was the nicest man I knew and we spent quite a bit of time in each other's company—never in a group of less than five people, mind. I thought he'd be happy for me when I met Torl. I…I didn't realize he thought we were courting."

"I'm sorry, Mama." Natua reached out to touch her mother's arm. She hadn't expected to be understood so readily. "Mama. If he'd asked you, before you met Papa, what would you have said?"

Kume shook her head. "I didn't see him that way. We used to go on picnics, large affairs with lots of young women and men—and a few parents, naturally. He always tried to sit next to me and, when he succeeded, I used to tease him that he was breaking the other women's hearts. I thought he was shy and just needed a nudge toward the right woman."

Natua nodded slowly. "Yes. I see what you mean."

Kume sniffled a little, then put away her memories to refocus on Natua's current problem. "Is that how you feel about him? Kal-oh?"

"No." It was Natua's turn to blush. "I never thought things out this way, but. When I met his mother, I knew I wanted her to like me. Then, at her shop last night, when I saw how her helper was looking at Kaloe, I didn't like it at all."

"Well, well." Kume arched her eyebrows. "It sounds to me like you're showing the first signs."

"Of love?" Natua shifted uncomfortably in her chair. She was a grown woman. Shouldn't she already know the answer to that question?

"Of more than friendship." Kume winked at her. "Keep tending the garden, dear. Pull the weeds and water the sprout. It won't be long before you'll be telling me instead of asking."

"Then. You approve? Of, um, us?" Strangely, Natua didn't blush at all this time.

"For now, yes. But I expect you to start bringing him by so I can get to know him better." Rising, Kume took Natua's hands and pulled her to her feet. Enveloped her in a warm hug. "Bedtime for you, I think. Hurry along upstairs. I've worn you out with all this talking."

Natua watched in mixed bewilderment and gratitude as her mother bustled off to the kitchen, where she heard Kume explaining that she would put together a tray.

"She works so hard, sometimes I worry about Natua. Thank goodness she's made some good friends, though. I hope they'll help her relax and have some fun."

Laughing softly to herself, Natua headed up the stairs. What a crazy, hectic, topsy-turvy day!

The next few days passed in a blur of meetings and interviews as Director Rysl familiarized himself once more with the day-to-day running of Itzuli Communications. Despite her best efforts, Natua found herself drawn into the process, leaving her with almost no time to consider Master Ganten's offer.

As tired as she was, she made a special effort at the end of each day to put in an appearance at the copy center—if only to see Kaloe. Lately they'd only been able to spend time together during the walk to her home. And today she had news.

"Hello, everyone!" Natua called out as she entered the room, inhaling the now-familiar scents of ink and paper. There were only five scribes there so late— including Kaloe. Oh, how she'd missed him and their easy camaraderie.

"There she is!" They stopped working to applaud.

"Alright, alright. Back to work, you yobs." The new supervisor, a pleasant-faced woman who easily walked the fine line between authority and camaraderie with the scribes, rose to greet her. "Welcome, Head Translator. What brings you here this evening?"

"Oh. I, um." Natua narrowly avoided looking at Kaloe. "N-nothing. I just dropped by to," she shrugged, hoping the action would look casual, "say hello to everyone. Won't take a minute."

"Carry on." The supervisor nodded and retook her seat.

Natua made a quick circuit of the scribes, careful not to spend too much time with any of them. There wasn't much to be said, really, though she enjoyed seeing how happy they all were. Etiquette seemed to dictate that she stop to speak with the supervisor as well, but then she took her leave.

"Have fun, everyone!" she teased, laughing kindly at the answering chorus of groans.

Having made good her escape, Natua crossed the street and walked past the next nearest building, where she paused to lean against it. Tipping her head back, she took a slow, deep breath, then let it out. She was far too old to feel this young and foolish.

Hearing footfalls approaching, she straightened, an expectant smile growing on her face of its own accord. It froze in place when three of the other scribes came around the corner instead of Kaloe.

"Evening, Translator." The first one to spot her bowed as she passed. "Everything alright?"

"Yes." Natua answered automatically. "I just...I just wanted to think for a minute before heading home."

They laughed, though not unkindly.

"Glad I haven't your job!" One of them chuckled. "All I take home are sore shoulders!"

They hadn't stopped walking and now they moved off, joking about the 'dangers' of working at a copy center. Papercuts were apparently quite high on the list.

Natua waved to the one who glanced over their shoulder—right as Kaloe appeared.

"Translator." He bowed circumspectly, conscious of the fact that not everyone would understand his decision to date a boss. Some would even report them to the higher bosses, exposing the relationship to an intense scrutiny that would kill it as surely as direct, scorching sunlight killed sprouting plants.

"Tetsu." Natua took her cue from him, returning his bow.

"They're gone." He slowed long enough to join hands with her, then hurried along to the next corner, where they would be safer from accidental sightings.

"We can't keep meeting like this." Natua blew out a breath. "Maybe I *should* take another job."

"Don't do that!" he objected reflexively. "We hardly see each other as it is anymore."

"It would make some things more difficult for us."

She squeezed his hand sympathetically. "But you will agree that it would be nice to not have to this from everyone."

It took him half a block to do it, but eventually Kaloe nodded. "Yes, that's true." Curious, he asked, "Where would you go, though? Jobs do not drop from the sky."

She bit her lip. "Actually, I've had two job proposals in the last few days."

He stopped abruptly to stare at her. "And you didn't tell me?"

"I can barely find time to consider them," she retorted. "Should I waste the little time I have with you in debating which job I might take?"

"Yes, you should!" Startled by his own vehemence, Kaloe dropped her hand to rake his fingers through his hair. "Natua." He turned to face her and rested his hands on her shoulders. "I love every minute with you. I enjoy trading silly stories about our childhoods, agreeing—or disagreeing—with our mothers, and building our relationship in general. But it isn't a waste of time to discuss a change that will affect us so drastically."

"I hadn't thought of it that way," she admitted. "I'm sorry. I thought it would be better for me to decide if I was going to take either job before I worried you."

Kaloe hesitated. "I see your point." Lifting his eyebrows, he asked, "Then you mention it tonight because you know which one you might accept?"

She nodded. "Master Ganten wants me to work as an interpreter at his company."

"An interpreter?" Kaloe interrupted. "But you don't have any experience with that."

"Which is part of why," Natua broke in before he could get wound up, "I don't think it's the right job. There's also a lot of travelling and so forth." She shook her head. "Mama and I are just starting to make a life here together. I can't go gallivanting around Marroi and leave her by herself."

Kaloe ran his hands down her arms to her elbows, which he shook gently. "Your mother need only be alone if she wishes it."

"Thank you." She meant it. But when Kaloe's gaze dropped to her lips, Natua retreated. "I'm starving. Come on, we can talk about the other job over a meal."

Taken completely by surprise, Kaloe was a few steps late in following her. "Hey, wait for me!" His long legs made up the difference quickly, allowing him to recapture her hand. "Where shall we eat tonight?"

"Well, since you insist on paying." She arched an eyebrow at him hopefully. Lurrakian restaurants were more expensive, and she didn't want to strain his budget any more than necessary.

"I do." He nodded emphatically.

"The usual place, then." Natua smiled.

It didn't take long to reach the restaurant and get settled at their table. Once the waiter had taken their orders, Kaloe looked at Natua expectantly.

"The job I think I'd like to take is at the palace. Leuna says she needs a private secretary." She'd received a formal offer in the mail and now she explained the duties entailed to Kaloe. "I would still travel a little, if she needed me with her on a state visit somewhere."

"But it would be completely different from camping with a transport pack train," he interjected. "Or even flying around from one tiny town to another. You'll need a whole new wardrobe, for one thing."

She blinked, then teased, "Does that mean you don't like my clothes?"

The waiter returned at just that moment, and while he gave no sign of having heard her remark, Natua couldn't help imagining all the ways he might interpret it.

"Maybe tomorrow we should eat supper at my house," she suggested once the waiter had gone. Why hadn't she thought of that before? It was an easy way to get a break from the monotony of this restaurant without emptying Kaloe's purse. Of course, they would be eating with her mother. Or… "You must bring your mother as well."

"We would love to come." Kaloe shook his napkin out. "And for the record," he dropped a slow, flirtatious wink, "I love everything about you."

Blushing, Natua slapped his forearm. "Eat your food."

He complied, digging into his dish with youthful gusto. Wiping his mouth after a few bites, he prompted, "So you'll take the job at the palace?"

"Yes." Natua nudged his knee with her own as she raised one hand to wave back at the boisterous group that had just entered.

"Hey!" The group's leader came over and plopped himself down beside Kaloe. "We missed you at the game, Tetsu."

Kaloe sat back as the rowdy fellow helped himself to the bread and cheese. The others joined them, plucking empty cushions from eating arrangements and bringing them over until they overflowed the original eating arrangement.

Natua, sensing that Kaloe was about to object, bumped his knee again. The only thing worse than being invaded would be to draw attention to the fact that they wanted to be alone.

Changing tactics, Kaloe threw a roll to one of the players and asked how the pilota game had gone. Whenever possible, he held hands with Natua under the table, but it was still a highly unsatisfactory way to spend an evening.

Realizing that the players would be hours eating and boasting, Natua finished her food more quickly than usual.

"You're not leaving!" One of the players who was also a scribe shot Kaloe a meaningful grin. "At least, not alone, surely?"

Kaloe clapped his hands to get everyone's attention. "For those of you who haven't already heard, there's big news at the copy center."

Natua froze in place, then relaxed as he announced the hiring of the supervisor.

Everyone had heard of Gusari and his termination, but clearly the scribes hadn't mentioned the brand-new supervisor to all of their pilota-playing friends, for now chattering swept through the group.

Kaloe beckoned to Natua and they escaped in the excitement.

"That was too close." Natua almost moved her hand away when Kaloe reached for it.

"Let them see." He tucked her hand into the crook of his arm. "You know I'm proud to be dating you. My only concern has been that it would cause you difficulty at work. Now that you're accepting another position, what do I care what those jabbering kraebirds think?"

She walked stiffly beside him for several steps before her tension began to ease. "You're sure?"

"I'd kiss you right here if I wasn't in a hurry to get you home." Kaloe spoke softly, his words for her ears only. He'd tried to kiss her a few times at her gate, but as yet she hadn't allowed him to.

"Oh." A sandstorm of emotions surged over her, threatening to smother her. The brief brush of his lips on the night of their supper at the palace had evoked such a strong response in her that she was reluctant to revisit it. She'd lived such an ordered life until now— boring was another word for it. Well, no matter what she called the past, the undeniable truth of it was that she was ill-prepared for the emotionally turbulent process of…of falling in love.

And yet, was it reasonable to try to date someone without getting…attached? Was it even honest? She didn't have to ask to know that Kaloe had given her full access to his heart. Why did she struggle so to reciprocate? She couldn't have it both ways. She couldn't keep her heart safe from harm *and* give it to him. Which raised the question of which was more important—protecting herself from the risk of pain? Or opening herself to the chance of a lifetime, pain included?

"You're awfully quiet." Kaloe slowed his gait, in case she'd eaten too much and was uncomfortable with the pace he'd set.

"Quiet is nice, sometimes. Quiet is an opportunity to reflect, to collect yourself." To face the awful fact that she was scared. She'd realized it just now. Plain old, unvarnished scared of the new feelings that being with Kaloe sent swirling through her.

"Have you been scattered today?" He hadn't meant it as a joke, but enjoyed her answering smile.

"I rather think I have. There's so much going on." She bit her lip. He deserved to know. It might change how he felt about her. "Kaloe."

"Hmm?" He slipped an arm around her shoulders to guide her around a rambunctious group of children. The slight tension in her shoulders bothered him, but he reminded himself to be patient. They'd covered a lot of ground in the short time of their relationship. He could slow to keep pace with her, especially when he planned for this journey to take the rest of their lives.

"I'm…." But no. She refused to have another intensely personal conversation in the middle of everyone else's lives. Slipping free of his arm, she caught his hand instead and tugged him into a side street. The relative quiet settled over her until she thought she could hear her heart pounding anxiously.

"Hey." Kaloe squeezed her hand, whether to reassure her or himself he couldn't have said. "What is it?" He deliberately avoided the negative assumption of asking, 'What's wrong?'

Lifting her eyes to his made all the difference for her. He was just so…open. The winds of fear that drove the shifting, stinging sands of indecision were suddenly still. The path to take was still obvious, but familiar in the sense that they had already traveled similar terrain in the form of their earlier, equally awkward discussions.

"Kaloe." She took a deep breath and raised their joined hands. "This scares me. *We* scare me." His eyebrows drew together and she stopped to let him speak. When he didn't, she continued, thoughts tumbling out. "I like it. I like kissing you. I love being with you. I just don't like..." The half-smile that had begun forming on his face froze and she closed her eyes to block it out before concern over his reaction got the better of her burst of courage. If she didn't say this now, however clumsily, she might never get it out. "I know how I feel about my life. I know how mad Gusari makes me. I know dragons scare me. I know I love my mother, no matter how frustrating she can get."

Opening her eyes, she risked meeting his eyes again. "But us, Kaloe. Every time we get closer, it reshapes my world. The sky changes color and the earth shakes. Sometimes I don't even recognize it anymore and it's, it's terrifying. It takes a while for me to get used to things and I am," she inhaled shakily as his hands settled on her waist, "*not* used to this." If she'd ever thought she was just humoring Kaloe in agreeing to date him, she now knew without a doubt that her heart was inextricably entangled with his.

"It's alright. I'd be worried if you were." He spoke softly, trusting her to hear him over the noise in the nearby street. "In truth, I'm delighted that all we share is as new for you as it is for me."

"You mean..." She stared up at him. "You feel the same way?"

"I find our time together exhilarating." Kaloe spoke slowly, a little reluctant to make the distinction. "I enjoy new things, new experiences. My world is more beautiful for the changes you make to it."

Her heart melted at the same time that her brain started looking for rocks to hide under. "Now I feel like a coward." She blinked furiously at the mortified tears stinging her eyes.

"No, darling, no, you must not feel that way." Throwing caution to the wind, and half afraid she would bolt away from him, Kaloe pulled her close and hugged her fiercely. It wasn't enough, not really.

He strained to hear what she said next, her words muffled against his shirt.

"You're…you're not disappointed?" Her embarrassment lessened when he tugged gently on her braid.

"How can I be disappointed in a woman brave enough to tell me the truth?"

Brave? Natua lifted her head from his shoulder to peek at him. Her stomach dipped when he shifted so that he was looking down at her as well. He was so close. She didn't even have to think about it. She just had to…want it.

Kaloe held perfectly still as she came up on her toes to press her lips shyly against his. Her cheeks were bright pink when her heels settled back on the ground and he couldn't resist teasing, "That wasn't so bad, was it?"

"What did I ever do to deserve you? Your patience?" She felt absurdly calm, as if the conversation—sealed with a kiss—had drilled down to the bedrock of her soul, the only proper place to lay a permanent foundation for their relationship.

"What would I, or this which you call my patience, be without you?" He winked playfully. "I know one thing for certain, though. Wherever you choose to go to work, you will still be found in translation." Kaloe smiled at his pun, thinking back to how he'd tormented her on her first day at the copy center.

He spent the rest of their walk doing a little pondering of his own. And made a decision. When they stopped at her gate, he wrapped her in his arms. Rested his cheek against her hair. Held her until her arms crept around his waist and she sighed softly. He felt ten feet tall, ready to take on the world to protect her—whether she knew she needed protecting or not.

But even wonderful things come to an end and he wisely straightened away at the first sign that she wanted to be released.

"Thank you, Kaloe." Natua smiled up at him, feeling more at peace than she had in days. "That hug…our talk. They were exactly what I needed."

"My pleasure." He smoothed her hair where it had rested against his chest, then opened the gate latch. "Sleep sweetly, and dream of us."

His words, his warmth, and the feel of his touch lingered long after she'd gone upstairs.

Kaloe continued enveloping her in hugs for the next several nights, almost as if he sensed how much they helped her. Those moments quickly became the highlight of her days, melting away the stress of informing Director Rysl and Master Ganten of her choice; of transferring her duties at Itzuli; and of taking up her new position at the palace.

"You don't have to wait," she told Kaloe on the morning of her first official day as Leuna's confidential secretary. "The dragon will be here any minute."

"I don't mind." He'd cut back on his extra hours specifically so he wait with her that morning. He hadn't expected to be invited to join the family for breakfast, but it was a delightful development.

"You're so stubborn. Are we going to go through this every morning?" She tried to poke him in the arm, but he dodged it, instead twirling her in an impromptu dance move.

"Of course not." He winked. "Well. Just until you accept my decision to be here."

"Actually. It might not be that long." She chuckled, then sobered. "There's some talk of moving us into the palace. In case there's emergency communication needed. In the middle of the night or something."

Kaloe whistled softly. "What an honor that would be."

"I suppose so." Natua scanned the sky that she

could see, faintly disappointed at his apparent approval. Didn't he realize how it would change things? "It's definitely ironic. I already struggle to leave work behind at the end of the day. This would make it fairly impossible."

Hearing her less-than-enthusiastic tone of voice, Kaloe stepped into her space. Waited, eyes on her face.

"He'll be here any moment," she protested, trying to step away. When Kaloe moved with her, she gave an exasperated huff. "What is it, Kaloe? Just tell me."

"I think it is you who should tell me," he countered gently. "I know you well enough to be sure you do not wish to live at the palace."

"And yet I may not have much choice." Natua scowled, thinking that he'd overlooked the obvious. "It's a city within a city, Kaloe. Work, food, entertainment, and housing—all bundled into that mountain your people use as a palace. I'd never have to leave it." She gasped and gripped his biceps as he pulled her tightly against him.

"Is that why you don't want to live there? Because you're afraid we wouldn't see each other anymore?" Kaloe's heart thumped painfully in his chest as he waited for her response.

Startled, Natua stared up at him. The intensity of his gaze made it difficult for her to think, leaving her to nod mutely. Her pulse tripped over itself as she wondered if… They were standing so close. Too close, some would say. She should…

"Do you actually believe I would allow that to happen?" Raising his hand to her chin, Kaloe tilted her head back. Pressed his lips to hers in a kiss that was both tender and wonderfully possessive. When his action went unchallenged, he slid his hand around to cup the back of her neck and kissed her again.

Natua's eyes blinked open slowly, and she looked at Kaloe—as well as she could with her cheek still against his. Finding her fingers tangled in his hair, she smoothed it while she tried to calm her racing pulse.

"Move to the palace. Move back to Lurrak." Kaloe kissed the curve of her neck, then her cheek and eyes as he straightened. "I'll still find a way."

"Kaloe, I."

He stopped her with another heart-jolting kiss. "I mean it."

She took a shaky breath and braced her hands against his chest. "I don't *want* to move away, you dolt." She felt his arms tighten and the distance between them became impossibly smaller. "And I'm not asking you to prove anything."

"Then I suppose I must be kissing you," he left a burning trail of kisses across her forehead, "because I want to."

"Y-yes." Coming up on her toes, she returned his kiss. Murmured breathlessly, "I suppose that must be it."

He tucked her in close, his chin resting against her temple as he treasured the moment. "I love you."

Natua shifted away from a lump in his tunic and considered the emotions rioting through her. Started to speak, then hesitated. "I love you, too." A palpable sense of rightness settled over her, as tangible as the warmth of sunlight on her skin. She felt his shoulders rise and fall, his contented sigh stirring her hair.

"How I have longed to hear you say that." Kaloe stroked her hair, exulting in the knowledge that she had given him the right to such a familiarity. Spotting a dragon in the distance, he nearly groaned aloud.

"What is it?" Sensing his increased tension, Natua drew back to look at his face. Instantly made the connection when she saw where he was looking. She waited, expecting to be seized by a dire compulsion to withdraw to a respectable distance before the dragon rider came near enough to really see them.

It never happened. Granted, they turned so that they could both watch the descent, but she found herself pleased to linger at Kaloe's side. Even to walk to the dragon with his arm still around her shoulders.

"Will you be working late tonight?" Natua asked as she prepared to mount.

"I can." Kaloe stood firm while she leaned on him for support.

"Then I'll see you there," she promised. As an afterthought, she added, "Don't wait past sundown. Today's bound to be a long day for me."

"Any day without you is a long one." Kaloe kissed the hand he held, then released it. "But if you're not back by suppertime, I'm coming to get you."

"Kaloe." Natua shook her head reproachfully. "Today will take as long as it takes."

"By suppertime," he reiterated firmly. "Or have you already forgotten that I promised I wouldn't let you become imprisoned in the palace?"

"Whenever you're ready." The rider sent Kaloe a friendly wink.

Caught mid-blush, Natua was just grateful the rider couldn't see her. Convinced now that Kaloe was serious, she sent him a meek nod before addressing the rider. "Let's go."

Kaloe retreated to a safe distance and watched them depart through his sheer gerri, raised to shield his eyes from the bits of debris stirred up by the dragon's powerful wings. How many times he would stand thus, he did not know. Nor did he care, so long as his days began and ended with the woman he loved.

Thank you for reading *Found in Translation*, I hope you enjoyed it!

I'm not sure how many of you have had the pleasure of reading a review of your own work.
Personally, I check for new reviews often and love reading them!
Please consider leaving a review on the site of your choice.

Thank you!

More titles by Lea Carter:

www.ingramcontent.com/pod-product-compliance
Lightning Source LLC
Chambersburg PA
CBHW070456200726
48293CB00007B/2240